W9-CDA-252

More praise for
The Dead Detective by William Heffernan
(the first novel in the Dead Detective series)

"*The Dead Detective* is a meaty story that offers an intriguing and conflicted protagonist, a darkly fascinating victim, solid police procedural detail, a knowing look at the Tampa Bay area and its politics, an unlikely murderer, and a creepy denouement that hints that Harry [protagonist] will be back."

—*Booklist*

"In his first new novel in seven years, Edgar Award–winner Heffernan delivers a readable, tidy police procedural that echoes any number of popular television series, from *The Mentalist* to *Criminal Minds*, whose many fans will find this series debut enjoyable."

—*Library Journal*

"After a lengthy hiatus, Edgar-winner Heffernan (*A Time Gone By*) makes a welcome return . . . Tough, troubled Harry Doyle will keep readers in line."

—*Kirkus Reviews*

"Heffernan has a classic lean, tough-guy style and effectively combines tense drama with the nuts-and-bolts details of investigation. And he knows the territory, from Tarpon Springs to Tampa."

—*St. Petersburg Times*

"We have a feeling that Heffernan is setting us up for more dead detective novels, which we welcome like the zealots we are."

—*Time Out Chicago*

"William Heffernan is one of the finest craftsmen in mystery fiction. The publication of a new Heffernan novel is an event worth cheering, and *The Dead Detective* is no exception. A mystery treat. A literary treat."
—John Lutz, author of *Slaughter*

"William Heffernan has written some crime fiction classics, and this much-anticipated return delivers a promising new protagonist, a plot with all the heat of its Florida Gulf Coast setting, and a finale that settles with beautiful, gentle menace. *The Dead Detective* is a veteran pro proving that he has much more to offer. Heffernan writes in a way that challenges the mind and the soul."
—Michael Koryta, author of *Rise the Dark*

"*The Dead Detective* breathes new life into the classic police drama. Jam-packed with strong characters and a powerful plot, this is as fine a book of its genre as I've read in decades."
—Reed Farrel Coleman, author of *The Devil Wins*

"They say that the dead talk to Harry Doyle. They know he can hear them because he was dead once, himself, murdered by his own mother and brought back to life by a sharp-eyed cop. Now Harry has become a detective himself and he's landed a case with echoes of his own haunted past where the dark forces of celebrity, sex, and religious mania conflate in shocking murder. Heffernan sends cold chills through the Florida heat with his singular new creation."
—Cathi Unsworth, author of *Without the Moon*

THE SCIENTOLOGY MURDERS

THE SCIENTOLOGY MURDERS

A DEAD DETECTIVE NOVEL

WILLIAM HEFFERNAN

Published by Akashic Books

Hardcover ISBN: 978-1-61775-535-4
Paperback ISBN: 978-1-61775-536-1
Library of Congress Control Number: 2016953894

First Printing
Akashic Books

Brooklyn, New York
Twitter: @AkashicBooks
Facebook: AkashicBooks
E-mail: info@akashicbooks.com
Website: www.akashicbooks.com

This book is for Terrence Timothy Heffernan, who left us in 2015.
I miss you, my brother.

I believe there are monsters born in the world to human parents.

—John Steinbeck

CHAPTER ONE

Palm Harbor, Florida

Harry Santos Doyle stared into the dead man's face. He had already removed the man's wallet; knew his name was Charlie Moon, knew he was twenty-eight years old, and that he lived in the house where his body was found. He also knew that the large butcher knife protruding from the center of his chest had probably cleaved his heart in two.

Doyle's partner, Vicky Stanopolis, squatted beside him. She, too, stared at the man. He was pale and flabby with a plump, round face and his blindly staring eyes still held a look of horrified surprise. His mouth was opened wide as though he wanted to scream out a final objection to his death. She glanced at Harry.

"Are you getting anything?" She waited, knowing he would answer when he was ready.

Seconds passed before Harry finally nodded. "I'm getting three words." He stared into the man's face. "*You old bitch.*" Harry shook his head. "When he said those words he was in great pain. I think they were the last words he ever spoke."

Vicky avoided Harry's eyes. She knew his history. She glanced through a doorway to an adjoining room. She could just see the crossed ankles of the elderly woman who had let them into the apartment. Vicky guessed the woman to be somewhere in her eighties. She was small and frail and Vicky had helped her to a chair before they went to examine the body. It was hard to imagine her plunging a heavy eight-inch butcher knife into a man's chest.

She turned to Harry. "Are you thinking Grandma?"

He nodded. "We better talk to her."

Harry Doyle was six one with enough lean, hard muscle to fill out a fairly large frame. He had wavy brown hair and penetrating green eyes but he was far from a pretty boy. There was a ruggedly handsome look about him, but one that also warned of someone who should not be pushed too far. Yet those features quickly softened when a sense of playfulness came to his eyes and a small, infrequent smile appeared at the corners of his mouth. Vicky knew that Harry's "gentler side," as she liked to call it, had a strong effect on her and it surprised her that he seldom used it while working.

Vicky by contrast was tall and slender with light brown hair that fell halfway to her shoulders, pale brown eyes that looked as though they could swallow you whole, a straight nose, and a mouth that seemed just a bit large, a bit sensual. Overall it gave off a soft look. In the six months they had worked together, Harry had learned that it was pure deception. The woman who had become his homicide partner—after spending four years with a sex crime unit—was as hard as nails when she had to be.

"Maybe you should let me talk to her," Vicky said.

"Are you implying that I'll scare her and you won't?"

Vicky grinned at him. "I could be."

Harry snorted at the idea. "That's only because she doesn't know you."

When they entered the adjoining room they found the elderly woman busily working a pair of crocheting needles, her fingers moving methodically, almost without thought. She had thin white hair and a heavily powdered face, a wasted attempt to hide the nest of wrinkles that covered her cheeks and forehead and neck. She had bright, clear blue eyes set deep in her head and Harry thought he detected a note of resigned fear resting there.

Vicky knelt in front of the woman, whose name was Delilah Moon. "I'm afraid you were right," she said. "Your grandson is dead."

The woman slowly nodded. "Good," she said.

The word startled Vicky, but she quickly caught herself. "Did he hurt you?" she asked.

Delilah Moon lifted her blouse displaying deep bruises on her stomach and ribs. "He hurt me whenever he was drunk and I wouldn't give him the money he always wanted. He was drunk most of the time, and I refused to give him money most of the time."

Harry knelt down beside Vicky. "Did you stab him, Mrs. Moon?" He spoke the words softly.

"I did." The old woman's jaw was set and Harry could tell it was something she felt no regret over, something she would have done again.

"How did you happen to have the knife?" he asked.

The woman began to rock in her chair and Vicky reached out and laid a hand on top of hers.

"After the last time he beat me I started carrying it around. If he got out of control an' I thought he was gonna hurt me, I'd wave it at him and he'd usually back off."

"And this time he didn't?" Vicky asked.

"That's right."

"Did he say anything to you when you stabbed him?"

The woman's mouth tightened and her lips pursed. "He called me a nasty name," she said.

"What did he call you?"

"He called me an old bitch." Her jaw tightened. "But he won't be doin' that no more. An' he won't be beatin' on me neither."

Harry called social services for a caseworker and left Mrs. Moon in the care of two female deputies and the corpse in the hands of the medical examiner. Then they went to the state attorney's office and laid out their case along with the lengthy rap sheet the victim, Charlie Moon, had assembled in his twenty-eight years on earth. The assistant state attorney, a short, fat man named Julius North, said his office would interview Mrs. Moon, but that he could see no reason why the elderly woman would be charged. "The newspapers would crucify me," he said. "Besides, it sounds like she did the county a favor by bumping the bastard off."

Back at the office, Harry and Vicky spent an hour writing up their reports, and it was just past ten p.m. when Harry's personal cell phone rang with a call from his adoptive mother, Maria Doyle.

"Hey, Mom, what's up?"

"Harry, oh, Harry." The fearful timbre in her voice immediately set his hair on end. "Harry, somebody shot Jocko. He's in Morton Plant Hospital in downtown Clearwater. They're just taking him into surgery."

Harry felt his legs go weak. Jocko was the only father he had ever known. "How bad is it?"

"Is very bad. They say he lost much blood."

"Do the Clearwater cops have somebody with you?"

"Yes, a nice young girl."

"I'll be there in twenty minutes."

Harry told Vicky what had happened and headed for the stairs.

"I'll go with you," she called after him.

* * *

With siren and lights they made the hospital in eighteen minutes.

"You go," Vicky said. "I'll secure the car and catch up."

Harry found Maria in the surgery waiting room, her face haggard; her hands in her lap nervously twisting a handkerchief. He sat beside her and placed an arm around her shoulders.

"Have you seen a doctor since they took him into surgery?"

"No, no one," she said.

"Where was he shot?"

"In the back. Two times. Then whoever does this pushes him in the water."

"The water? Where was he?"

"When they found him, he was hanging onto a ladder in a little marina downtown."

"Why was he at a marina?"

"You remember Joey O'Connell?"

Harry nodded. Like his adoptive father, O'Connell was a retired Clearwater cop, who left the job on a disability. O'Connell had been shot in the spine while trying to stop an armed robbery. Harry knew that Jocko visited him every week.

"What about Joey?" Harry asked. "What does he have to do with this?"

"Not him, his daughter."

Maria was a short, stocky woman with graying black hair, warm brown eyes, and a round face filled with lines from her perpetual smile. She also ran his and Jocko's lives like a marine drill instructor, or at least tried to. But it was an effort always filled with an irresistible love. Harry hated seeing her so frightened and in so much pain.

Vicky came in and sat on the other side of Maria, taking hold of her hand. "Any news?" she asked.

Maria shook her head. "Thank you for coming. You take good care of my boy."

"I try, but it isn't easy."

Maria gave her son a reproachful look. "Tell me about it," she said. "I try for almost twenty years. Does he listen?"

Harry ignored the comment. "Tell me about O'Connell's daughter."

"A nice girl," Maria said. "She's maybe twenty-two, twenty-three years old. Her name is Mary Kate." She shook her head sadly. "Some time last year she joins up with these Scientology people and a little while later she tells her father and mother that she can't talk to them anymore, because they don't belong to her church." She shook her head again and drew a long breath as if that summed everything up. "Then last week Joey calls Jocko and asks him to find her, tell her she should come home. He thinks maybe these church people are keeping her a prisoner."

"Why didn't Joey go to the police? He knew Jocko was retired and didn't have the authority to do anything, or even pressure anybody."

"He told Jocko that he didn't think the regular cops could do anything. But Jocko said he thought it was because Joey was ashamed. He didn't want his friends in the department to know what happened to his daughter."

Like everyone else in the Tampa Bay area, Harry was familiar with the Church of Scientology. It was a massive, highly secretive organization—to many, more cult than church—that had made Clearwater, Florida its spiritual headquarters. Over the years, church leaders had bought up more than half the buildings in the downtown area and turned it into a private enclave that discouraged anyone who tried to breach their guarded domain. Some claimed that resistance at times turned violent, although church officials vehemently denied it. Yet to many the separation was clearly visible and unmistakably aggressive. It was as though an impregnable wall had been built around the majority of downtown Clearwater.

Harry turned to the patrol officer who had been assigned to watch over Maria. She was in her early forties, tall and slender, with a plain, unremarkable face and the look of a cop who had seen more than she cared to remember. Her name tag identified her only as *Moore*.

"Patrolwoman Moore, where did they find Jocko?" Harry asked.

"Like your mother said, he was in the water in this small marina just west of that old elementary school on Osceola Avenue. The school was shut down a couple of years ago and the Scientology people are supposed to be buying it. Rumor is that the marina's part of the deal. Anyway, it was a guy who keeps his boat there who heard the shots and found your dad. The detectives and forensics are still at the scene and will probably be there for quite a while. They could give you more info."

The doctor, still in surgical scrubs, came out half an hour later and sat with them. His name was Josephs and he spoke directly to Maria.

"The surgery went well and your husband is in intensive care. He's in critical condition mostly because of the extensive loss of blood he suffered. In addition to the bullet wounds he also had a collapsed left lung and some broken ribs, but I have every confidence he's going to survive. The next twenty-four hours will be critical."

"Can I see him?" Maria asked.

"Yes, but I can only allow one visitor." He turned to Harry. "Are you his son?"

"Yes."

"I'm afraid you'll have to wait until tomorrow." Dr. Josephs turned back to Maria. "You should go home after you see him. Get some rest and we'll call you if there's any change."

"No. I stay," Maria said.

Harry saw that her jaw was set and knew the doctor was wasting his breath. He had seen that determined look too many times, all the way back to his childhood. He turned to the doctor. "It's no use arguing with her. Trust me."

Dr. Josephs studied the floor and nodded slowly. It was a situation he had faced before. "I'll want someone to stay with her . . . just in case he takes a turn for the worse."

"I'll stay with her." It was Patrolwoman Moore. She held Harry's eyes. "Jocko was a mentor to me, and a friend. I know you want to get to the scene. Let me do this for you."

Clearwater detectives were still canvassing the surrounding area when Harry and Vicky arrived at the marina. The lead detective was a sergeant named Max Abrams. He was a contemporary of Jocko's and knew Harry well. He was also a transplant from the New York City Police Department who had left that job after ten years of service and opted for warmer climes. He still carried the Brooklyn accent of his birth.

"Hey, kid, how's the old man doin'?" Abrams was a short, stocky man with receding salt-and-pepper hair, a wide nose, and large lips. He looked totally ineffectual until you noticed the steel in his hard gray eyes.

"He's out of surgery, still critical, but the doc thinks he'll make it," Harry said. He inclined his head toward Vicky. "This is my partner, Vicky Stanopolis."

Abrams nodded to her, then turned back to Harry. "It'll take more than two slugs in the back to take Jocko out. You have any idea what he was doin' down here?" He waved his hand, taking in the largely unoccupied marina.

"He was doing a favor for Joey O'Connell."

"What kind of favor?" Abrams asked.

"He was trying to locate Joey's daughter. Seems she joined up with the Scientologists, and Joey was worried they had some kind of hold on her. Supposedly she had told her parents she couldn't have any contact with them because they didn't belong to the church. Joey asked Jocko to find her, see what was going on, and try to get her to come home."

"You have any idea what brought him here specifically . . . to this marina?"

"Just one thing and I can't verify it." Harry glanced around the sparsely occupied marina. "The cop staying with my mom said the Scientologists were trying to buy this place, along with the abandoned school up on Osceola Avenue. That's the only connection I know of."

"You ever meet the daughter?"

"Once, but it was quite awhile ago. She was just a teenage kid. I met her at Joey's house but didn't pay much attention to her. She just sort of breezed through while I was there with Jocko. Her name is Mary Kate."

"I'm sure Joey could give us a picture of the kid," Abrams said. "I don't expect much cooperation from the Scientologists if she did hook up with them. They never cooperate with the cops unless it's in their interest. They just shut you down whenever you ask any questions about their church or anybody who belongs to it. You ask me, they're an overall pain in the ass." Abrams hesitated, and then looked Harry in the eye. "You plan on looking into this yourself . . . on your own time . . . kind of unofficial like?"

"I'm thinking about it. Will that be a problem for you, Max?"

"The department won't like it, but it won't bother me. Just do it quiet like and don't get me in trouble with my bosses. If you can do that I'll share what I get with you, and you do the same. Where do you want to start?"

"I'd like to talk to the boat owner who found Jocko."

Abrams inclined his chin toward two men farther down the dock. "He's talkin' to Jimmy Walker, my bright young partner." He grinned, turning the sarcasm into a joke. "Come with me and I'll introduce you."

Abrams led Harry and Vicky down the dock. When they were twenty feet away he called Walker over and introduced him. "Harry is Jocko Doyle's son," he explained. "He's also a homicide dick with the sheriff's office. He wants to look around a little bit, just to put his mind at rest, and I told him it would be okay."

Walker was tall and thin with a hooked nose and protruding Adam's apple. His brown hair was cut in a high and tight military buzz and Harry guessed it hadn't been long since he'd started on patrol.

"Fine with me," Walker said. His brown eyes narrowed. "But the captain ain't gonna like it, he finds out."

"You're right," Abrams said. "So we won't bother him about it. Understood?" He waited for Walker to nod agreement. "Any problem comes up, I'll take the heat." Abrams gestured toward the man Walker had been interviewing. "Whatshisname, he give you anything new?"

"His name's Edward Tyrell," Walker said. "He's a stockbroker and his story's pretty much what he told you. He had just brought his boat back in and was washing it down when he heard what sounded like two shots. So he goes to see what's up and he spots Jocko in the water hanging onto a ladder. He hauls him out and calls 911. End of story."

"Okay, you go back to the car and write up your report. Harry wants to thank this guy for saving his dad. I'll introduce him."

Harry grinned as he watched Walker head off. "Nice maneuver."

"Hey, what can I tell you? I only inherited the kid a week ago. Everything's a learning experience for him. Today he learned when to mind his own fucking business."

* * *

Edward Tyrell was a tall, trim, well-built man who clearly put in plenty of time at the gym. He had sandy brown hair, a straight nose, blue eyes that could only be described as vibrant, and very white, capped teeth. Vicky immediately dubbed him "the movie star" in her mind. Harry thought he looked too slick by half.

"Mr. Tyrell, we met earlier," Abrams began. "This is Detective Harry Doyle and his partner, Detective Vicky Stanopolis. The man you pulled out of the water, retired Sergeant Jocko Doyle, is Harry's father." He gave Tyrell a smile that lacked any warmth and Harry figured that Max didn't cotton to the man either. "Harry's got a couple of questions."

"Sure," Tyrell said, flashing a broad, very white smile. "Anything I can do to help."

"First, I want to thank you for pulling him out. I don't think he would have made it if you hadn't." Harry extended his hand.

"Happy to help." Tyrell took Harry's hand, squeezing it harder than necessary.

"So tell us how you happened on him."

Tyrell placed his hands on his hips and nodded down the dock. "I had just brought my boat in and was washing her down. She's the fifty-three-foot Hatteras yacht three slips down. Well, I was on the other side of the boat so I didn't see anything, but I did hear what sounded like two small explosions, sort of loud popping sounds. So I went to look. I thought some kids might be setting off fireworks and that's not too cool to do around boats, what with all the fuel on board. But there's no one there and as I'm walking back I hear this moaning and I look down and there's this guy hanging off a ladder. So I hauled him up."

"Did he say anything to you?" Vicky asked.

"He was out cold as soon as he hit the dock. That's when I saw he was bleeding and called it in to 911."

"Could you show me exactly where he was?" Harry asked.

Tyrell walked them to an empty slip where a finger dock jutted out into the water. A ladder ran down the side of the dock and now, at close to low tide, stopped just a foot above the water. At high tide the ladder would extend well into the water.

"How deep is it here?" Harry asked.

"At high tide it's about eighteen feet," Tyrell said. "At dead low you're talking about twelve to fourteen—still plenty, even for a large-keeled sailboat. It's a good marina for large boats."

"Have you heard anything about the Scientologists buying it?" Harry asked.

A veil seemed to fall over Tyrell's eyes, but he quickly pushed it away. "Not a word. If they do, I hope they let me keep my boat here." He forced another broad smile. "Like I said, it's a helluva marina for a big boat and great access to the gulf."

Harry walked to the edge of the slip Jocko had been pulled from and knelt, staring into the water. Almost a minute passed before he stood and turned back to Max Abrams.

"You need to get some divers out here, Max."

"Divers?"

"Yeah, and you need to do it now."

An hour later the divers brought up the body of Mary Kate O'Connell. They placed her on the dock, her pale, colorless face and faded blue eyes staring blindly at the men who stood in a semicircle above her. Harry knelt down next to her and listened but the words that came to him were garbled. He thought she looked grateful to finally be out of the water.

* * *

Harry Santos had died when he was ten years old, murdered by his mentally disturbed mother. He and his six-year-old brother, Jimmy, were drugged; then dragged into the garage of their home and left there with the engine running in the family car while their mother went off to her church. An alert neighbor heard the car and called the police. Two Tampa patrol cops broke into the garage and dragged the boys outside. Neither had a heartbeat and neither was breathing. CPR eventually brought Harry back, but it was too late for Jimmy, who was younger and smaller. When Harry's mother was sent to prison, he was placed in foster care with Jocko Doyle, a Clearwater police sergeant, and his Cuban-born wife, Maria. The couple adopted him a year later.

After graduating from the University of South Florida, Harry Santos Doyle joined the Pinellas County sheriff's office. Five years later, when he was promoted to homicide detective, the story of his boyhood death came out. Cops being cops, they quickly dubbed him "the dead detective," a moniker that took on an eerie connotation when they later learned that the dead seemed to speak to him.

Chapter Two

The room was lit by a solitary desk lamp which allowed the man seated behind the desk to lean back in his heavy executive chair and keep his face in shadow. It pleased him to do this, because he knew that those he spoke to from this vantage point were immediately disoriented and unable to gain control of the conversation. It was a carefully orchestrated setting. It was ten o'clock in the morning, but heavy curtains had been drawn across the windows, keeping a sun-filled Florida morning at bay.

The man leaned forward, bringing his sharp features into the light. "It seems you were unable to carry out a very simple, very straightforward task." His voice was low and steady, and his eyes made no attempt to hide his displeasure. "Would you say that assessment is . . . accurate, Edward?" he asked with contempt as he again receded into the shadows.

"There were unanticipated problems," Edward Tyrell said. "And the man you sent didn't react well to—"

"The man *I* sent? So this regrettable situation is my fault. Is that what you're telling me?"

"No, of course not. It's just—"

"It's just what? Just like the excuses you make when the investments we allow you to choose for us fail to earn the income you project." Tyrell started to speak but the man raised a hand that demanded silence. "This is more than a small financial failing, Edward. This could easily prove to be a disaster." He waved his hand, dismissing everything that had been said, and then leaned forward again, bringing himself into the small cone of light. "Tell me, Edward, what did you believe your task to be? What was it you were supposed to do for us?"

"The girl was supposed to be brought to my yacht and then taken out past the twelve-mile limit, where we were to rendezvous with the church's cruise ship, *Freewinds*."

"And what did you think would happen to her once she was aboard *Freewinds?*"

Tyrell twisted nervously. "I had no idea. It wasn't something I was told."

"Well, let me tell you then." The man inhaled and continued: "It had been determined that the girl was 1.1. We had ordered a disconnection, but her family was still reaching out for her. They had even gotten a retired police sergeant to search for her. Their intent was obvious, so we decided auditing was the best solution for the young woman and we wanted that auditing to be done somewhere where she could not be located until it was finished—ergo, *Freewinds*." He stared into Tyrell's face. "Auditing, Edward; not elimination. And we certainly never envisioned the elimination of the retired police sergeant who was trying to find her."

Edward quickly translated what he had been told. The girl was 1.1, a very dangerous and wicked level of spirituality for Scientology members: someone who perhaps engaged in casual sex, or even homosexual activity, or who had openly expressed opposition to church teachings. In this case the young woman had been ordered to separate from her family, i.e. *disconnection*, and was going to undergo *auditing*, or extensive spiritual counseling, aboard *Freewinds*, which was one of several seagoing vessels owned by the church.

"I didn't know any of that," Tyrell said. "Your man had just gotten her on board. She noticed the engines were running and asked why. When I told her we were going out on a short cruise she got nervous. Your man tried to calm her by explaining that we were going to rendezvous with a church-owned ship, but it had the opposite effect. She panicked and jumped back onto the dock. Your man was on her before she got very far, and the next thing I knew he was throwing her body into the water.

"Then he heard something and ran around the side of the vessel in the next slip and I saw what the problem was. A man was jogging down the dock, and even worse, he had a pistol in his hand. He ran to the place where the girl had gone into the water and knelt down to see if he could find her. That's when your man came out from the vessel he had hidden behind and shot him twice. Before I knew what had happened, two people appeared to be dead and the man you had sent was heading down the dock."

"And that's when you discovered the retired police officer was still alive and pulled him out of the water?"

"I had to. When I went to the slip where both bodies had been thrown in, he was there hanging onto a ladder. He stared at me, saw me. What else could I do?"

"And then you called 911."

"Yes. I had no choice. There were two other boat owners in the marina and I wasn't sure what they'd seen."

The man was silent for several moments. "Let us hope this retired police officer moves on to a new and better existence. Otherwise I fear we will have further problems."

"I'm afraid we already have those problems."

"Why is that?"

"The injured cop's son is a sheriff's department detective and he's investigating what happened to his father." Tyrell shifted his weight nervously. "I did a computer search on the son. He's a dangerous man."

"That's unfortunate. It's unfortunate for us and it's unfortunate for this dangerous detective. Give me all the information you have on him."

When the church offices opened for business the next morning, the man was still seated behind his desk, the room still darkened by the heavy curtains, the only light coming from the solitary desk lamp. The man's name was Regis Walsh and he was in charge of discipline for the Clearwater church and reported only to the church's national leader, who was based in California. Walsh, however, regarded himself as sole arbiter when it came to discipline and had not reported to the church's national leader, or to anyone else, in more than six months.

The door to the office opened and Kenneth Oppenheimer, Walsh's first assistant, slipped into the room. "So, we need someone close to this detective," Oppenheimer said.

"Like a second skin. I want to know his plans before he's even certain of them himself." Walsh handed Oppenheimer a thin file that summarized everything he knew about Harry Doyle.

Oppenheimer weighed it in his hand and frowned. "I better get busy. Fortunately we have some members who work in the sheriff's office."

Walsh raised his eyebrows and stood up behind his desk. He was tall, almost regally so, and slender. His brown hair formed a widow's peak and his blue eyes were piercing—together with his sharp nose this gave his face the look of a raptor. He had not known the sheriff's office had been infiltrated and this fact pleased him. But it was not surprising. A number of years back, when the Internal Revenue Service was giving the church fits, IRS files had suddenly disappeared, allegedly destroyed by church members who had been embedded in the IRS. The agency had eventually granted the church's request for tax-free status.

Walsh smiled at Oppenheimer. It made him look even more raptor-like and had an even more chilling effect. "Work your magic, Kenneth," he said.

Chapter Three

Harry returned to the hospital and found that his father's condition had improved. His mother was asleep on a waiting room sofa and someone had given her a blanket and pillow. Patrolwoman Moore was seated in a chair close by and she stood when Harry entered. "Jocko's better," she whispered, as she led Harry away from his sleeping mother. "He's still listed as critical but the nurse assigned to him told me he's been improving steadily. Your mom finally fell asleep after she heard that."

"He's a tough guy," Harry said. He looked back at his mother. "So is she."

"Did they come up with anything at the crime scene?" Moore asked.

"They found Mary Kate O'Connell's body. She was in the water, not far from where Jocko went in. We're guessing he was going after her when he was shot."

"This shooter's a piece of work," Moore said. "He shoots a retired police sergeant and drowns a retired cop's kid. That's putting a big bull's-eye on your back. Who's notifying Joey O'Connell?"

"Max Abrams. He and his partner, a guy named Walker, caught the case."

Moore nodded, indicating her approval.

"Thanks for staying with my mom," Harry said. "I can take it from here."

Moore took a business card from her pocket and wrote a number on the back. "That's my personal number. Don't hesitate to call if you need me."

"Thanks." Harry glanced at the card and saw that Moore used the initials M.J. as her first name. "What does M.J. stand for?"

Moore smiled. "Just M.J."

"Good enough," Harry said.

It was nine o'clock before Harry and his mother were allowed into the intensive care unit. Jocko Doyle lay in bed with tubes coming from every visible orifice. He was as pale as Harry had ever seen another human being, and had it not been for the heart and respiratory monitors he would have checked his father's pulse to make sure he was alive.

Slowly, Jocko's eyes opened and flitted between Harry and his wife. "I feel like crap," he growled around the tube that was taped at the corner of his mouth.

While his mother moved in to stroke Jocko's head, Harry smiled down at him. "That's what happens when you let somebody pump two bullets into your back. What happened to the idea of ducking? That's what you always told me to do."

"He snuck up on me." A faint smile toyed with Jocko's lips. "I must be getting old."

"I'm working the case with Clearwater PD thanks to Max Abrams. Can you tell me what the shooter looked like?"

Jocko nodded and Harry could tell the effort to talk was taking its toll. "He was a weird-looking guy, a very pale complexion; tall and wiry, but strong. He had snow-white hair, but he was no more than thirty, so the hair really stood out."

Harry spent the next half hour with Jocko, then left him in Maria's care and headed toward the marina where he kept his boat. Two months earlier he had sold his beach house to the builder who had been pestering him for years. The decision to sell had been forced by his birth mother's release from prison and—despite a condition that forbade her from coming within one hundred feet of him—her regular appearances at the end of his street and on the beach that bordered his house.

Complaints to the parole board were met with inaction—*The parolee in question has the right to use public streets, parks, beaches, and places of business,* they wrote in response to his complaint. Harry's solution was simple. He sold his small oceanfront house and bought a forty-eight-foot trawler—a boat large enough to serve as a comfortable home and one he could untie and move to a new marina whenever needed. It also left him with more than a million dollars in the bank and the security of knowing he could leave his job whenever he chose.

At present, the boat was docked at a small private marina just across from downtown Clearwater, only half a mile from his former home. The marina was fairly secure, due mostly to an extremely nosy dockmaster, who regularly paraded up and down the docks wearing a pith helmet and complaining about any minor infraction he found—a dripping water line, a gasoline container left on the dock, anything he could find from a long list of "violations" that the marina published and gave to each boat owner. Harry had heard other boat owners referring to him as "the dock Nazi." But he provided Harry with one definite advantage: he also questioned anyone on the docks who he did not recognize. The dock Nazi would be a welcome barrier to Harry's mentally disturbed mother when she eventually found him again.

Harry walked down the main dock to the Grand Banks trawler he had christened *Nevermore*, in a nod to his favorite author and an expression of his intent to escape the woman who had killed him and his younger brother Jimmy. The boat, now ten years old, had received tender care from the original and only previous owner. It had two staterooms and two heads, each with its own shower, a sizable galley with a three-quarter fridge, a full oven, sink, microwave, and even a hidden washer and dryer, located three steps down from a large salon furnished with a sofa, two reclining chairs, and a large-screen television set. It was every bit as roomy and comfortable as the small beach house he had sold. The sole difference, as far as Harry was concerned, was that instead of having a view of the ocean, he now floated on it.

After boarding, Harry went straight to the chart table and began writing down his notes on the case. As he was finishing, a voice floated in from the dock.

"Hey, boat guy, permission to come aboard?"

He turned and saw Vicky. "Permission granted. And it's not *boat guy*, it's *captain.*"

"Yeah, sure, Popeye, anything you say." Vicky stepped on board and came through the open hatch. "How's your dad?"

"He's still listed as critical, but he's going to make it. He's a tough old bird."

"And your mom?"

"She's a wreck, but now that she has him to fuss over, she'll be okay too."

Vicky looked around. It was her first time aboard the new trawler. "Pretty nice boat you've got here, detective." She walked aft, then back to the chart table. "I met this strange little guy on the dock. Said his name was Tully and that he ran the place. He was wearing a pith helmet and wanted to know where I was going. I flashed my shield, told him I was looking for Harry Doyle, and he pointed me in the right direction."

"That was the dock Nazi," Harry said. "At least that's what people here call him. His official title is dockmaster and he likes to find things to complain about. Now, with you flashing your tin, he probably thinks I'm a felon."

"He doesn't know you're a cop?"

"I never give out any more information than I have to."

Typical Harry Doyle; it brought a smile to her lips. "Well, you look like a felon, so he probably thought so anyway." Her smile widened. Vicky was wearing jeans that she filled out beautifully, a pale tan blouse under a lightweight green jacket, just long enough to conceal the Glock on her hip. "Anything new?" she asked.

"Jocko gave me a description of the shooter. Tall and skinny, about thirty with snow-white hair. Other than that, you know everything I know."

"I may have come across something."

"What's that?"

"It might be a good idea to check out Mary Kate O'Connell's sex life."

"Why is that?"

"I was thinking about her last night, about how and why she got tied up with Scientology, and I remembered this girl from my old neighborhood in Tarpon who got mixed up with this guy who was a church member. To make a long story short, she ended up joining too and was a member for a couple of years, then finally told her family that she couldn't see them anymore unless they joined her church. That did it for her family and they staged an intervention that included a Greek Orthodox priest—a big, burly, bearded one who accosted her on the street in downtown Clearwater, right in the middle of all the Scientology buildings . . . told her to get her little Greek tushie back home so her family could talk to her."

"And she went?"

"I take it you've never been confronted by a Greek priest. You bet she went, and once her family and that priest got through with her, she was home for good. All this happened a couple of months ago."

"Interesting story, but what's the point?"

"The point is, I went to see her and told her about Mary Kate. Turns out she knew her, or knew of her. She told me there was some talk going around that Ms. O'Connell had been accused of being gay."

"Accused, like in a crime?"

Vicky nodded. "In Scientology, at least according to this woman, gay people are labeled as 1.1. That means the church feels they've reached a dangerous level of spiritual corruption and need to be audited."

"What's that?" Harry asked.

"Well, according to what I've read online, it's some kind of spiritual counseling involving weeks of isolation and talks with church auditors or ministers who use some special tool called an E-meter to try to find and correct problems. Sometimes, in the most serious cases, it's supposedly done aboard one of the church's ships by a member of Sea Org, which is someone who has reached that special level in the church. It's like a religious order."

Harry let out a long breath. "I've got to read up on this church, find out what the hell I'm dealing with."

"Lucky you, they've got a bookstore downtown."

That evening Harry was well into the second of three Scientology books he had purchased when Vicky returned to the boat.

"You're going to love some of the tenets of this religion," he said as she stepped onto the boat.

"Tell me."

"Okay. First, did you know that mankind's problems began seventy-five million years ago when dinosaurs were still roaming the planet and Earth was known as the planet Teegeeack?"

"No, I guess I missed that in my high school history class."

"Well, according to our Scientology friends, man existed at that time and Earth, or Teegeeack, was part of a seventy-six-planet confederation ruled by a tyrant named Xenu. Much like today, the confederation faced a serious overpopulation problem with a lot of nonproductive people sucking up its resources." A small smile appeared. "Seems like Xenu solved the problem by trapping the *excess people* in a frozen compound made up of glycol and alcohol. The people were then transported to Earth, where they were placed at the base of some volcanoes." The smile widened. "Old Xenu must have been a Republican, because he had H-bombs, more powerful than any we have today, dropped into the volcanoes, killing these excess people and releasing their spirits, which they called *thetans*. Then they attached themselves to other humans. Later, when those humans died, they moved on to new human hosts and kept perpetuating themselves. Ergo life everlasting or something like that."

"And they get people to believe that?" Vicky asked.

"Not much stranger than the parting of the Red Sea, or a virgin birth, or angels versus devils, or Christ's ascension into heaven. I grew up believing all of that."

"Do you still?"

Harry grinned at her. "At least I question things now. Apparently, the true believers in Scientology accept their tenets, or at least give serious lip service to them."

"Who dreamed up all that stuff?"

"A science fiction writer named L. Ron Hubbard, the guy who founded the church. He was later rumored to have said that the easiest way to become rich was to found your own religion."

"I love it."

"Yeah, well, love this too. According to what I've read, today they're one of the richest and most powerful religions on earth . . . and the most secretive. And, if you cross them, you better watch your ass."

"I guess little Mary Kate missed that last part."

"She sure did," Harry said. "And so did my dad."

The next morning, Harry poured a cup of coffee and went up on deck to plan out his day. Across the floating dock a thirty-four-foot Morgan sailboat was maneuvering into the slip just opposite. The young woman at the helm clearly knew what she was doing as she guided the sailboat bow first into the slip.

Harry stepped off his boat, crossed the dock, and called for a line. The woman threw him one and he quickly secured it to a starboard-side cleat; then called for another. Again she threw one and he secured the port side.

"Thanks," she called over her shoulder, as she tied the stern lines.

"Happy to do it," Harry called back. Actually, it was a common courtesy expected among boaters who shared docking space at a marina.

He lingered, watching the woman as she expertly secured her vessel. She was perhaps five foot six, he noted, dressed in tan shorts and a pale blue T-shirt, both of which displayed a curvy yet trim figure. She had red hair and green eyes and her first words took him by surprise.

"You must be the cop." She smiled at the look on his face, which Harry thought probably made him look like a dumbstruck hick. "The dockmaster told me I'd be across from one. He seemed to consider it a selling point."

"Folks around here call him the dock Nazi."

She laughed at that. "Yeah, I can see why they might. He's a curious little guy. Asked me question after question." She smiled again, revealing very white teeth. "I'm Meg Adams."

"And I'm Harry. Harry Doyle."

"And you're a cop, like the dock Nazi said."

"Detective, sheriff's department," Harry replied.

"And you live aboard?"

"Yes."

"Me too."

Harry shook his head slightly and peered down the dock toward the dockmaster's office. "Did our beloved dock Nazi happen to give you any other information, like maybe my shirt size?"

She laughed lightly. "He probably would have if I'd asked for it."

"I wonder if it's you or if he's just a . . ."

"Nosy little twit," she said. Her smile widened. "It's probably a little of both. At least I hope so. I'd hate to think my feminine charms had nothing to do with it."

A boyish grin was Harry's only response. "Look, when you finish what you have to do, if a cup of coffee appeals, you know where to find me."

"Keep the coffee warm, I'll be finished up here in fifteen or twenty minutes."

Harry returned to his boat. It was ten o'clock, late enough to call his mother at the hospital. He checked the coffee to make sure it was still warm, then called the intensive care unit. After explaining he was Detective Doyle, Jocko's son, the nurse said she would get his mother. A minute later, Officer Moore came on the line.

"This is M.J. Your mom's asleep and I didn't want to wake her. I got the okay to come back and sit with Jocko and help your mom where I can."

"That's terrific. I can't tell you how much I appreciate that. How's Jocko?"

"They say he's holding his own; not out of danger yet, but heading in that direction. He looks a helluva lot better than he did yesterday."

"Jesus, that's good to hear. Please pass the word to your bosses about how much I appreciate you being there. It's a big help to my mom and it will give me more time to look for the son of a bitch who shot Jocko." Harry paused. "No, on second thought, maybe you better forget the last part. I don't want to put Max Abrams on the hot seat with the brass."

"Don't worry," M.J. said, "I learned a long time ago when to keep my mouth shut."

"Thanks. When my mom wakes up, tell her I'll be there later, and I promise I'll keep in touch with you and let you know how things are going on my end."

"If you need my help finding this creep, let me know."

"I will."

"Permission to come aboard," Meg Adams called out.

"Permission granted. The coffee's still hot."

Meg came through the starboard hatch, her red hair giving off a fiery flash as she moved from sunlight to interior shadow. She was still dressed in the clothes she had worn on arrival, the pale blue T-shirt and tan shorts that seemed to accent her every curve.

"How do you take your coffee?" Harry asked, as he placed a heavy mug next to the coffee pot.

"Black. I'm easy."

Harry poured a cup and took it to the chart table where his own cup waited. He motioned for her to take a seat and raised his cup. "Welcome, easy lady."

"Easy . . ." She drew the word out, playing with it, then added: "At least as far as coffee goes."

"It's a start," Harry said, trying to keep the banter alive, but Meg let him know the subject had run its course.

"Have you been here long?" she asked.

"Not long. Until you showed up I was the new guy on the dock."

"What brought you here?"

"I had a house about a quarter of a mile north off Mandalay Avenue. I thought I'd like to try living on a boat, so I sold the house, bought this"—he tapped his hand against the chart table—"and here I am."

"And you're pleased with your decision?"

"So far I am. And you, what made you decide to live aboard a boat?"

Meg hesitated, deciding, Harry thought, what she wanted to reveal and what she did not. She offered him a not-quite-regretful shrug. "A relationship that didn't work out," she said. "He kept the apartment and the furniture. I took the boat."

"A thirty-five-foot Morgan in exchange for some furniture. Sounds like a shrewd trade to me."

"He never liked the boat. We bought it because *I* wanted it. Poor guy, he got sea sick every time he came aboard. Even if we were tied up at the dock he'd get sick." She looked out the window at her boat. "But I loved it. And . . . the apartment was about to go condo and he wanted to buy in. It's a high-rise on Sand Key with a great view of the gulf, but you have to deal with an elevator every time you want to go down to the pool or the beach, which means you have to deal with other people whether you want to or not." She glanced at him to see if he understood what she was saying. "I just started to loathe that elevator and knew I didn't want to live that way." She smiled now. "Picky, huh?" She brushed back a lock of hair that had fallen across her forehead. "It also didn't help that my relationship with my guy friend had gone very, very flat. So I opted for the isolation and a boat. A boat gives you all the privacy you want. You see who you choose to see. People can't just wander around a marina's docks without eventually being challenged."

Harry nodded. *All true*, he thought, *unless you're being stalked by a crazy woman.*

Chapter Four

Regis Walsh stared up at the man who stood before him. The white hair he was used to seeing was gone now, replaced by a blond dye job that was obviously from a bottle.

"I sent you a directive to appear before me and explain your actions," Walsh said. "It took you a long time to respond, much too long."

"I thought it would be safer if I changed my appearance first." Tony Rolf raised a hand toward his head and then continued, "Too many people saw me. And even though they weren't close enough to see my face, I knew the white hair would give me away."

"Let's get to the point," Walsh snapped. "Why did you kill the girl?"

Rolf bristled at the question. Muscles in his neck bulged freakishly and then traveled down into his arms and hands. It was almost as though a switch had been thrown, sending a current through his body. Walsh cautioned himself to tread carefully with this man.

"I didn't kill her," Rolf said, his words coming out in a near growl. "I was waiting on Tyrell's boat so we could take her out to the *Freewinds* for auditing. When she saw me she freaked out and accused us of trying to kidnap her. Tyrell attempted to calm her, but she jumped off the boat and started running down the dock. I ran after her and grabbed her arm. She twisted away, lost her balance, and fell. Her head hit the dock hard and she rolled into the water. I started to go after her, when I saw a man running toward us. He had a gun in his hand, so I went to the nearest finger dock and ducked behind another boat for cover. When

I looked out he was reaching down into the water where she had gone in." Rolf stiffened and a hint of pride came into his voice. "He must have seen me out of the corner of his eye, or sensed me there behind him. He started to turn. The gun was still in his hand, so I shot him and he went in the water too." Rolf set his jaw in open defiance. "The man was shot in self-defense. The girl caused her own death trying to get away. She was 1.1. You told me so yourself. She was homosexual scum."

"We didn't know that. We only suspected it. We wanted her audited, not dead," Walsh replied. "And we certainly didn't want a retired Clearwater police sergeant shot. Why were you even carrying a gun?"

Rolf stared at him with a mixture of confusion and anger. His lank, wiry body had stiffened again. "I always carry a gun. Have you forgotten? Oppenheimer arranged for a permit that allows me to carry a concealed weapon. He said you wanted me to be armed."

Walsh's face reddened. "I wanted you to be *able* to carry one . . . *when necessary*."

"And wasn't it necessary this time?" Rolf demanded. "Think of what we'd be dealing with if that retired cop had rescued the girl and then had his buddies at headquarters arrest Tyrell and me. That disgusting lesbian would be down at police headquarters right now, telling them how Tyrell and I work for the church and how we were trying to kidnap her and take her out of the country. Think about that scenario."

Walsh glared at him, but kept his voice soft and low. "No, *you* think about this, just as you should have thought about it last night." He jabbed a finger at his desk. "Consider that she ran away and you let her go. Did you think we'd never find her again? She had no place to go except her father's house. Without us she had no job, no income, no anything. She had forsaken it all at our direction, and to prepare herself for a chance to join Sea Org. Her life was what we had made it. So . . . we could have found her whenever we wished, and knowing she was frightened, we could have done it in a much less intimidating way. Do you understand all of that?"

Rolf shuffled his feet, less certain of his position now. "But that retired cop would have had her . . ."

"And what would he have had? What would he have had except a hysterical young woman?"

"I don't know," Rolf conceded.

Walsh let out a weary breath. "All right, let's try again. The girl is dead. Now we have a new problem—namely, the retired cop's son. He's taken a leave of absence from his job at the sheriff's office to investigate his father's shooting and the girl's death. He is living in a marina only a quarter of a mile from where we sit. I have all the particulars about him, his boat, his finances, and his record as a cop. They call him 'the dead detective,' by the way, because he once died when he was a child. The details about that, along with everything else, are in this dossier." He handed a thick manila envelope across the desk. "Read it, learn it, and keep watch on this man. We will have others watching him as well."

Rolf took the dossier and turned to leave.

"One more thing: lose the gun. It can be used as evidence against you if the police get hold of it. And see Ken Oppenheimer before you leave. He has something for you that will make your task easier. And I hope you're not superstitious. Some of this dead detective's fellow cops claim he can communicate with the dead." He began to laugh, a rarity for him. His laughter followed Rolf out of the office.

Harry had just left the hospital. Max Abrams had been there with a police artist, who had guided his father through a drawing of the man who had shot him. When they finished, Jocko, though still weak, was certain they had a picture that looked reasonably like his white-haired assailant. He and Max both took photocopies of the drawing and headed for the center of the Scientology compound in downtown Clearwater.

Here, Scientologists of all ages bustled from building to building. Harry had seen them whenever he had business in the nearby courthouse, but he'd never paid much attention to them before; he had just smiled at them dressed in their "sailor suits," each one looking sincere and dedicated and always in a hurry to get somewhere. They had reminded him of the White Rabbit in *Alice in Wonderland*, racing along and telling everyone within earshot that he was "late for a very important date." The image always brought a smile to Harry's lips as he finished the rabbit's words in his mind: "No need to say hello, goodbye, I'm late, I'm late, I'm late."

Now he realized these people were much more. His recent reading had explained that Scientologists who wore the sailor attire were members of Sea Org and each of them, no matter what else they did in life, worked for the church, much like the nuns and brothers in the Catholic faith. Sea Org was as close to a religious order as Scientology had, and according to its leaders, once a member reached the level of Thetan III, he or she had a degree of spiritual understanding that exceeded both Jesus Christ and Buddha.

Harry explained it to Max Abrams.

"What about Moses?" Max asked.

"Not even in the ballpark," Harry said.

There was a sneer in Max's voice. "That's what *they* say. Did any of them ever talk to a burning bush?"

"I didn't see anything about that," Harry replied, fighting off a smile. "You'll have to ask them."

* * *

Max and Harry didn't have a court order to enter Scientology property, so they decided, for the time being, to question passersby on public sidewalks. At Max's suggestion Harry had attached his badge to his belt, so he could avoid verbally identifying himself as a detective working the case. Harry took up a position outside a Starbucks on Fort Harrison Avenue that was kitty-corner to Scientology's lone church in the area. Fort Harrison was the main drag that went through the sprawling structures that made up Scientology's primary buildings. Max located himself on the opposite side of the street.

Armed with the artist's sketch of the white-haired man, Harry approached anyone carrying a Scientology book, along with all those dressed in Sea Org attire. Most insisted they didn't have time to answer questions, validating his "I'm late, I'm late" image. Some stopped and looked at the sketch and asked if he was a police officer, then, when he said he was, hurried off. Others refused to talk to him at all. Out of the few who did, several said the sketch resembled a white-haired man they had seen around Scientology's main office building, but that they had no idea if he worked there or who he was. At last he hit on a young woman who said he might be a man she saw coming out of the office of church discipline; she said she remembered it because the office always seemed a bit "spooky" to her, and the white-haired man she saw coming out of it was "spooky-looking" as well.

When Harry told Max, they decided to move ahead immediately and question everyone who worked in the office of church discipline.

The receptionist in the lobby of the main office building was an attractive middle-aged woman wearing a modest business suit that still managed to show off her trim figure. The nameplate on her desk identified her as Lorraine Beck; the look behind her cool green eyes said she'd be a difficult lady to get past.

"I got this," Max said as they moved up to the reception desk. He opened his coat to make sure the shield hanging from his neck was clearly visible. He glanced back at Harry and saw his badge was still on his belt.

"I'm Detective Sergeant Max Abrams of the Clearwater Police Department and this is Detective Harry Doyle of the Pinellas County sheriff's office. We'd like to see the person in charge of the office of church discipline."

Lorraine smiled up at him. "Do you have an appointment?"

"No, we don't, but this is police business involving a murder we're investigating," Max said.

"Do you have some kind of court order?" Lorraine asked, still smiling. She had auburn hair that added to the effect of her green eyes and it made her look quite pretty for a woman of her age, Harry thought. She also looked like one tough broad. "I'm afraid the church is very insistent about things like court orders," she added.

Max tapped his badge. "This is an active murder investigation and our prime suspect was seen leaving that office. So this is all the court order I need. Now, you will tell me who is in charge of that office and tell me how to get there or I will place you under arrest for impeding a police investigation. Then I will handcuff you and call for a patrol car to take you to police headquarters where you will be booked, strip-searched, and placed in a holding cell. So which will it be, Lorraine, me and my partner on the elevator or you in the pokey?"

Lorraine's jaw dropped and she fumbled with the glasses that were lying unused on her desk. She put them on and took a sheet of paper from her desk that appeared to have a list of extension numbers on it, found the one she wanted, and dialed it. After a brief, hushed conversation she turned back to Max. "Someone will be right down to see you," she said, struggling to retain her composure.

Two minutes later the elevator doors opened and a slender man in his early thirties exited and walked over to Lorraine's desk. He was dressed in a tailored shirt and silk necktie and his short blond hair and suntan spoke of weekends on a sailboat, the perfect image of a yuppie, Harry thought, right down to the cell phone attached to his belt. He looked at Harry and Max, taking in their badges, then smiled at each of them in turn. "I understand we have a problem," he said. "My name is Jim Gleason and I'm in charge of problems." The man smiled at his little joke.

"You work in the office of church discipline?" Max asked.

"Public relations."

Max looked back at Lorraine. "That doesn't cut it, Lorraine. You better start getting your personal stuff together."

"Just a minute, officer . . ." Gleason started to say more but Max's raised hand cut him off.

"It's sergeant," Max snapped, "and Lorraine has received a lawful police directive and has refused to comply."

Gleason feigned outrage. "You can't be telling me that you're going to arrest a woman who's a mother and a grandmother, just because she's following church directives for her job." He raised his chin toward a nest of framed family photos on Lorraine's desk.

"I'll arrest Lorraine and anyone else who tries to impede a murder investigation," Max said. "That means you too, Mr. Gleason. Now let me put this simply: We have evidence that a man who matches the description of the murder suspect we are trying to apprehend was seen leaving the office of church discipline. We intend to speak to everyone in that office and *anyone* who tries to impede that effort is committing a crime and will be arrested *forthwith.* You got that Mr. Gleason?"

"Just a moment." Gleason turned his back, took out his cell phone, and took several steps away from the desk. He spoke briefly into the phone, then listened. When he finished the call he returned to the desk. "I just spoke to our legal office and was told to cooperate."

"And . . . ?" Max said.

"I will take you to the office immediately."

As they moved toward the elevator Max leaned in to Harry and whispered: "How'd you like that?"

"I especially liked the *forthwith,*" Harry whispered back.

As the elevator doors closed Harry saw Lorraine reaching for her phone. He nudged Max with his elbow. "The warning call is going out."

"Of course it is," Max said.

Gleason remained quiet. *Smart man,* Harry thought.

The elevator doors opened on the seventh floor and as they exited Gleason directed them to a set of double doors across the hall. "The office of church discipline occupies most of the floor," he said. "This is the executive wing. I think we should start here."

As they entered the office an attractive young secretary greeted them. "Mr. Walsh is expecting you," she said. "Please follow me." She led them to another set of double doors that were made of cherry and polished to a high gloss. She opened the door and stood aside.

The interior of the office was lit by a single lamp on an oversized desk, leaving most of the room dark. Max located a switch just inside the door and turned it on, flooding the room with light.

"I prefer to keep the room darker." The words came from the man behind the desk.

"I prefer to see who I'm talking to," Max said. "And who might be standing in the shadows."

"So be it. My name is Regis Walsh and, as you can see, there is no one standing in the shadows." He smiled. "And you gentlemen, I take it, are Detective Sergeant Max Abrams and Detective Harry Doyle." Walsh now stood behind the desk. "Welcome. How may I help you?"

Harry studied Walsh and found a tall, slender, imposing man with dark hair swept straight back from his forehead. He had piercing blue eyes and sharp features. He made Harry think of a bird of prey dressed in an expensively tailored gray suit. Standing behind his oversized cherry desk, he cut a figure of power and his eyes had not left Harry since they entered.

Now he turned them on Gleason. "Thank you, Jim. You can get back to your other duties. I'll take good care of these gentlemen." He turned his attention back to Harry and Max. "Please take a seat, gentlemen, and tell me how I can help you."

It was a far cry from the way they had been treated in the lobby and the change in attitude was so abrupt that Harry found himself momentarily confused. He glanced at Max. He, too, seemed somewhat nonplussed.

Max began by telling Walsh about Mary Kate O'Connell's death, allegedly at the hands of a young white-haired man. "We've been told the young woman was a member of your church," he concluded.

"Yes she was," Walsh said. "She was a struggling member."

"What do you mean by *struggling*?" Harry asked.

Walsh leaned back in his chair. "As I recall, she was having difficulty with her family. They were urging her to leave the church and return home." He raised both hands and let them fall back to his desk in a gesture of helplessness. "Unfortunately, this is not uncommon. Frankly,

I think we do a poor job in helping family members, who do not belong to the church themselves, understand the principles of our faith. There is simply too little outreach. In Ms. O'Connell's case I believe the difficulty was with her father."

"He's a retired Clearwater cop," Max said. "He went out on a disability riding a wheelchair."

"Yes, I know," Walsh said. "But I believe he was being helped by another retired Clearwater officer, who was trying to bring Ms. O'Connell, who was well past the age of consent, back to her childhood home."

"That would have been my father," Harry interjected. "He was shot twice in the back by this white-haired man as he was trying to rescue Ms. O'Connell. She had been knocked unconscious and thrown into the water by this man. My father witnessed the attack; saw her thrown into the water when she was unconscious. When he tried to rescue her he was shot from behind and left for dead."

"I'm sorry to hear that," Walsh said. "I take it he's still alive. What's his prognosis?"

"He's still critical, but he's going to make it." Harry paused and stared at Walsh. "He's under police guard at the hospital. We like to take care of our own."

"I'm pleased to hear he's improving."

"Let's get back to the white-haired man," Max said. "He'd be in his late twenties, early thirties, tall, wiry build. Another church member told us that a man matching that description was seen coming out of this office. Do you have a man working here who matches that description?"

"We do," Walsh said. "His name is Tony Rolf, but I'm afraid he's not here now. There was some trouble with his family—a mother who has become quite ill. He took a leave of absence to care for her."

"When was this?" Harry asked.

"Just the other day," Walsh said.

Harry and Max exchanged glances.

"Fits the time frame," Max said to Harry. He turned his attention back to Walsh. "This Rolf guy, what's his job here?"

"He helps locate church members who we're having trouble reaching."

"You mean he brings them in whether they want to come or not?" It was Harry this time.

"No, nothing like that." Walsh leaned forward, elbows on his desk; hands together, the index fingers forming a steeple. "He would be sent out to contact someone we had been unable to reach by phone, e-mail, or letter."

"Was he sent out to locate Mary Kate O'Connell?" Max asked.

"Not to my knowledge. But feel free to ask others in the department. They might know something I don't. I suggest you start with Ken Oppenheimer. He's my assistant and he basically runs day-to-day operations. His office is just down the hall."

Harry doubted that Oppenheimer would provide anything new. Despite Walsh's claims, he was certain nothing happened in this department that escaped his notice. "Do you have an address for Mr. Rolf's mother?" Harry asked.

Walsh offered a regretful shrug. "I do not. But again, feel free to ask others."

"Do you have Rolf's address?" Max asked.

"That I'm sure we can give you. I'll have my secretary look it up now." He picked up his phone and asked for the information. "We'll have it in just a moment," he said. Then Walsh peered at Harry. "You're the officer they call the dead detective, are you not?"

Harry gave him a hard, unwavering look. "You're well informed."

"It's something I always strive for. Is it true . . . that you can speak to the dead?"

The secretary entered the room, interrupting them, and handed Walsh a piece of paper. He rose from his chair and passed it to Max. "This is the address we have on file for Mr. Rolf. He may have moved and not informed us. That does happen from time to time."

Max and Harry started for the door. Halfway through it Harry turned back to Walsh. "Sometimes they speak to *me*," he said.

"What?" Walsh said.

"The answer to your last question," Harry said. "There are times when the dead speak to me."

When the elevator doors closed, Max turned to Harry. "Why'd you tell him that . . . about dead people talking to you?"

"He was trying to spook me out by letting me know how much he knew about me," Harry said. "I thought I'd return the favor."

They decided to put off questioning others in the church office and go directly to the address they had for their white-haired suspect, Tony Rolf. The address, which was only a few blocks away from the church compound, turned out to be a two-story house that was within walking distance of the marina where Mary Kate O'Connell had been murdered.

The landlady, who occupied the first floor, was a heavyset woman in her late fifties with a world-weary look in her eyes. She identified herself as Ruby Lee Dixon, and told them she owned the building. Max showed her his shield and asked if Tony Rolf lived there.

"Upstairs. But he ain't here now."

"Do you know where he is?"

"Don't have a clue," Ruby Lee said. "Came by early this morning and told me he'd be away for a while. Said he'd mail me next month's rent." She shifted her weight and put a hand on her hip. "Long as I get the rent, I don't care where he goes or for how long. It's his apartment until the rent stops comin' in." She paused. "He in trouble with the cops?"

"Not that we know of," Max said. "We think he might have witnessed a crime. It's kind of important that we talk to him."

"Can we take a look at his apartment?" Harry asked. "There might be something there that'll tell us where he is."

Two cats eyed him suspiciously from two corners of the room.

Ruby Lee also seemed uncertain. "Well, I don't know," she said. "It's his place, after all—when the rent's paid, that is." She paused again as if arguing with herself.

One of the cats approached Harry purring loudly. Ruby Lee watched it as if it were some type of omen. Harry bent down and scratched the cat's neck. The second cat came to him to get some of the same.

Harry looked up at Ruby Lee. "You can come up with us, make sure we don't take anything."

Ruby Lee continued her internal argument. Finally she said: "Well, I suppose it'll be alright. My cats seem to trust you. Shoot, if you can't trust your local police, who can you trust? The entrance is around back. Let me show you."

She led them through the first floor and into the kitchen, where she took a key from a drawer and then continued out to a rear porch, where wooden stairs led up to the second floor. She handed Harry the key. "Them stairs is too much for me. You go ahead."

When they entered the three-room apartment both men stopped and took in the small living room, then moved on to the single bedroom, the eat-in kitchen, and the bathroom. Each room was more immaculate than the one before it.

"I've never seen a bachelor pad this fucking clean," Max said. "I bet you couldn't pull a single print off anything in this place."

Harry looked carefully at each room as they worked their way back to the living room and wondered if that was the reason for such cleanliness, or if Tony Rolf was simply a neat freak who chose to live this way. He thought of his boat and the house he had lived in over the previous five years. Clean, yes; immaculate, far from it.

"Let's toss the place, just in case," Max said. "I'll start at the back with the bedroom and bath. You start here in the living room and we'll meet up in the kitchen. Be thorough, but let's not make it obvious the place was searched."

"You got it."

Harry started with a small desk in a corner of the living room. There was a stack of blank paper on the desktop, a pen, but no computer. Harry searched the desk drawers where he found two Scientology texts, one appearing to be a bible of sorts, the other dealing with unacceptable behaviors. He leafed through the latter and found several dog-eared pages dealing with homosexuality. According to the book, Scientologists considered homosexual contact of any sort the most aberrant of behaviors, one that called for intense and long-term auditing, a form of counseling that involved confessing one's missteps. If auditing was successful, meaning that the church member banned homosexuality from his or her life, a return to normal church activities was permitted. If auditing failed, the member would be banned from the church for the remainder of his or her life.

He picked up the bible-like book and opened the cover. Inside he found a manila envelope that held half a dozen eight-by-ten photos that appeared to have been taken without the subject's knowledge. Harry flipped through them. They were all the same person: Mary Kate O'Connell.

Harry left the photos on the desk and started on the rest of the room. There was little to search, a handful of books, all written by L. Ron Hubbard, including a heavily underlined copy of *Dianetics*, which detailed the principles and practices followed by Scientologists.

Max gave Harry a thumbs-down gesture as he returned to the living room, indicating he had found nothing of value. Harry pointed to the pictures on the desk.

"They were tucked away in a Scientology bible that was in the desk," he said. "It ties our boy directly to the murder victim."

Max flipped through the photos and his face broke into a smile. "It sure as hell does. I'll get a subpoena to seize them, along with anything else that looks even vaguely suspicious."

Harry left Max to handle the subpoena and returned to the hospital, where he found his father out of intensive care and relocated to a private room. M.J. Moore was seated in a corner and she raised her finger to her lips.

"He just fell asleep," she whispered. "Your mom left a few minutes ago."

"How is he?" Harry asked.

"The way he's terrorizing the nurses, I'd say he's in peak form."

"I'm not terrorizing anybody," Jocko said with a raspy croak. "And I'm not asleep. I was just faking it so Maria would go home." He turned his head toward Harry. "So, did you find this back-shooting, white-haired creep yet?"

"Max Abrams and I just finished tossing his apartment. We found some candid photos of Mary Kate tucked away in a Scientology bible. Max is going to name him as a person of interest and see if that shakes anything out of the Scientology tree."

"You confirmed that he's a member." Jocko spoke the word as fact, not a question.

"Even better," Harry said. "He works for the office of church discipline."

"What the hell is that and who do they discipline?"

"Whatever and whomever they want to," M.J. offered. "I've had to deal with them a half-dozen times. They're a law unto themselves and no other law applies. At least that was my experience."

"So what leads do you have that'll help you track down this son of a bitch?" Jocko asked, his voice painfully weak.

"Only that he left to take care of a sick mother. So far nobody seems to know where the sick mother lives."

"If he's a Scientologist they know where every member of his family lives, who they work for, and what they had for dinner last night," M.J. said. "That's an exaggeration, but only a slight one."

Harry put his hand on his father's shoulder. "Here's what I need you to do. When you feel up to it, I want you to close your eyes and try to picture this guy; concentrate as hard as you can on his physical appearance. You gave us good information the first time around, but we need anything else you can come up with—scars, tattoos, anything at all. I'm assuming he's done something about his hair—dyed it, shaved it off—he'd have to be pretty stupid to leave it as it is. So think about him, try to visualize him, see if you can come up with something new."

"I'll try. I'm just so damn tired."

Harry lightly squeezed his shoulder. "Just rest for now; you can try later when you feel stronger."

It was five o'clock when Harry got back to the marina. As he walked down the dock he realized for the first time what a beautiful day it was. Clear cobalt skies stretched out into the Gulf of Mexico, which lay in a flat calm disturbed only by the wakes of passing boats.

That's where you should be, Harry told himself. *You should take the boat out, run it into deep water, drop anchor, and watch the sunset; let it heal your mind.* He drew a long breath. *Yeah, play it smart. Don't let everything that's happened eat you up. You're going to need a clear mind to solve this thing, a clear mind to stand up to the powerful people who are going to be working against you.*

As Harry approached his boat, Meg Adams came up on the deck of her sailboat. She watched him move down the dock and smiled. She was dressed in tan shorts and a blue denim shirt tied off at her midriff, revealing a narrow, well-tanned waist.

"I'm about to cook dinner. You interested?"

"I am if you can cook it on my boat."

She tilted her head to one side, questioning what he had just said.

"I'm going to take the boat out; anchor a few miles off shore and watch the sunset. Are you up for that?"

"Help me carry the food over," she responded.

An hour later Harry dropped anchor two miles west of Anclote Key. While Harry made sure the anchor was set, Meg went below to the galley to get dinner started. Harry joined her once the boat was secured and was greeted with an approving nod.

"Very impressive for a bachelor," she said. "The galley is well equipped, orderly, and surprisingly clean."

"You expected some roach-infested hellhole?"

"Let's just say I've seen a few bachelor kitchens."

"You've obviously dated the wrong kind of bachelor."

"Obviously."

"Now what can I do to help with the cooking?"

"You cook too?" she said mischievously.

"You're going to find out that I have a myriad of talents."

"And a good vocabulary too." She started to laugh. "I don't need any help at all. It's going to be a simple meal, fettuccine Alfredo with sautéed shrimp." She paused. "But you *can* open the wine. I noticed you have a lovely pinot grigio chilling in the fridge. That will do very nicely. And I wouldn't mind a glass while I cook."

They ate at the small dining table in the boat's lounge and then took the remaining wine up on deck to await the sunset.

"This is what life should be about—floating on the water on a comfortable boat, sipping a glass of wine, and waiting for the sun to set. Now there's a pretty simplistic concept, one that challenges any approach to the real world." She turned to look at Harry and added, "But who needs the real world?"

"I'm afraid *I* do," Harry said. "It's what I'm paid to do."

"And did you earn your pay today?"

"Yes, I did."

"How so?"

"I found out where the killer of a young woman lives, where he works, and what he looks like. He's hiding out now. But before long I'll find him. That's the real world of Harry Doyle."

"Well, I hope you succeed. Life is much more agreeable when the monsters that kill people are locked away." She raised her arm and pointed toward the horizon. "There goes the sun."

They were quiet as they watched the sun seemingly slip into the gulf, leaving an orange-red glow in its wake.

"My mother told me that I cried when I saw my first sunset. She said I thought it had fallen into the ocean and would never be back again."

"Where was that?" Harry asked.

"Carmel, a little town in Northern California. It's where I grew up."

"I've been there," Harry said. "Not for any length of time; just passing through. It's the town where Clint Eastwood was mayor for a short while, right?"

"He was indeed, for one two-year term, from 1986 to 1988. I was three when he gave it up and went back to films," Meg said.

So you're twenty-nine, Harry thought. About the same age as Vicky Stanopolis, who grew up on the water in Tarpon Springs, a small fishing village dominated by Greek sponge divers. It was a far cry from Carmel, which was one of the most affluent areas of Northern California.

"Is your family wealthy?" he asked. "Everyone I met in Carmel seemed to be."

"Afraid so. My dad was in the computer industry when it took off. He owned a piece of the company, so he was set for life. Then he went into the security business and that took off as well. He passed away when I was in college at Stanford. His will made sure his wife and only child were well provided for."

"So you don't have to work."

Meg shook her head. "Sometimes I feel guilty about it. But the feeling passes quickly."

Harry laughed, amused not so much about what she said, but how she said it. He found himself attracted to Meg. He was also very attracted to Vicky, but that was something he would never really admit to himself, and certainly not to her. She was his partner and off-limits.

The glow in the sky had begun to fade and Harry decided it was time to return. "Let's head in," he said.

"Let's clean up the galley first."

Harry agreed and they got to work in the galley. It was an easy cleanup—Meg washed and Harry dried.

When they finished Meg turned to him. "God, it feels like we're an old married couple."

The galley was small, close quarters for two people. Meg raised herself up on her toes and slipped her arms around his neck. "Are you ever going to make a pass at me?" Her voice had a huskiness to it that immediately aroused him. He had been living like a monk for several months, ever since the woman he'd been seeing moved back north, back to her abusive former boyfriend. *You're never here,* she had said. *And even when you are, you're not.*

Harry looked down into Meg's face. "I guess I am going to make a pass. But I'm warning you right now, cops make bad boyfriends."

"If you are, then I'll just throw you out." She raised her lips to his and within seconds they were going at each other with an unbridled passion that surprised both of them, pulling off clothing as they moved down a passageway toward the main stateroom.

They were naked when they reached Harry's bed and he laid her on it and began moving his lips slowly along her body.

She reached down and cupped his face between her hands. "Do that the next time. Right now I need you inside me . . . Please, please, please," she whispered.

An hour later they lay next to each other, exhausted but finally satiated. They had made love a second time more slowly, then a third. Meg had been as eager and hungry a lover as Harry had been himself.

Too long between drinks for both of us, Harry told himself.

"I don't know if I have the energy to take the boat in," he said.

"Good." She pressed up against him. "Let the sun wake us and we'll go in then."

"Sounds like a plan."

Chapter Five

Regis Walsh looked across his desk at his assistant, Ken Oppenheimer. It was seven a.m., the time of their regular morning meeting. "So where are we with our dead detective?" he asked.

Oppenheimer smiled. Like Walsh he was a tall man, but he was far from the lean, fit man he had been when Walsh had hired him ten years ago. He ran a hand through his thinning sandy-brown hair. "Rolf is working at the marina where our friend keeps his boat. He's well disguised now, so I doubt our once-dead detective will be able to pick him out. And as you know, we have others watching him as well."

"How did you arrange the job at the marina?" Walsh asked.

Oppenheimer's smile widened. He knew Walsh would appreciate what he was about to tell him. "The dockmaster proved easily bribable. I told him I worked for an organization that was negotiating to buy the marina and we had decided we would like him to stay on. I suggested that he hire Rolf as an assistant, but there was no need to pay him, since he worked for us. I'm sure once Rolf is on the payroll his salary will find its way into the dockmaster's pocket each week. Do you know what the people who keep their boats at the marina call him?"

Walsh shook his head.

"They call him the *dock Nazi.* He's little more than a joke to everyone who rents slips there. Mostly he parades around in a pith helmet and flip-flops looking for things to complain about. He's so easy to corrupt it's almost laughable."

"And perfect for our needs," Walsh said. "I think our detective friend would be quite mortified if he knew how easily we've put the man he's searching for right next to him."

"I'm glad you're pleased," Oppenheimer said.

"Can you reach Rolf easily?"

"Yes, he has one of the cell phones I keep in my name. I told him to throw his away and only use the one I gave him. I also told him that he was not permitted to give the number to anyone."

"Give me the number. I want him to meet with me late tonight. I'll call him myself."

Oppenheimer wrote the number on the back of a business card and handed it to Walsh.

Harry brought the boat into its slip at seven a.m. He had awakened just before dawn, thrown on a pair of shorts and a T-shirt, raised the anchor, and headed in, leaving Meg asleep in his bed. Traffic had just started to form its regular morning madness on the Clearwater Memorial Causeway as he tied the boat up and went down into the galley. The clothing they had left scattered on the floor had been picked up, telling him that Meg was probably showering in one of the two heads. He checked which one she was in, then went to the other to shave and shower.

When he came out, wrapped in a towel, he found her in the galley cooking bacon. She raised her chin toward the Keurig coffee maker. "I just put on a cup of French Market for you so grab whatever you put in it."

Harry squeezed by her, kissing her on the back of the neck. "Thanks for making breakfast."

"I figured I owed it to you. Just consider it a display of gratitude for the way you rocked my socks last night."

"You rocked a few socks yourself."

"I sure hope so." Meg turned, rose up on her toes, and kissed him softly on the lips. "I want you to come back for more." He reached around her and started to pull her toward him but she spun quickly away. "But not now or I'll burn the bacon."

"God forbid," Harry said. "I hate overly crisp bacon."

Tony Rolf squatted next to an electrical box on an empty slip. The slip was located on a pier with a clear view of Harry's boat. Rolf watched as Harry and a woman came out of the main cabin, climbed down, and stood talking on the dock. He had watched Harry bring the boat in early that morning. He and the woman had clearly spent the night out on the water. He studied the woman closely, studied the way she dressed. Her clothing was clearly provocative—short shorts that barely covered her, a shirt tied at the midriff obviously intended to show off her bust. Of course the detective had probably seen her naked. The slut wouldn't have missed the opportunity for that.

The woman boarded her sailboat and climbed into its main hatch, as the detective headed down the dock toward the parking lot. He decided to follow the detective, see where his investigation was taking him. He cautioned himself to do it slowly, carefully, to make sure he wasn't seen. It would be better to lose him than have his eagerness give himself away. He knew Regis Walsh would never forgive him if he blew his cover and lost the chance to continue spying on the detective. No, he had learned long ago that Regis Walsh was not the forgiving type.

When Harry reached the parking lot he found his partner Vicky Stanopolis leaning against his car.

"Hi, sailor," she said.

"Why didn't you come down to the boat?" he asked.

"I did. But I heard voices and since one of them was obviously a woman I decided not to interrupt . . . Harry Doyle, you're blushing."

"I am not," he snapped. "I got a lot of sun yesterday."

She started to laugh, partly because of how guilty he looked, partly to hide the jealousy she could feel growing inside her. She pushed it away. "You said we had a busy day today."

"We do. To start with, the Clearwater PD's sending another police artist to work with my dad. I want to check in on that."

"I thought they already did that."

"They did, but he was still so groggy they want him to take another shot at the guy's facial features. Then, as long as I've got you here, I'd like to meet this woman you know, the one who told you that some Scientologists had accused Mary Kate of being gay."

"Her name is Lilly Mikinos and finding her shouldn't be a problem," Vicky said. "She works in her parents' shop on the Sponge Docks."

"Are you sure she'll be there?"

"You really don't understand Greeks. Unless there's been a death in the family, they'll all be there trying to squeeze a few more bucks out of their business."

The police artist seated next to Jocko's bed was halfway through his sketch when Harry and Vicky arrived. Jocko, appearing more animated than at any time since he'd been shot, had regained most of his color and was eagerly responding to the artist's questions. It told Harry he would soon be demanding to be sent home.

"Hey, Pops, you look good," Harry said.

"You do," Vicky echoed. She bent down and kissed his forehead.

"Yeah, for a dumb ex-cop who forgot how to duck," Jocko rasped.

"Now I know you're truly on the mend," Harry said.

"How's that?" Jocko asked.

"Your cranky disposition is back. I'm gonna call Mama and tell her to get over here to keep the nurses safe."

"Tell her to bring my cigarettes," Jocko said.

Harry shook his head and laughed, then turned to the police artist. "How's the sketch of the perp coming?"

"We're getting there—"

"I don't like it," Jocko interrupted. "It doesn't look anything like the guy."

"It will. It just takes time." The artist extended a hand to Harry. "I'm Jeremy Jeffords. I work out of forensics."

"Harry Doyle, the son of this tough old billy goat and also a detective with the sheriff's office."

"Yeah, Max Abrams told me about you."

"Can I see what you've got so far?" Harry asked.

Jeffords handed over his sketch pad. Harry stared at it, studied the drawing of the man's face—the long narrow jaw and nose, eyes that were close set, a mouth that seemed to hold a hidden sneer. "Not a very pleasant-looking guy, but definitely somebody who might shoot you in the back." He passed the sketch to Vicky. "This is my partner, Vicky Stanopolis," he explained.

"Yeah, but it doesn't look like the guy who shot *me*," Jocko insisted. "I liked the first sketch better."

"We'll get there," Jeffords replied. "Just take it slow and easy like your doctor said."

"We're going to move along," Harry said. He turned to Jocko. "Did you come up with anything else about this guy?"

"I remember a tattoo, but I can't remember where it was on his body. It was a knife, a stilleto. I think it was on his forearm but I can't remember for sure. It's drivin' me nuts."

"Don't worry about it," Harry said. "What you gave me is terrific. Just relax and let whatever else there is come to you."

"Yeah, yeah," Jocko said.

Harry leaned over and kissed him on the forehead. "I'll talk to you later." He turned back to Jeffords. "Don't work him too hard."

They drove north eight miles to Tarpon Springs. When Harry was a child his mother had brought him and his brother here. Back then, a quarter of a century ago, the road from Clearwater to Tarpon Springs weaved through seemingly endless orange groves and horse farms. Now it was bordered by one walled housing development after another and rush-hour traffic clogged every road, including Route 19 that had been widened to four lanes to accommodate all the new housing. Needless to say, all the horses and orange trees had fallen victim to this version of progress along with the bulging bank accounts of fat-cat developers. But Harry knew that blaming the developers was only the easiest answer. A fishing boat captain he knew said air-conditioning was the true villain. It allowed people to live in subtropical climates year round, rather than just the winter months. Air-conditioned homes, air-conditioned cars: it made paradise available to all.

Harry thought back to what he had learned over the years about Tarpon Springs. In 1876 this small coastal area with numerous bayous flowing into the Gulf of Mexico began to attract wealthy Northerners in search of winter homes. These newly arrived residents spotted tarpon jumping out of the waters and named it Tarpon Springs. At the turn of the new century sponge beds were discovered off the coast of Tarpon

Springs and a local entrepreneur, John Cocoris, recognized its potential as a major sponge-harvesting area. Cocoris promptly recruited sponge divers from his native Dodecanese Islands in Greece and by the 1930s this new industry was generating millions of dollars a year.

Today, even with the sponge industry greatly diminished, the "Sponge Docks" remained the focal point of Tarpon Springs, a place where boats still unloaded the remaining sponges to professional buyers, and Greek-owned shops and restaurants catered to a continuing stream of tourists.

"Where is the shop we're going to?" Harry asked, as they turned onto Dodecanese Avenue.

"It's almost directly across the street from the Sponge Docks," Vicky said.

Harry drove past the shops and restaurants that lined both sides of the avenue until he reached the Sponge Docks and its row of gaily painted sponge-diving boats with their strings of freshly cleaned sponges hanging from bow to stern. He pulled to a stop next to a bronze statue of a sponge diver, his massive brass hard hat held heroically in the crook of his arm. Parking wasn't permitted on that stretch of road, so Harry flipped down his visor to display an *Official Sheriff's Business* card. "Let's go find Lilly Mikinos," he said, as he slid out of the car.

Vicky led him across the street and into a shop offering a plethora of clothing and baubles and seashells and sponges and what all, each item identified as coming from *Tarpon Springs, the Sponge-Diving Capital of the World.*

They found Lilly at the rear of the store unpacking a new delivery of T-shirts, each bearing the name *Tarpon Springs* with a diving helmet below and the word *Spongers* beneath that.

Vicky greeted Lilly in Greek, jabbered away for a few moments, then turned to Harry and switched to English. "This is my partner, Harry Doyle," she said.

Lilly looked Harry over and smiled, then spoke to Vicky in Greek. Whatever she said brought a faint blush to Vicky's cheeks.

Vicky quickly changed the subject, switching back to English and bringing up Mary Kate O'Connell's death.

"I read about it in the paper," Lilly said in English. "So sad, but then her whole life was sad."

"Why do you say that?" Harry asked.

Lilly looked around and called to a woman on the other side of the store. "Mama, I'm going outside to take a short break." The woman waived her hand dismissively and Lilly turned back to Harry and Vicky. "Let's go across the street to the docks. This place is going to fill up with customers before you know it."

They followed Lilly across the street. She appeared to be in her mid to late twenties, close to Vicky's age. She was a small woman, barely an inch or two above five feet, with a slender figure and large brown eyes beneath wavy black hair. She had a long, slender nose and a wide mouth, and she was dressed in tight tan jeans and a loose-fitting white T-shirt emblazoned with a large red heart.

They stopped near one of the sponge boats tied up to the seawall. Two young men were working on the deck, checking out a compressor that would send air into the diver's helmet by way of a heavy rubber hose. Harry noticed that they also took the time to check out Vicky and Lilly.

"So, tell me why you feel Mary Kate's life was so sad," Harry said.

Lilly didn't hesitate; it was as though she had been waiting for someone to ask her that very question. "People who come to Scientology are desperately seeking answers," she began. "And most have been seeking those answers for years. But it doesn't matter what the questions are, Scientology promises that you will find the answers if you follow what they teach."

"*Do* people find the answers they're looking for?" Harry asked.

"The church tells them they have. I just don't know if they do or not; if I did or not. But I do know there are rules, strict rules that you have to follow. And there are taboos that are simply not permitted."

"Like homosexuality?" Harry asked.

Lilly nodded. "Yes, that's a biggie for them. If you're suspected of homosexual behavior you're labeled as 1.1. You can also find yourself labeled 1.1 if you're involved in casual heterosexual sex, or if you refuse to disconnect with your family."

"Does everyone have to disconnect from their family?" Harry asked.

Lilly thought for a moment. "Eventually, yes, unless the family follows their child into the church. You see, the religion is for believers only, and if you're a believer you don't associate very much with anyone but other believers, not on a personal level. Oh, you can work with nonbelievers, if necessary. But you don't socialize with them too much; you never talk about church matters with them, unless you think they can be converted. And in those cases, you bring in help from the church."

"Was Mary Kate considered to be 1.1?" Vicky asked.

"I think so, and I think it might have been justified." The words seemed to offend her as she spoke them. "Justifiable for them," she added. "Based on what they believe."

"Did you think Mary Kate was gay?" Vicky asked.

"I suspected that she was, yes."

"Did she come on to you?" Harry asked. It was the question everyone had been circling around.

"I think so. Oh God, who knows? It was nothing terribly overt. But it was a definite feeling I got. Maybe it was because I knew other people who thought she was gay. I mean she was so goddamn needy. She seemed to want to be close to everyone, to be protected by everyone." She folded her arms across her chest, creating a barrier. "You do know that everyone in Scientology is watched, right?"

"I've read about people being watched after they leave the church," Harry said. "Cars supposedly parked near their homes that follow them wherever they go; same for people who write about the church, or simply go around asking too many questions."

"Yes, there's that," Lilly said. "But the people inside the church are also watched. There's a whole department that keeps track of us."

"The office of church discipline," Harry said.

"That's right. When I left the church and came home there were people all over the Sponge Docks keeping track of me. Then I'd see them parked near my house. It was pretty scary being watched like that."

"No one spoke to you?" Harry asked.

"Just one time. A woman entered the shop and asked if I was coming back to the church. That's the way she said it: *coming back to the church*, as if I had defected or something. You see, they don't let go very easily."

"Do you still see them? Up here, I mean."

"Every so often I see someone who looks familiar." Lilly shrugged. "But Tarpon is a popular place for tourists, so who knows?"

"Was Mary Kate being watched?" Harry asked.

"Oh yes. And she knew it was happening. She said there was a scary-looking guy with white hair and very pale skin who watched everything she did and it really scared her. I knew who she was talking about. We used to call him 'the albino,' and whenever he was around everyone seemed nervous."

* * *

Tourist activity had increased and Tony Rolf used it to get closer to the three people he was watching. He stepped inside the Hellas Bakery, bought himself a pastry, and took a table near the front window.

He knew both women Doyle was talking to—he had seen the detective's partner on other occasions. Like Doyle, she did little to conceal the large automatic pistol she wore on her hip, leaving no doubt that she was a cop. The other woman had taken a bit longer to place. Then he remembered the great stir she had caused when some bearded Greek priest dressed in a cassock had approached her on the street right in the heart of the church's Clearwater compound and demanded she return to her parents' home. *And she had gone with him.* In an act of open betrayal she had walked away from the church.

Now what was she up to? They were undoubtedly talking to her about the woman he had been forced to kill. Had she been one of her lovers? Did she know something about him? Since she had been a member of the church it was quite possible that she knew he worked for the office of church discipline, as many members did. She might even have known from the woman herself that he had been assigned to her case. But she couldn't have known that he was assigned to take her out to the cruise ship *Freewinds* for auditing. Even the O'Connell woman hadn't known that until just before she died. But what *did* this Greek woman know, especially about him? And what was she telling these two cops?

He knew he had to find out, and he had to do it quickly.

He waited until the shops began to close, then took a position near a small gyro shop at one end of the Sponge Docks. From there he could drink a soda and watch the front of the Mikinos store from which Lilly should soon emerge. He had already checked the rear of the shop for a car but found none. He had called his office and learned that the home address they had for Lilly was only a few blocks away on Athens Street. She would be walking, unless someone picked her up, and if so she should be turning onto Athens Street minutes after she left the family shop. He only hoped she would be alone.

Chapter Six

It was nine twenty before Lilly left the shop. Two older women had left before her, apparently leaving Lilly to close up for the night. Tony Rolf had moved across the street and positioned himself to the right of the door as if studying items in the window display. When Lilly stepped out and turned to lock the door he rushed up behind her, placed one hand over her mouth, and used his body to push her back into the store.

She spun out of his grasp and turned to face him. A look of fury filled her face, which quickly turned to confusion and then to fear.

"You remember me?" he hissed.

Lilly looked at his hair. It was blond now and it had initially confused her. She had thought at first that the assault was a simple robbery attempt and she had been ready to fight him off, or at least to try.

"I asked if you remember me."

"I remember you. You're from the church. You're the one we used to call the albino."

"What were you telling those cops today? Did you tell them something about me?"

"I don't know anything about you."

"I think I spoke to you once. I think I asked you about that dyke Mary Kate. Did you tell them that?"

Anger flared over the slur, but Lilly fought to control herself. "That's all I knew about you. That you asked about Mary Kate, and that other church members thought you were creepy."

"But they didn't feel that dyke was creepy, did they?"

Lilly felt another flash of anger, a rush of adrenaline that momentarily overcame her fear. "How do you know she was a dyke? Or did you just decide she was because she turned you down?"

Rolf's eyes widened and color came to his pale complexion. "Are you suggesting I tried to initiate something sexual with her? Are you implying that I'm 1.1?" He moved forward, using his body to push her back until she was pressed against a display case.

Lilly's mind raced with possibilities for escape. Without warning she drove a knee into his groin. It wasn't a solid hit, but it was enough to move him back, and she spun away and raced to the back of the store where her family kept a baseball bat to use against would-be robbers. She heard a loud growl and looked back over her shoulder. Rolf was moving toward her, his eyes wild, and she saw the flash of a knife in his hand.

She reached the storage room where the bat was kept and grabbed it, swinging it as she turned to face him. The first blow hit his arm and he howled in pain and she raised the bat again. He lunged at her and she felt a sharp blow to her stomach, then another to her chest.

Rolf stopped and watched her.

Lilly looked down at her shirt and saw dark stains spreading out from her stomach and chest. Confusion came to her face and she looked up at Rolf as if he might tell her what was wrong. "What have you done?" she asked, no longer sure to whom the words were directed. Then her eyes began to cloud and she started to fall. She never felt herself hit the floor.

Harry got two calls to his cell phone, one after the other, before he had poured his first cup of coffee. First Max Abrams and then Vicky; both told him that Lilly Mikinos had been murdered in her family's Tarpon Springs shop.

Abrams picked up Harry at the marina ten minutes later and headed for Tarpon Springs.

"I recognized the name when it came through this morning and realized it was the same woman you were going to interview yesterday," Abrams explained. "Do you think her murder has any connection to our case?"

"It's possible," Harry said. "It's also possible it was just a robbery that happened after Vicky and I talked to her."

"You actually think it could have been a coincidence?"

"Yeah, I know," Harry said. "I don't believe it either. But if it wasn't, it raises an ugly possibility."

"That somebody followed you."

Vicky was already there when they arrived at the Mikinos store. She looked pale, shaky.

"One of Lilly's aunts called me this morning to tell me what happened," she told them. "She wanted to know if Lilly's murder had anything to do with our meeting yesterday."

"What did you tell her?" Harry asked.

"What *could* I tell her? I said I didn't know."

"What do you think?"

"It had to, Harry. Nothing else makes sense."

"Not a coincidence?"

"Don't believe in them."

Harry glanced at Abrams. "I don't think we could sell that idea to anyone," he said.

* * *

They met with the two Tarpon Springs detectives who had caught the case and filled them in on their meeting with Lilly the previous day, along with the fact that she had been a friend of Mary Kate O'Connell, the victim in the case they were investigating.

Max had brought several copies of the latest sketch that the police had produced along with the caveat that it didn't have the wholehearted endorsement of Jocko Doyle. "But it's the best we've got," he said.

The Tarpon detectives were treating the case as a murder resulting from a robbery, based on the fact that the cash register had been cleaned out, but said they would show the artist's sketch around the Sponge Docks and keep a two-way line of communication open until the case was resolved. Vicky, Harry, and Max then headed to the medical examiner's office to see what had been learned from the preliminary examination of Lilly's body.

The ME's office was located in a nondescript two-story building a short distance from the sheriff's office on Ulmerton Road. They found Lilly's body in the main autopsy room being prepped for a postmortem examination. The body was naked and an autopsy technician named George Rios was going over it inch by inch, looking for any DNA evidence the murderer might have left behind.

"What's the story, Georgie?" Harry asked.

Rios looked up from his work and smiled. "Harry, Vicky, Max, you guys on this case?"

"Max is," Harry said. "Tarpon is handling this murder, but it's connected to a murder in Clearwater. That's Max's case. Vicky and I are just interested parties."

"Which Clearwater murder was that?" Rios asked.

"Mary Kate O'Connell."

"I don't remember that one," Rios said. "Musta come in on my day off."

"Did you find anything on your preliminary exam?" Max asked.

"Nothing significant. But I understand we found some hair on her clothing that could give us some DNA. We also found some clothing fibers. I haven't cleaned out her nails yet. There could be more there. I'm hoping for some tissue samples if she fought the killer." He shrugged. "Who knows?"

"Who's the doc handling the post on this one?" Max asked.

"Angela Sugarman. She's due to start in about fifteen minutes."

"We'll wait," Harry said. "Thanks."

Harry stared at the pale, lifeless body, the muscles slack, the back darkened by lividity. The eyes were partially open and he tried to look into them but they had already begun to cloud over. One word seemed to be coming from Lilly's corpse but it didn't make sense to him.

Vicky had been uncommonly quiet and when Harry glanced over at her he found that she, too, was staring at Lilly's body. He found it strange looking down at the young body after just speaking with the woman the previous day. He could only imagine how Vicky felt. Vicky had known Lilly most of her life and had set up the meeting that may have led to her death. Now she was peering down at her on an autopsy table, all of it just settling in her mind, becoming real to her.

Harry slipped an arm around Vicky's shoulder. "You doing okay?"

"No," she responded in barely a whisper. "I remember going to her birthday party when she was seven years old. Looking at her now, I feel like shit." She turned and gave him the hardest look he had ever seen on her face. "And Harry, I'm telling you now: I want this bastard bad and I don't care what it takes to get him."

* * *

Dr. Angela Sugarman arrived for the post with the air of a diva moving to center stage. She was a short, heavyset woman somewhere in her late forties with a doughy face that softened her large, sharp nose and broad forehead. Her blond hair clearly had help from her hairdresser and her nails bore the signs of a recent manicure. She knew Max and Harry and quickly introduced herself to Vicky. "I've seen you around the building several times but I don't think I've ever worked one of your cases." She paused. "You look angry. Is everything okay?"

"I knew the victim," Vicky said. "I grew up with her."

"Then you shouldn't be here for the post. That's not the last memory you want to have of your friend." Dr. Sugarman raised her chin toward Lilly's corpse. "This looks like a pretty clear-cut case. We have two entry wounds from what appears to be a wide-bladed knife; one to the heart, one to the liver. Each would have been fatal. You wait in my office or call me in an hour and I'll give you the results." The woman's words left no room for argument. Vicky was being dismissed.

Harry put his arm around her again. "Come on, I don't need to see this either. I've seen enough autopsies to last me a lifetime. Max can fill us in."

Max came out an hour later to find Harry and Vicky seated under a tree near to where they had parked their cars. "You guys look like you're waiting for a picnic lunch to be delivered," he said.

"What did Sugarman find?" Vicky asked, dismissing Max's attempt at levity.

"Nothing that wasn't obvious. The murder weapon is a six-inch-long double-edged blade that's two inches wide in the upper part then tapers to a sharp point, just long enough to reach every vital organ in the body. There were some contusions indicating that she fought her attacker, and like Rios told us, they found some hairs on her clothing. They were blond—blond from a bottle."

"What was the underlying color?" Vicky asked.

"White," Max said. "According to the lab report, the original color of the hair was pure white."

"Like an albino," Harry said, then turned to Vicky. "That was the one word I got from her: *albino*."

"So it was that son of a bitch Rolf," Max said.

"Let's find him. Let's find him now." The tone of Vicky's voice was so fierce that it sent a shiver down Harry's spine.

Chapter Seven

Tony Rolf sat in the small salon of his sailboat home. An empty box of Just For Men hair color sat on the chart table before him. He had returned to the boat after his encounter with the woman, making one stop at Walmart on the way. There he bought a baseball cap, the hair dye—a medium brown—and a tanning lotion to use on the exposed portions of his body. Now he studied the results in a handheld mirror. An entirely new person looked back at him. He added a Tampa Bay Rays baseball cap to complete the new look and smiled at the result.

Across the marina Harry walked slowly toward his boat. He had invited Vicky to come with him, offering to cook her dinner, but she had declined, telling him that she needed to be alone, needed time to think everything through.

As Harry neared his boat a voice called out: "Hi, stranger."

Harry followed the sound and found Meg Adams sunning herself on the forecastle of her sailboat. She was wearing a bikini small enough to make Harry forget—at least for the moment—all the unpleasantness of the day. "You look absolutely fetching."

"That was the intention," Meg said. "Want a drink?"

"Very much, thank you. Do you have something strong, like Jack Daniel's?"

"Only wine, I'm afraid. But good wine, if that makes a difference."

"I have Jack Daniel's . . . your boat or mine?"

"I like yours. It's roomier."

"Then grab a bottle of wine for yourself and come join me."

Meg stood, making the bikini she was wearing even more alluring, and slipped on a T-shirt that went almost to her knees. It was a tease, he thought, one that forced him to remember what lay beneath.

Harry waited while Meg collected her wine, and together they boarded his boat and made their way to the galley. Harry poured a heavy dose of Jack Daniel's over ice, then held up Meg's wine to the light.

"Châteauneuf-du-Pape," he said. "You weren't kidding when you said a bottle of good wine. I've seen this go for $350 a bottle."

"This isn't quite that good a year," she replied. "But it wasn't a bad one either. I think this set me back about fifty-nine bucks."

"So you're serious about the wine you drink."

Meg waited while he uncorked the bottle and allowed it to breathe. "Wine is one of the things I take *very* seriously," she said.

"What are the other things?"

"You discovered one a few nights ago; now you've learned another."

"And . . . ?"

"And now you'll have to wait and see what else you can learn."

Meg took her glass and entered the salon. When Harry followed he found her tucked into one end of the sofa with her legs curled beneath her.

"Let's play house," she said teasingly. "How was your day, darling?"

"You don't want to know."

"That bad? Then sip your drink and forget about it."

Harry paused a beat, then said, "You pay pretty close attention to what's going on in the marina. Have you noticed anyone paying close attention to me?"

"Other than the women I've seen checking you out?"

Harry ignored the tease. "This would be a man, slender, about five eleven, medium build, blond hair, extremely pale complexion."

"You're serious, aren't you?"

"Deadly serious," he said. He filled her in on the deaths of Mary Kate O'Connell and Lilly Mikinos.

"And this guy works for the Church of Scientology?"

"Yes, he works for the office of church discipline. I've heard that the church keeps close watch on its members and have people whose job it is to confront those who stray across the line, whatever that line is."

"A few years ago I took one of their courses, sort of on a lark, and I didn't see any of that. Of course, all the people in my class were like me—they were just beginners."

Harry struggled to hide the alarm bells that had suddenly gone off. "And you didn't go on with it after that first class? Scientology, I mean."

"No, although I admit there was quite a selling job by church members. They really push you to take the next level of courses. And I've got to tell you, they are pretty pricey. But it just wasn't for me. It was too rigid, too dogmatic. The members that I met were so insistent that the church's way of life was the *only* way you could live, and I'm too free a spirit to ever buy into that."

"How about the other people in the class, did many of them go on to another course?"

"Oh, yes, I'm sure many of them did—at least half, I'd say." She watched Harry's eyebrows rise. "Most of the people I met were very needy. They were searching for something that was going to turn their lives around. And that's what Scientology promises to do."

"Hey, I'd like to turn my life around . . . especially after today."

"Then sign up." She offered up an impish grin. "After a year you'll have more wisdom than Buddha. It's guaranteed."

* * *

Regis Walsh sat behind his oversized desk, his chair tilted away from the only illumination in the room. He heard a light knock on the door and pressed a button on his desk that buzzed it open.

Tony Rolf stepped through the door and closed it behind him.

"Take a chair, Tony."

Rolf's eyes darted around the darkened room.

"You're always so cautious, Tony."

"That amuses you?"

There was an edge to Rolf's voice that Walsh did not like. He chose to ignore it for the moment. "It doesn't amuse me, it surprises me. This should be the one place that you feel safe."

"I don't feel safe anywhere." Rolf paused, then added, "Or with anyone." He stepped forward slowly and sat in the chair he'd been offered.

"That's a very disturbing statement. You should know that you've always been a very valued and trusted member of our small family. We've all relied on you during difficult times."

Rolf stared at him but remained silent. Walsh found it unnerving, something he was unaccustomed to feeling in his own office. "Don't you have anything to say?" he demanded.

"I'm just thinking."

"Thinking about what?"

"About all the criticism you heaped on me when things didn't go perfectly."

"It was only the death of the girl and the shooting of the retired police officer that upset me. It all seemed unnecessary and it presented some potential difficulties for the church—serious difficulties."

"It's hard to judge if something is necessary or not when you're sitting behind your desk and not out there when it's happening."

Walsh glared at him. "Don't presume to lecture me, Tony. Not about this or anything else where the good of the church is concerned."

"What about the good of Tony Rolf?"

Rolf was glaring right back at him and it caused Walsh to visibly squirm in his seat as he realized how dangerous the moment was. "I'm always concerned about that—always."

"How would you feel if I told you it was necessary to kill another 1.1 last night?"

"Who?" Walsh's voice was little more than a whisper.

"A turncoat bitch named Lilly Mikinos. You remember her? It was a little more than a year ago. A Greek priest showed up in the center of our community and took her away. And we did *nothing.*"

"Why did she have to die?"

Rolf seemed momentarily confused by the question. "She had been talking to that cop, Doyle, and his female partner. When I confronted her about what she had been telling them, she attacked me, screamed at me. She knew who I was, even with the dyed hair, and I knew she would turn me in to those cops as soon as she could." His voice had been rising with each statement. Now it became soft again. "I knew she'd even drag the church down just to get me. There was that kind of hatred in her eyes. I've seen that hatred before in the eyes of rabid animals and I knew there was only one way to stop her."

Walsh was silent for almost a minute. "I want you to leave the marina," he finally said. "It's too dangerous for you there. I'll arrange for a church apartment where you can lay low for a while. Then we'll put you on the *Freewinds* and get you out of this area."

Tony stared at him. "*Freewinds?* Where Mary Kate O'Connell was supposed to go for auditing?" He gave Walsh a knowing look that ended in a bitter smile. "I'll have to turn you down on that. I don't need an ocean voyage."

Again Walsh found himself squirming in his chair. He felt he had to get them off the subject or risk . . . what? "Let's just put that conversation aside for now," he offered. "We can talk about it later. What's important is finding a way to keep you safe." Walsh picked up his phone and placed a call to Ken Oppenheimer. "First let's get you into a safe apartment or house."

Oppenheimer entered Walsh's office at seven the following morning. Like Walsh he was unshaven and groggy from lack of sleep. "He's in a house in Safety Harbor," he began as he took a chair, "and he seems quite paranoid. He made some obscure comment about the house being better than *Freewinds* that I just ignored. Frankly I'm a bit concerned about his stability."

Walsh snorted, and told Oppenheimer about his earlier meeting with Rolf.

"Jesus," Oppenheimer said. "That's two murders and one attempted murder. And we're getting very close to being accomplices, if we aren't already." He ran a hand over his face. "Have you thought about turning him in to the police?"

"I'm afraid it's too late for that. We sheltered him after the first killing. We could probably argue that he was only a suspect then and we helped the police as much as we could, but now . . . I think we've lost that argument."

Oppenheimer leaned forward, clearly anxious, and asked: "What have you got in mind?"

"I think we have to get him the hell away from here. Either that or . . ."

"Eliminate him?"

Walsh shook his head. "I don't even want to discuss that possibility."

Oppenheimer nodded his head slowly. It was clear they were already discussing it. It was also clear that it might be the only way he and Walsh would survive this madness Rolf had created.

Chapter Eight

Tony Rolf stood in front of the massive floor-to-ceiling window that looked out onto a secluded garden. The house Oppenheimer had hidden him away in was only a short walk to Safety Harbor's main thoroughfare, but it might as well have been tucked away in the rural reaches of the county for the privacy it offered. Oppenheimer had explained that it was the home of a senior Scientology administrator who was on temporary assignment to a church office on the West Coast.

Oppenheimer had warned him to stay out of sight and to leave the house only in an emergency, but Rolf had no intention of obeying that directive. He needed to scout the area, find escape routes; locate one or more cars he could steal if the need arose. And he was certain it might. This detective who was pursuing him was a dogged son of a bitch and he knew that sooner or later Detective Harry Doyle would have to be added to the body count. There was simply no way to avoid it.

Harry Doyle awoke with his body spooned around a naked Meg Adams. It was dawn and the first rays of a rising sun were seeping through the starboard portholes of his stateroom. He had been dreaming about an albino man who was relentlessly following him and in the dream he had wondered how that could be, how had he never noticed. It was almost as though the albino was some kind of ghost who remained invisible to him.

Meg pressed back against him, driving the albino away, and he kissed her shoulder, eliciting a purr.

"You awake?" he whispered.

"Almost," she breathed back.

A voice called out his name from the dock and his body stiffened. He slid out of bed, grabbed a bathing suit and T-shirt that lay nearby, and pulled them on. Out on deck he saw her standing there, a beatific smile spread across her face.

"Harry," she said in a soft, soothing voice. "Oh, I miss you, Harry."

Harry stared into the face of his birth mother, Lucy Santos. Psychiatrists at the prison where she had spent the past twenty years had determined that she was no longer insane, no longer a danger to herself or others. She was normal now, they had said, capable of caring for herself, ready to be paroled back into society. Harry looked down into her eyes. The madness was still there, would always be there for him. He still had the letters she had sent him, one every year, each posted to arrive on the anniversary of the day she had killed both him and his six-year-old brother Jimmy, letters that always held words of love, and always ended with her wish that he would soon be with Jimmy basking in the glory of their Lord, Jesus Christ. He had sought and received a court order directing her to remain three hundred feet away from his domicile at all times, an order she ignored just as the court ignored his efforts to have it enforced. As he looked down at her now he felt not an ounce of pity, only revulsion. She was fifty-two and nothing remained of the beautiful young mother he remembered. She looked older, tired, beaten down. The lines in her face were carved deep and her once-lustrous black hair was mostly gray. Prison had not worn well on her. He pushed those thoughts aside and took out the cell phone he had brought on deck and dialed the marina office. When the dock Nazi answered he simply identified himself and said: "My mother is standing on the dock next to my boat. Get down here and get rid of her; call the cops, do whatever you have to do, just do it now."

Harry pulled up in front of Vicky's Tarpon Springs apartment located just a few steps from Spring Bayou, where every year dozens of young boys dove for a cross as part of the Greek Orthodox celebration of Epiphany. Vicky once told him she had dated a boy who had actually captured the cross, which supposedly insured him of a year of good luck. The first time she entered the boy's car after his victory, he had reached for her chest. She told Harry she smacked him in the face and told him he wasn't *that* lucky.

Harry had called the sheriff's office and had learned that Vicky had called in sick.

Now, as he approached her door, he could hear a news report playing on the television. He rang the bell and waited.

"Who's there?" Her voice came through the door with a harsh edge.

"It's Harry."

The door opened and Vicky stood there dressed in jeans and a T-shirt. Her face was drawn and haggard; she was wearing no makeup and Harry thought she looked very vulnerable, like a young girl. He pushed the thought of vulnerability away. This was not his partner, not Vicky.

"You look like shit," he said.

"Thanks. You always know how to lift a girl's spirits. Got any other smooth lines you want to bestow on me?"

Harry reached out and wrapped his arms around her, pulling her to his chest. "Go wash your face and I'll take you out for breakfast."

* * *

They went to George's Breakfast Station on Pinellas Avenue, a favorite of Harry's for a good greasy breakfast or a fast gyro sandwich. George greeted them at the door. He was a short, slender Greek somewhere in his sixties, who worked in the restaurant from dawn to well past dusk. He had a big smile spread across his face; nothing made him happier than a customer coming through his door.

"Harry," he said, "I haven't seen you in a long time. You must not be eating good."

He looked at Vicky in a way that she recognized. She got it from her mother all the time. It said: *Eat, you're too skinny*. "Go sit down; I'll make you a good breakfast," George said instead.

They sat in a sunlit window that overlooked a parking lot and the liquor store next door and ate their breakfasts. Not exactly a garden spot with soothing surroundings, Harry thought. But it had been a damned good greasy breakfast just as he liked it—eggs over easy, corned beef hash, and home fries, with toast and coffee, lots of it. Vicky had gotten a thick Greek omelet with feta cheese, onions, and tomato, with an English muffin and tea. And she had eaten it all.

"How was your breakfast?" Harry asked.

"Fantastic. If I ate here every day I'd be a nice, plump little Greek girl, just like my mother always wanted me to be."

Harry leaned back and looked her in the eye. "Okay, so where do we go to find that albino bastard?"

"Someone is hiding him out. Probably somebody in that office of church discipline where he works. I say we shake that tree, shake it hard, and see what falls out."

"I don't think Walsh—the big boss there—will rattle. But let's try his assistant, a guy named Kenneth Oppenheimer."

"Should we bring Max along?" Vicky asked.

"Yes, we should definitely bring Max. When it comes to rattling someone's cage, there's nobody better than that guy."

"I'll call him and ask him to meet us at Oppenheimer's office. He'll love it."

Max was waiting in the lobby when they arrived at the Scientology building that housed the office of church discipline. Harry briefed him on what they wanted to shake out of Oppenheimer's tree.

"Win or lose this is always a nice way to start the day," Max said.

They entered the lobby and found Lorraine Beck—the same receptionist Max had bullied into submission a few days earlier—seated at her desk, a false smile of welcome spread across her face.

"Hi, Lorraine," Max began. "We're the same cops who were here earlier this week, remember?"

"I remember," Lorraine said, her smile cracking slightly.

Max gave her his own false smile. "Well, dear, we're going up to that office again—same reason as last time—and I wanted to let you know so you could call ahead and not end up in trouble for letting us by."

"Thank you," Lorraine said.

Max gave her a wink and the three of them headed for the elevator as Lorraine reached for her phone. When they entered the elevator Max looked back at Lorraine and shook his head. "This place reminds me of that famous book my class read in high school. It was about a place where everybody was always being watched and had to do whatever the boss man—a guy called Big Brother—said."

"George Orwell's *1984*," Vicky said. "My high school English class had to read it too."

"Yeah, that's it, *1984*. I feel like I'm walkin' around in George Orwell's fuckin' world. That's what all this Scientology shit reminds me of."

When they exited the elevator they were immediately confronted by a smiling middle-aged woman. "I'm Mrs. Ryan. Mrs. Beck called from the lobby to say you were coming up. What can we do for you officers?"

"We'd like to see Kenneth Oppenheimer," Harry said. "Mr. Walsh suggested that he'd be a good person to talk to. I'm Detective Doyle. My two colleagues are Detective Stanopolis and Sergeant Abrams. Please tell Mr. Oppenheimer that we need to see him *now.*"

She gave Harry a smile normally reserved for small boys who have just suggested something outlandish. "Well, detective, Mr. Oppenheimer is very busy this morning; he has a *very* full schedule. You may just have to wait or come back later."

Max stepped forward so he was just inches away from the woman. "Lady, I'm going to tell you something and you better listen very carefully. I want you to go into Mr. Oppenheimer's office right now. And when you get there you tell him this: *There are three cops out here who need to talk to you now*. If he's too busy to do it here, he can grab his coat because we'll be taking him down to police headquarters to talk to him there."

"But, but—"

"No buts, lady. This is a multiple-murder investigation. People are starting to drop like flies. So get in there and tell him." The woman began to leave, but the words he directed at her back brought her up short: "And lady, if you ever use that simpering smile on us again, I promise you that you'll find yourself sitting in the back of a squad car."

When the woman left, Abrams turned around and found Harry and Vicky grinning at him. "You keep forgetting the *forthwith,*" Harry said.

* * *

Kenneth Oppenheimer was pure cordiality when they entered his office moments later. He directed them to a sitting area away from his desk and offered them coffee or tea, which they declined.

Oppenheimer was a tall man with thinning hair and a body that had begun the downward slide from fitness to fat. He had enormous hands that appeared far better suited to the outdoors than working behind a desk. To Harry he seemed an amalgamation of contrasts. He chose to work in his shirtsleeves, leaving the jacket of his dark gray suit hanging on a coatrack behind his desk, but his silk tie was drawn up tightly to his neck and the cuffs of his shirt were held together with gold links that had clearly set him back a few dollars.

"Mrs. Ryan tells me you are here about something quite urgent," he said. "What can I do to help you?"

"We need to find Tony Rolf ASAP," Max said.

"Does this involve the death of Mary Kate O'Connell and the shooting of the retired police officer?" Oppenheimer asked.

"Along with the murder of another former member of your church—a young woman named Lilly Mikinos, who was stabbed to death in Tarpon Springs last night." It was Harry this time and he paused a moment, holding Oppenheimer's gaze. "And by the way, that retired police officer is my father." His tone seemed to momentarily unsettle Oppenheimer.

"I'm sorry to hear that. I hope his recovery is going well."

"He'll make it," Vicky said. "And we believe he'll be able to identify Rolf as the man who shot him when he tried to save Mary Kate O'Connell."

"The idea of Tony doing all that is so inconceivable," Oppenheimer said. "He worked with us for several years, at least five if not more, and we never had one complaint from the church members he tried to help.

And believe me, we often get complaints. People have great difficulty accepting the errors of their ways."

"Is that what *auditing* is—getting people to understand—"

"Yes," Oppenheimer cut in. "The auditor's work involves helping people understand how their individual behaviors might be interfering with their ultimate goal, which is to reach a certain level of mental and spiritual clarity, which will allow them to put aside their problems, worries, and bad memories, and thereby lead more perfect and more satisfying lives. It's a state of being that we call *going clear.*"

"Well, let me make something *clear* to you," Max said. "You better get the word out among your minions that *anyone* who knows where Tony Rolf is and fails to tell us, or who just knows anyone else who knows where he is and fails to tell us that, is gonna find themselves charged with aiding and abetting a murder, and that is something that carries heavy time in prison and that could even make them an accomplice in any future crimes this fruitcake commits. You got that, Mr. Oppenheimer?"

"I do, sergeant. And I assure you, if I learn anything about Mr. Rolf's whereabouts, I will contact one of you immediately."

As they entered the elevator Max turned to Harry. "That lying fuck. He knows where that white-haired prick is. I'd bet my pension they've got him stashed somewhere, just waiting for things to die down so they can slip him safely out of town."

"*Freewinds* is our best option," Regis Walsh said.

"Where is the ship now?" Oppenheimer asked.

"She's stopping at various ports in the Bahamas. We could call her back but it might arouse suspicion with the Coast Guard. All her ports of call have been filed with the proper authorities. If we wait and let her schedule play out it will be another week before she's back." He gave Oppenheimer a long, level stare. "Can we keep Tony secure for that long?"

"If he does as he's been told and keeps himself out of sight, there won't be a problem. Six months ago I would have had complete faith in him doing just that. Today, I don't know. He's gone a bit around the bend recently. I should have spotted it but . . ." He shrugged. "My only excuse is that I've been preoccupied with other church business."

Walsh kept staring silently across his desk. *Results, not excuses*, was his business mantra.

"Perhaps I should put other matters on the shelf and concentrate on Rolf until we can get him out of here."

"That sounds reasonable, given the current predicament," Walsh said. "I can't think of anything that would bring more harm to the church than to have one of its employees dragged into a murder investigation."

"Yes, I can see that." Oppenheimer knew full well that should the latter happen, it would be on his plate alone. Walsh had made that clear.

Chapter Nine

Tony Rolf took a long sip of his beer. He was seated at the bar of a small French restaurant just off Main Street in Safety Harbor. The dinner crowd was thinning out and there was only one other patron at the bar, a reasonably attractive blonde somewhere in her early forties. He pushed away his plate which held the remnants of a steak sandwich and fries and gave her a more thorough appraisal. She was tall and slender and had long shapely legs accented by her dress, with high cheekbones and a mouth fixed in a permanent pout. She wore a wedding band but she was clearly alone. Separated, or perhaps with a husband traveling on business. Either way, she was out on her own.

Rolf signaled the bartender and ordered another draft of Carlsberg. "And please ask the lady if I can buy her a drink."

The bartender leaned in close and whispered: "She probably thought you'd never ask. Every time her husband travels she's in here looking for a sympathetic shoulder."

"I have two of those." When the woman accepted his offer, he moved down and took a seat next to her. "My name is Tony," he said. "I hate to drink alone."

"I'm Janice Rand and I'd be happy to have a drink with you." She smiled and he thought he sensed a touch of desperation. A woman long off the pedestal she had once been placed on, he guessed. One who was eager to find approval wherever she could.

He thought about the woman he had killed twenty-four hours earlier. She had actually attacked him; screamed at him; tried to physically hurt him. There had been little choice but to harm her in return and he had enjoyed using the knife, seeing the shocked look in her eyes as it sliced deeper and her life began to slip away. But this woman would offer no threat, although he would not take her back to his hideaway.

That would be foolish. No, he'd just have a drink here, perhaps two, and see where it led. He smiled inwardly, realizing that he didn't care if it led anywhere or not. He needed the diversion.

Rolf reached out and let his finger run across the back of her left hand. "Separated?" he asked.

Janice offered up another smile, a bitter one this time. "I might as well be separated. My husband Pete travels all the time. He's a construction engineer. He works for a company that builds roads and bridges and other stuff all over the world." She looked away, then turned back to him. "I sit at home with a fifty-inch TV to keep me company and occasionally treat myself to a night out."

Rolf offered her what he considered his most compassionate look. It could be an interesting night, he decided.

When he returned to his hideaway two hours later, Rolf felt a growing rage building inside. It was caused by two factors: first was the not-too-subtle rejection Janice had handed him when he had suggested they return to "her place" for a nightcap, and second was the note he had found on the hideaway's front door telling him to call Ken Oppenheimer right away.

The bitch, he thought. Feeling rejected by her husband, she had flirted outrageously, played him along until he was prepared to take the obvious next step, and all of it just to give her the opportunity to reject *him*. He had wanted to wrap his fingers around her throat in the restaurant parking lot. But there were other people leaving at the same time, so he had just spun on his heels and marched off, the little boy dutifully chastised.

And now he came to find that Oppenheimer had been at the hideaway—no doubt checking on him—so now he would have to deal with him as well. The entire evening had turned to shit. He picked up his iPhone and pressed *Oppenheimer* on the screen, struggling to keep his temper in check.

Oppenheimer definitely put it to the test with his first words: "I thought I was clear that you were not to leave the house."

"I wanted a steak and there were none in the fridge, so I went out to a restaurant," Rolf snapped back.

"That's your excuse for blatantly disobeying me?"

"That's it." He listened to the silence on Oppenheimer's end, then continued: "Look, no one recognized me; no one even has a picture of me. I've changed my appearance. That dead detective cop could have been sitting at the next table and he wouldn't have known who I was. Christ, I lived and worked in the same marina and he never spotted me. And I've changed my appearance again since then. You're worrying about nothing."

"I need to know that you're doing what we tell you to do," Oppenheimer spat out, emphasizing each word.

"And I need to know what you're doing to help *me*," Rolf replied in kind.

Oppenheimer played the silent card again. When he finally chose to speak his tone and demeanor had become softer and more deliberate: "We need a few more days before we can move you safely."

"Where do you plan to send me?"

"That hasn't been decided; perhaps one of our facilities in the

Bahamas or on the West Coast. That's being worked out now."

"Will I have any say in where I go?" Rolf's voice dripped with sarcasm.

"Of course you will, Tony. It's something we'll discuss and decide together."

"If you're sure that's the way it will be, then I'll sit tight."

Oppenheimer hesitated. "You know you were wrong about one thing, Tony."

"What was that?" He paused, thinking. "The old cop, right? Is he still in the hospital?"

"Yes, he's there under police guard. But I understand he'll be going home soon."

"I'm happy for him."

"He remains the one danger to you. Don't forget that."

After disconnecting from the call, Tony Rolf threw back his head and laughed. It was the first time he had laughed in days, perhaps longer. They were all the same, these self-serving bastards who ran the church. They hinted at what they wanted; never came right out and said it; never said anything that might come back to bite them later. *Well, don't worry, Mr. Oppenheimer. Tony Rolf knows what's good for him, and from now on that's the only road he's going to follow.*

Chapter Ten

Harry Doyle awoke at seven the next morning seething with anger. He showered and shaved quickly, managing to cut himself on the chin, then brewed a cup of coffee in the Keurig coffeemaker and called Max.

"I just wanted you to know that I'm heading over to the church office and I plan on raising a fair amount of hell with those bastards."

"Did we wake up on the wrong side of the bed this morning?" Max responded.

"Am I sounding like some pissed-off little kid?"

"Just a bit," Max said. "Plan on getting there at nine and I'll meet up with you. That way, if you have to bust somebody you can do it legally."

Harry let out a small laugh, directed mostly at himself. "See you at nine."

Max was waiting outside the building when Harry arrived. "So what happened to push that bug so far up your ass?"

"I woke up thinking about what you said yesterday," Harry said. "Hell, I probably spent the night dreaming about it . . . how these smarmy bastards know where this white-haired geek is hiding, how they're smiling to our faces and giving us the finger behind our backs and waiting for a chance to slip him out of town. Well, that's not gonna happen. He tried to kill Jocko, the only father I've ever known, the man who took me in as a fucked-up little kid and helped me recover from the mess of a human being I was after my mother tried to put me six feet under. No way, Max. That white-haired prick belongs to me. He's going down for what he did, and I'm the one who's gonna take him down."

"Good enough for me," Max said. "Let's go upstairs and start breaking some balls."

Max had already commandeered an empty office and had begun calling in members of the church discipline staff when the door to Ken Oppenheimer's private office opened and he and Regis Walsh strode into the outer office.

"May I ask what is going on?" Walsh demanded. His eyes settled on Harry.

"We're questioning your staff to see if they know the present location of Tony Rolf," Harry said. "Unless I'm mistaken, you gave us the okay to do that."

"No, you're not mistaken. But circumstances have changed."

"How so?"

"Since we last spoke I've had occasion to speak with our attorney. It's her view that no questioning of staff should take place unless she, too, is present." Walsh gazed at the staff now assembled for questioning. "I'm advising each of you to ask that an attorney be present when you're questioned by the police. The church will provide one at no cost to you."

Harry stared at the floor. He had no doubt that every member of Walsh's staff would do exactly what he had suggested. He looked up at Walsh. "Did your attorney say when she'd be available to join us?"

Walsh offered up a small smile. "At ten o'clock tomorrow morning. She told me to inform you that she would seek a restraining order if you tried to move ahead before then."

Harry glanced at Max who was standing near the door of the small office they had confiscated. Max gave an abrupt nod and turned into the doorway. "Have every member of your staff at police headquarters at ten a.m., and that includes you and Mr. Oppenheimer as well," he said.

"I thought you would do the questioning here," Walsh said.

"That's when we were all being nice. You just changed the rules and nice went out the window." Max gave Walsh a good imitation of his small smile, then continued on out the door with Harry on his heels.

"You're a very mean man," Harry said, as they headed for the elevator.

"So I've been told. But somebody likes me." Max handed Harry a folded piece of paper. "One of the secretaries slipped me this."

Harry unfolded the paper. It read: *I overheard two executives talking. They said Tony Rolf was hiding in Safety Harbor.*

"Did you ask her which executives?"

"She won't say," Max answered. "I don't want to push her . . . yet. I want her to think the policeman is her friend. Later, if she still won't say . . . then we'll see."

They spent the afternoon canvassing Safety Harbor's restaurants and bars, hitting the day staff first, then waiting for the night staff to come in at five and starting all over again. They hit pay dirt at the third restaurant, a small, pricey French place just off the main drag.

The night bartender was a well-built kid with a deep tan, somebody who evidently never missed a day at the gym or the beach. He studied the picture for over a minute, then hemmed and hawed at first, before finally saying he was sure it was a guy who had been at the bar the night before.

"It's a lousy drawing, that's all. The guy's face was thinner, his nose sharper, and his hair darker—but I'm pretty sure it's him." He hesitated. "Yeah, it's definitely him. No doubt about it."

"Was he alone?" Max asked.

"At first, yeah, but he put a move on one of our regulars, a lady who lives here in town. Her name is Janice Rand."

"You have an address for her?" Harry asked.

"No, but her husband's name is Pete. He's a big-shot engineer who works on international stuff. I'm sure you guys can find him."

The bartender was right, and within half an hour Harry and Max were standing outside a stately white house overlooking upper Tampa Bay. Harry pressed the ornate brass doorbell and the door swung back so quickly it made him wonder if the woman who opened it had been standing in the foyer waiting for the bell to ring. She began talking before Harry or Max could even show her a badge.

"I'm Janice Rand. Are you the two police officers who were asking questions about me at the restaurant?"

"We are," Harry said. "But you're not the subject of our investigation. We're interested in the man you had a drink with."

"Does my husband have to know I was having a drink with him? He gets home from South America next week."

"Does he know the man?" Harry asked.

"No, definitely not."

"Then he won't hear it from us." Harry said. "We can't guarantee the bartender won't tell him. He called you to tell you we were coming?"

"He's an old friend. He won't say anything."

"Then you have nothing to worry about."

"Good." She gave an exaggerated shiver. "The man you're asking about"—she shivered again—"he was strange. Not at first. But as time went by he just got weirder and weirder."

"How so?" Max asked.

"First off, his hair was dyed."

"Are you certain?"

Janice raised a hand and touched her own blond tresses. "I pay a fortune to have this done professionally. Believe me, I know the difference. This guy's hair was strictly a bottle job and not a good one at that."

"Did he ever give you a name?" Max asked.

"He said his name was Tony Robertson. But I was sure it was as phony as his hair. He kind of stumbled over the last name like it was unfamiliar to him."

"If he's the man we think he is, he's very dangerous," Harry said. "He's already killed two people. Does he know where you live?"

"I never gave him my address. He kept suggesting we come here and when I turned him down he got very upset. He called me a tease."

"Did he offer to take you to the place where he was staying?" Max asked.

"He said he couldn't, that it wasn't his place; that he was just visiting." Janice clasped her hands and began twisting them together. "I mean, I wasn't planning on going with him anyway. It was his way of pushing to come here. But after that first drink I knew I was dealing with a creep."

"Did he say where his place was?" Harry asked.

"No, but he didn't have a car, so I assume he walked to the restaurant."

Damn, Harry thought. *So close but still no cigar*.

They thanked her and Max gave her a card with a number to call if she saw him again.

Janice reached out and touched Harry's arm. "And, like you said, my husband doesn't have to find out about this."

"We have no need to talk to him."

Janice let out a sigh of relief.

"Lady wouldn't have to worry if she just stopped stepping out when her husband's out of town," Max growled as they climbed back into their car.

"Maybe he should take her with him," Harry said.

"And who are all those lovely señoritas going to play with if he does that?"

Less than a mile away Tony Rolf stood before the floor-to-ceiling window that dominated the living room of his hideaway. He had slept poorly, all his senses awaiting a knock on the door that would bring his world crashing down. He had defied Oppenheimer and refused to keep himself hidden away. The woman had been a mistake. Women were always a mistake for him. He was a freak of nature, an albino, and all the things he had done to hide it—the hair dye, the tanning solution, the tinted contact lenses—were for naught. It hadn't fooled the women he had encountered. Somehow they had sensed the falseness of it all, the falseness of *him,* and they had been repulsed rather than attracted.

His own father had told him he repulsed people. He wasn't sure how old he was when his father first said that, but he knew it was before he had started school. He knew because he remembered his mother taking him to school on his first day and recalling his father's words and how he had expected the other students and his teacher to hate him. And, of course, they had, just as his father had said they would. His father had never said that he, too, was repulsed by him, or hated him, but he didn't have to. Some things, he had learned, were simply true whether spoken or not. He remembered how his father had told him that one day he would end up in the hands of the police. It was his birthday and he had just turned nine when his father spoke those words. If his father could see him now, hidden away in this small, isolated house, cowering whenever a car drove by—ah yes, seeing all that, his father's face would be creased with a broad smile. But, of course, that was impossible. His father's face no longer existed; nor his smile, nor anything else about him. All that remained of the man was a rotting skeleton buried in a Los Angeles cemetery. He had survived his son's first attempt to kill him. As a nine-year-old he had set a fire outside his father's bedroom door, on the night of that birthday twenty years ago to the day.

His mother had escaped the fire. She had slept in a separate bedroom at the end of a long hallway. When she had awakened the entire opposite end of the hall was engulfed in flames and she had run to her son's empty bedroom, then outdoors where she found him standing in the backyard watching the house burn. His father had stumbled out a few minutes later.

Police and fire investigators quickly determined that the fire had been set by someone and just as quickly fixed their sights on his mother, after learning that she slept apart from her husband. But his mother was having none of it. She told them to talk to her son, and when they did, one investigator smelled the faint odor of charcoal lighter fluid on his pajamas. But he had not been a fool, even at the tender age of nine. He had feigned shock and stood mute before the investigators. It had caused a split among them, with two believing he had set the fire, and three clinging to the belief that his mother had, then had splashed her son with lighter fluid to throw suspicion on him; they believed the shock of it had left the boy mute.

How clever you were, even then, he thought now. *And you will need all that cleverness to rid yourself of the one person who can identify you. But you'll take care of that problem soon . . . very, very soon.*

Harry and Max spent the rest of the afternoon searching the neighborhood of Safety Harbor. They started at the obvious central point, the restaurant where Tony Rolf had last been seen, then began their canvass east and west of that central point, then north and south, going a half-mile in all directions. It was exhausting and it accomplished nothing.

They were both tired and frustrated when they packed it in at seven that evening. Max headed home to his wife and a late dinner and Harry made a stop at the hospital to see his father.

Jocko Doyle was sitting up in his bed watching the Tampa Bay Rays in a close game with the Yankees.

"How are the Rays doing?" Harry asked as he entered the hospital room.

Jocko held his nose with two fingers. "The owner just won't cough up the bucks he needs to spend to compete. I mean Hal Steinbrenner's a cheapskate compared to his father, but Stuart Steinberg just won't spend *period.*"

"He says the Trop is usually half empty; that he can't spend what he doesn't bring in," Harry said.

"And why is that?" Jocko challenged. "If your mama and I wanted to go to a game, it'll be a hundred bucks for two decent seats; then I got to pay thirty bucks to park my car and another thirty for a couple of sausage sandwiches and a beer and soft drink. That's a hundred and sixty bucks. What working stiff can afford that more than once a month? And Steinberg bitches that the seats are empty. I say make going to a game affordable and they won't be."

"So I guess you're feeling better," Harry said.

"Why, because I'm bitching about stuff?" Jocko smiled, acknowledging the truth of it. "Yeah, they say I'll be headed home this week. And how's the hunt for that albino son of a bitch going?"

"We had him pinned down in Safety Harbor, then he vanished. He's getting help. We're pretty sure it's coming from one or more people in Scientology, but proving it is something else."

"I'm the only one who can identify this clown as the shooter, right?"

"That's right. And the answer to your next question is no, you are not going to be used as bait."

"Why the hell not?" Jocko demanded. "We can set a trap for him and nail his sorry ass."

"No." Harry tried to stare his father down but got nowhere. "Let us do our job. We'll get him."

"And what if he shows up here?"

"We have the guard outside your door and extra security at all entrances. Nobody's going to get in here."

"I wish that albino bastard would make it in here. I might have a little surprise for him."

"Like what?"

"Like maybe he'd run into one pissed-off ex-cop who's not as helpless as he expects him to be."

"You know, you should have been born Latino." Harry shook his head.

"Oh yeah, and why is that?"

"Because you've got enough machismo for two Irishmen."

* * *

Meg Adams was seated in a lawn chair set up next to her boat. Harry noticed that she was reading on her Kindle when he made his way down the dock at nine that night.

"Hi sailor," he said, "what are you reading?"

Meg looked up and smiled. "A detective novel. The hero is tall and handsome and he beats up bad guys. Is that what *you* do, Harry?"

"That's about right. You want to see my rubber hose?"

Meg raised her eyebrows and put on a look of feigned innocence. "I think I already have," she said.

"Ouch. I walked right into that one."

"Yes, you did. And did you have a good day, Detective Deputy Sheriff Doyle?"

"Let me put it this way: it was one of those days . . . the kind that makes me wonder why I ever became a cop."

"Anything Mama can do to make it all better?"

"I am going to jump into the shower. There is a bottle of Jack Daniel's in the galley. You could pour me a stiff one over ice and hand it to me."

"Aye, aye, captain."

Harry stood under the shower letting the water beat down on his neck and shoulders, trying to let the day's tensions drain away. The shower door opened and a hand holding a glass of amber liquid appeared before his eyes, followed by a naked red-haired woman with an impish grin on her face.

"Anything else, captain?"

Harry took a long sip of his drink, then another. "I can think of one or two things," he said as he set the empty glass on the soap tray and slipped his arms around Meg's waist.

"Only one or two?" she said, rising up on her toes and biting his lower lip.

Tony Rolf slipped into a rear door of the hospital laundry. Inside the noise was deafening as a dozen massive washing machines and dryers churned away. He had done this before when fallen-away Scientologists were hospitalized but still needed tending.

He had always enjoyed the frightened looks on their faces when he entered their rooms wearing hospital scrubs and let them know who he was. They were all *SPs*, of course, those who had been deemed *suppressive persons* who were trying to disrupt the order within the church, trying to raise doubts among weaker members, turning each of them into a *potential trouble source*, or *PTS*.

He looked around the laundry. Back in the day there was always a church member who worked in the hospital who would be there waiting to help. But those visits had been authorized by the people he worked for; not like now. Now he was going after the old cop alone, solely to protect himself. Sure, Oppenheimer had hinted at it, but there had never been a direct order to go after him, or any offer of help.

Rolf remained in the shadows. He was dressed in a black T-shirt and black jeans and it made him nearly invisible when he remained out of brightly lit areas. He quickly observed that recently laundered items were placed in rolling carts ready for delivery to their appropriate locations and he could see where the fresh scrubs were stacked. He moved boldly to the cart that held them. He had learned long ago that when dealing with low-level employees, the trick was to act assertively. They were disinclined to challenge anyone who they assumed held a higher rank. And in the case of laundry workers, that was just about everyone.

He grabbed a full set of scrubs—pants, shirt, shoe coverings, mask, and head cover. Then he made his way out of the laundry and entered the rear of the main hospital building. It felt like old times as Rolf headed to the physicians' locker room and slipped inside. The room was empty, and he quickly checked for unlocked lockers. On the fourth try he found one. The doctor had even left his name tag and stethoscope hanging inside. He snatched them up and quickly changed into the fresh green scrubs he had taken. He went to a telephone in the locker room and dialed the operator. Using the doctor's name whose name tag he now wore, he asked for the room number of John Doyle, stating he had been asked to evaluate his condition. With the information in hand he checked his watch—nine thirty. He would wait until ten when the rooms would be dark and the halls largely deserted.

At 10:05 Tony Rolf approached the police officer seated outside Jocko Doyle's room. He was dressed in the green scrubs, including face mask and head covering, and he put a note of urgency in his voice.

"Officer, there's a man in the staircase who has a knife. He looks like he plans to use it."

"Which staircase?" the cop asked.

Rolf indicated with his head that it was behind him. "Come, I'll show you."

When they reached the staircase door the officer extended his arm, indicating that Rolf should stay back, and pushed open the door. He stepped into the stairwell, his hand now shifting to his weapon, as Rolf swung the sap he had taken from his pocket.

The officer lay sprawled in the stairwell, his weapon clattering down the stairs. Rolf thought about retrieving it and immediately rejected the idea. He had his knife; a gun would just raise an alarm and make his escape more difficult. He returned to the hallway that led back to Jocko Doyle's room.

* * *

Jocko's bed was elevated to a sitting position and his head rested against a pillow. He was reading a magazine.

"You should be sleeping," Rolf said. "I thought I'd have to wake you."

"What do you want, doc?" Jocko asked.

"I've been asked to evaluate your condition. It seems they want to get you out of here."

"I couldn't agree more."

Jocko had just put down his magazine when he heard an all-too-familiar sound. He reached under the sheets and came up with a Smith & Wesson snub-nosed revolver—his old off-duty weapon. "Since when do doctors carry switchblades?" he asked as he pointed the gun at Rolf's chest. "Nice to see you again, punk."

Rolf skidded to a halt.

Before Jocko could react, Rolf spun around, ducked down a bit, and raced for the door. Jocko lowered his weapon and aimed at the man's legs. He was able to get off one shot before Rolf reached the hallway and raced away.

Jocko eased himself out of the bed and moved slowly into the hall—no Rolf, no blood on the floor. He had missed the son of a bitch. He saw that the uniformed cop who had been guarding him was gone as well.

Nurses ran toward him from the nursing station.

"The guy who shot me just came back to finish the job," he said. "Call hospital security and Clearwater police. Tell them he's dressed in hospital scrubs. And see if you can find the cop who's been sitting outside my door. He may be hurt."

A nurse pointed at the gun. "Why do you have *that?* It's not allowed in the hospital."

"Never mind that!" Jocko shouted. "Just do what I told you! If you don't do it right now the son of a bitch will get away."

Harry's phone rang at ten thirty. He was lying next to Meg; they were both naked and drowsy with postcoital bliss.

"Yeah?" he said hoarsely into the phone.

Max's voice came across the line: "You better get back down to the hospital. Our boy tried to off your father again. But don't worry, Jocko's okay." Max filled Harry in on the details. When he got to the gun and the shot Jocko had fired, Harry cut in.

"Where the hell did he get a gun?"

Max began to chuckle. "Seems like he asked your mother to bring it to him and she did." He paused a moment. "Good thing she did. It's probably the only reason Jocko's still alive. The hospital folks are a touch pissed off, to say the least. They say he shot up their hospital."

"Tough shit," Harry said.

"My sentiments exactly."

"What happened to the cop who was guarding him?" Harry asked.

"They found him in a stairwell. He took a bad blow to the head. He's in his own room now with a concussion. I'm just about to go in and interview him."

"Thanks, Max, I'll be there as quick as I can."

Harry arrived at the hospital twenty minutes later. He went straight to his father's room, where he found him talking to an agitated hospital administrator.

"Hi, Dad, are you okay?"

Jocko brushed off his concern. "I'm fine, except I missed the asshole. I was trying to hit him in the legs. It was a piss-poor shot. I better get down to the range and put in some time."

Harry fought back a smile. The hospital administrator interrupted. He was a tall, angular man with a narrow face set off by a long nose. He reminded Harry of a rat.

"We can't have this," he began.

"What's your name and what are you doing in my father's room, talking to him in a raised voice?" Harry countered.

"My name is Joel Morgan and I work for the hospital. We were discussing Mr. Doyle's discharge of a firearm in this hospital."

"Well, I'm Harry Doyle, *Detective* Harry Doyle. I'm his son and an investigator on this case. And if my father had *not* discharged a firearm in this hospital, he'd probably be on a slab in your morgue right now."

A new voice came from the doorway: "And if he *was* on a slab in your morgue, this hospital and its lax security would be largely responsible. So don't let me hear any more shit about him protecting himself with a legal, licensed weapon."

"I beg your pardon, Mr. . . . ?"

"Detective Sergeant Max Abrams. I just got through interviewing our injured patrolman. He told me that he was lured away by a man who identified himself as a doctor, who had the credentials saying he was a doctor, and who was dressed in hospital-issued scrubs. But it turns out he wasn't a doctor. He was a murder suspect who apparently was able to get scrubs and a hospital ID and access to this floor. Where he was then able to assault the police officer guarding Sergeant Doyle and then make another attempt on Sergeant Doyle's life. So what I want from you is an explanation of how all that was possible before you say one more fucking word about Sergeant Doyle saving his own life and possibly other lives in this hospital by discharging a licensed, legal firearm as a murderer armed with a knife was attacking him."

Morgan attempted to formulate a reply. "I . . . I . . . I . . . can't explain it . . . other than to say it must have been someone who . . . who had intimate knowledge of how the hospital . . . functions. Maybe he was someone who once worked here."

"I'll give you the man's name and you can get on a computer and tell me if he ever worked here."

"I'll get on it immediately," Morgan said, clearly eager to leave the room.

Harry watched him go and then glanced back at his father. Jocko was a tough old bird, he thought, and he wished he had seen him work during his prime. "You think you've caused enough trouble?" he asked in a playful voice.

Jocko waved a hand at him, dismissing his words. It made Harry smile; he was just so damned happy his father was still alive.

A middle-aged nurse entered the room. She was slender and attractive and her blond hair was tucked under her cap. "I'm here to check out Wyatt Earp." She kept a straight face and continued her routine: "I've got to run a few basic tests to see what damage he did to himself when he turned this place into the O.K. Corral."

"I'm fine," Jocko snapped.

The nurse stared at him. "Look, I'm really tired, Wyatt, and I'll be happy to pass you by. All you have to do is show me your medical degree."

Jocko shook his head. "Don't pick on me. I've been shot. And somebody just tried to knife me."

"Poor baby. There's a guy down the hall with a failing heart and he just grabbed my butt."

This forced Jocko to smile. "Go ahead, do your worst."

Chapter Eleven

Tony Rolf slipped in a side door of the main Scientology office building. Oppenheimer's office was on the seventh floor, but Rolf avoided the elevators by taking the stairs instead. He was still shaken by his encounter with the cop. The lousy old bastard had been waiting for him. And he had been *armed.* He could still feel the rush of hot air as the bullet had gone between his legs. A few inches higher and the cop would have blown his balls off.

He made it to the seventh floor without encountering anyone and used the key they had given him to open the outer office. He didn't have a key to Oppenheimer's inner office, but he didn't need one. The set of picklocks in his back pocket would do the job.

He had fled the scene at the hospital in a panic before realizing that no one was pursuing him. He had gone directly to the doctors' lounge and retrieved the street clothes he had left there, changed, returned the doctor's ID to the locker he had taken it from, and used his cell phone to call a cab. He was at Scientology headquarters a half hour later.

Inside Oppenheimer's office he fell into the soft leather couch and closed his eyes. Oppenheimer, he knew, would not arrive until six, his usual hour. That would give them time for a little chat, perhaps one with Regis Walsh as well.

By one a.m. the Clearwater PD had a new officer assigned to guard duty outside Jocko's room and a two-man squad car was keeping a tight surveillance of the exterior of the hospital complex. Jocko had insisted on keeping his weapon. The hospital capitulated, but only after he assured them the weapon would only be used under the direst of circumstances.

"What do they think I'm going to do, shoot into the goddamn ceiling every time the Rays win a ball game?" he groused to Harry.

"Okay, Wyatt, just don't shoot any nurses, especially the cute ones," Harry said.

"Any more of that Wyatt Earp crap and you better be prepared to dance," Jocko replied.

Meg was still on his boat and wide awake when Harry got back. "I wanted to know how your father was," she explained.

Harry told her about the albino's attempt on his father's life, how the guy had taken out the police officer guarding him only to discover that his father was armed and waiting for him.

"This is the second time he's tried to kill a cop, plus the two women we know he killed. Every cop in the state is looking for him. He shows his albino ass anywhere, he'll either be lying on a slab in the morgue or sitting in jail."

"Doesn't sound like he has much of a chance," Meg said.

"Not if I find him first, which is what I intend to do."

"Why is it so important that *you* find him?"

He looked at her with astonishment. "Twice now that bastard has tried to kill the only man who ever tried to be a father to me. I intend to make sure he doesn't get a third chance."

Meg returned to her sailboat and Harry used the opportunity to grab a few hours of sleep.

When he awoke he found Vicky in his galley brewing coffee. "I heard about Jocko," she said. "So I took some vacation time so I could help you." She raised her nose and sniffed the air. "Smells like a woman's been here." She inclined her head toward the dock. "The sailboat lady?"

"Would you really respect me if I was the kind of guy who kissed and told?"

"Depends on who you're kissing."

Harry let that one lie. He noticed that Vicky was blushing.

"What are you doing here?"

Tony Rolf awoke to the sound of Kenneth Oppenheimer's voice. The words took a moment to register, as he stared up at the hulking body that was looming above him.

"You're supposed to be at the house in Safety Harbor. Did something happen?"

He could hear the fear in Oppenheimer's voice and the sound of it sickened him. In the past few hours he'd subdued one police guard and faced down another cop who had sent a bullet whizzing between his legs. And here was his supposed protector wetting his pants because he'd found him sleeping on his office sofa.

"I went after the old cop—the one who could put me away for dealing with that 1.1 O'Connell woman." He gave Oppenheimer a detailed account of what had happened. "I escaped without any problems but I couldn't push it any further and take a chance they could trace me to the safe house."

"I'll get you back there before the rest of the staff gets in."

"What about Walsh? Maybe I should talk to him."

"I'll tell him you're interested in talking to him. If he agrees, he can come to the house in Safety Harbor or reach you by phone."

"Tell him it's important to me. Tell him he can either grant me that courtesy or he just might find me waiting in *his* office some morning."

Oppenheimer stared at him, wondering if he should say anything. He knew that Rolf was armed with a knife, perhaps even the same weapon he had used to kill the woman in Tarpon Springs. There was no need to push him, no need to put his own life in danger, he decided. He'd get the man out of here and let Walsh handle it.

"If he's hiding in Safety Harbor it has to be in some church-owned property, or a house or apartment that belongs to a church member." Vicky tapped the side of her nose. "We need to talk to somebody in the city clerk's office."

While Vicky headed to city hall, Harry and Max expanded the search zone they had started the day before. It was Friday morning and the neighborhoods were quiet. A few mothers pushed strollers and carriages to nearby parks, and numerous retirees were out doing yard work or headed to local hardware stores and garden centers or to one of the local restaurants for breakfast. All in all, it made for easier interviews than normal. Harry and Max each had copies of the police artist sketches of Rolf.

On his twelfth interview Harry got his first solid lead of the day. Jimmy Drake was a seventy-five-year-old retired chief warrant officer. The US Army had been his home for thirty years, until he realized that those who ran it were going to keep sending him to Vietnam until he finally came home in a box. After a third tour he retired and took a job with a major pharmaceutical company where he spent another fifteen years, retiring at sixty-five with two pensions topped off by a monthly Social Security check. Now his garden occupied most of his time, and his pensions provided the means for his second great passion: frequent visits to the areas many upscale restaurants.

Harry learned all of this in his first fifteen minutes of conversation. Jimmy Drake lived alone and he was obviously starved for conversation. He was also a thoroughly nosy neighbor, the kind all cops dream of finding.

"These Scientologists, they're everywhere. They're not just in downtown Clearwater, you know," Jimmy said. "They're here too. See that house across the street? It's owned by a guy named Drummer. He's one of them." Harry turned to look at the house. Jimmy reached out and took his arm as if preparing to restrain him. "Oh, he's not there now. Those kooky bastards he works for just sent him and his wife out west for a couple of months—some special training or something. Probably gonna meet up with some spaceship or something. I see lights on over there at night, but it could be set up on a timer. I have one of those for my place if I go out of town."

"Do you know any other Scientologists who live here in town?" Harry asked.

"No, but I know they're here," Jimmy insisted. "I see them coming to Drummer's house, socializing, you know? Parties, barbeques, and stuff like that. Then I see them around town later. And according to all those articles I read in the *Tampa Bay Times*, even though it's not Scientology's official policy, these guys are only supposed to socialize with other members of their church."

"So you never saw any of your other neighbors going over there?"

"Not a one, never. And he sure as hell never invited me." Jimmy let out a derisive snort. "And if he had, I sure as hell wouldn't have gone. Bunch of fuckin' kooks, that's what they are."

Harry caught up with Max just as he was finishing a call on his cell. He quickly filled Max in on what Jimmy had told him.

"We'll check out the house, see if anyone's there." Max held up his cell phone.

"Now I got one for you." He took the sketch of Rolf out of his suit coat pocket and held it up. "You remember our police artist buddy, Jeremy Jeffords. Well, I just got a call from my regular partner, Jimmy Walker. I asked him to do a little digging. It always bugged me that Jocko said the sketch Jeffords did was bullshit. Guess what Walker found out?"

Harry's face lit up. "You're kidding me."

"No, I'm not," Max said. "Jeffords is a member of the church, a dyed-in-the-wool fucking Scientologist."

Harry's cell rang; it was Vicky wanting to know their location. Harry told her and a few minutes later she pulled up in her car.

"Been waiting to hear from you guys," she said. "Have you come up with anything?"

Harry updated her on Max's new information.

"Son of a bitch," she said.

Harry nodded toward the house behind them. "That joint is owned by a Scientologist, according to a neighbor I interviewed. He and his wife are supposed to be out of town for a few months on church business."

"A perfect place for our boy to be stashed," Vicky said.

"Let's go shake the doors and look in the windows," Max said. "See if we can flush this bird."

Tony Rolf stayed far back in the shadows as he listened to them knock on the front door and ring the doorbell. One of them even tried the door to see if it was open. Then someone went to the back door and did the same. He had been watching the cops as they gathered outside his little hideaway. He knew all three by sight, given the time he had spent watching Harry Doyle. Now it seemed that this dead detective and his friends might have him cornered. He slipped into the master bedroom and then the adjoining bath. He placed a call to Oppenheimer and waited for him to answer. The cell rang five times and went automatically to voice mail. He left a detailed message, then put his phone on vibrate so any return call wouldn't give away his presence in the house.

He listened intently as one of the cops moved around the perimeter, covering all the windows, making as much noise as he could. He was certain the other two were watching the front and rear doors. They didn't know he was there, he thought, or they would have forced their way inside. Instead they were trying to panic him, flush him out one of the two doors.

He tried to remember if he had left any clothing on a chair or the bed. No, he was certain there was nothing they could see that would give them a reason to force their way inside.

Oppenheimer called back two hours later, explaining that he had been in a meeting that had just ended. When Rolf told him what had happened, there was an eerie silence on the line. Rolf knew that Oppenheimer was calculating the threat, especially the threat to himself. "You'll have to be moved," he said.

"That boat we were trying to get Mary Kate O'Connell on, the one that investment clown owns; that's where I want to go."

"Edward Tyrell's boat . . ."

"That's it. I couldn't remember his name. I can get out of here myself. It'll be safer than having you meet me. As soon as I hear that Tyrell is at his boat I'll slip out of here, grab a cab, and meet him there. You can tell him whatever you want, but just make it clear that I'll be staying on the boat until you move me to a new location."

He could hear the relief in Oppenheimer's voice as he agreed to the plan. It would keep his hands clean if everything went south. If the cops nabbed him as he fled the house, Oppenheimer could deny any involvement. His ass would be safe, the fucking coward. And it wasn't just Oppenheimer. He knew Walsh was in the background pulling the strings for his puppets—Oppenheimer, Tyrell, and who knew how many others. He hoped that someday he would have a chance to pay all of them back.

Oppenheimer called him again at eleven that evening. Rolf had been watching the street and he was certain the cops were gone. A lone patrol car went by the house every hour, but that seemed to be the only surveillance. Still, he wouldn't take any chances. He'd jump the fence of the neighboring house and cut through their yard to the street—he'd taken that route before and it had worked well—then head straight to the restaurant at the corner of Main Street where he'd order a beer and call for a cab. Fifteen minutes after the cab arrived he'd be aboard Tyrell's fifty-three-foot Hatteras yacht. Rolf smiled to himself. It was going to be nice staying in a hideout that could move at high speed if necessary.

Harry returned to his boat and immediately got on his computer. Meg stuck her head into the salon and requested permission to visit. Harry waved her in.

"What are you up to?" she asked.

"We think we may have flushed the albino out and that he'll try to get out of Safety Harbor tonight, so I'm checking with all cab companies that service the area for any fares carrying single males."

"What if he goes with a friend from the church?"

"Then we're screwed," Harry said. "But I don't think anybody inside the church is going to stick their neck out that far."

"Sounds like a long night. I'll get us a good bottle of wine from my private stock."

Tyrell was waiting for Rolf on the dock.

"You'll be going aboard a friend's yacht in another marina," Tyrell explained. "The owner, who is also a client, is out of town on an extended business trip and he asked me to keep an eye on the boat for him. He should be gone for the next three or four weeks and you should be out of the area by the time he gets back."

"Whose idea was this?" Rolf demanded. He could see that Tyrell was extremely nervous and Rolf was enjoying it.

"It was Mr. Walsh. He feels the police may be able to trace your movements. If they do and it leads to this marina, my boat will be an obvious place to look for you."

"I want to talk to him," Rolf said.

"And he wants to talk to you. He asked me to tell you that he'll call you later tonight."

Rolf was pleasantly surprised when he saw the new boat. It was a few years older than Tyrell's but just as large and comfortable. The Hatteras Yachtfish was a serious sportfishing boat, fitted with outriggers and all the gear needed to pursue and catch major game fish, from blue marlin on down to dorado and wahoo. But it also offered luxurious accommodations with three staterooms, each with a private head and shower, a comfortable salon and dining area, and a well-equipped galley. It was docked in a small marina a quarter-mile across the channel from the marina where the so-called dead detective kept his boat—*so near and yet so far.*

Rolf smiled to himself and looked at Tyrell. He was tall and slender, with a gym-fit body that reeked of money right down to his perfectly capped teeth. And he was ready to wet his pants. The man couldn't wait to get away from him. "This will do very nicely," Rolf said, making a circular motion with a finger to take in the entire vessel. He held out a hand. "Keys."

"Well, you'll only need keys for the salon door; you won't be taking her out," Tyrell said. There was a tremor of fear in his voice.

"I want a full set of keys." He gave the guy a hard, unblinking stare.

Tyrell swallowed hard. "Yes, yes," he said. "On second thought, that makes better sense."

Kenneth Oppenheimer entered Walsh's dimly lit office. He had been tersely summoned, which was always a bad sign, so he had dropped what he was doing and had gone directly to the office's rear door.

"When you saw Tony Rolf, how would you describe his mood?" Walsh asked.

"Volatile."

"Volatile in what way?"

"In every way; I was uncomfortable being in the same room with him. I had no idea what would set him off and I didn't know if he was armed, but I assumed he was. After all, he's killed two women, and he's tried to kill that retired cop twice now."

Walsh leaned back in his plush executive desk chair. "Tony has served us well over the years. Don't you feel we owe him some loyalty . . . If it was your decision, what would you do?"

"I'd get rid of him, one way or the other."

"Kill him?"

"No, of course not," Oppenheimer said. "I'm not a killer and I don't condone it from others."

"There's an interesting word in the church's lexicon. It's called *un-*

mock. It means to have a person or thing disappear, become nothing, cease to exist."

"Cease to exist as in death?"

"Mr. Hubbard never elaborated on the word. I think it's fair to say it was left open to interpretation."

Tony Rolf sat in one of the salon's plush chairs and drummed his fingers on a side table. Walsh should have called him by now. He glanced at his watch; it was nearly eleven. They all thought they could put him off, make him wait. But when they wanted him to do something, it had to be done lickity-split. That stupid expression, it had been one of his father's favorites. But so was: *You little freak*. That was reserved for when he addressed his only son, the albino, the child whose very existence disgraced him.

His father was convinced his mother had cheated on him with some degenerate who had passed on the inferior gene. None of the doctors the boy went to could convince him he was wrong, and whenever he went on a bender—which was often—he would come home and beat his mother and then him, just on general principle.

He still remembered the day his father had stopped hitting him. He was fourteen and his father was fat and flabby and fifty. That afternoon Tony had gotten a roll of nickels at a bank and wrapped it with tape. A street thug he had befriended had showed him how. Then he held the roll of taped nickels in his right hand and closed his fist around it. His street friend had called them "a poor man's brass knuckles" and said it would allow him to hit with the power of a professional fighter.

This time, when his father had finished with his mother and turned on him, he was ready. He hit him flush on the jaw with every ounce of strength he had, and the fat bastard had gone down like a bag of wet laundry.

He was on him as soon as he hit the ground and one blow was followed by another and another, as years of hatred and frustration poured out of him. After half a dozen blows his mother wrapped her arms around him and struggled to pull him off.

"Stop, Tony, you'll kill him, you'll kill him!"

He had turned and glared at her. "I want to kill him," he hissed. "I want it more than anything else in the world."

When he went to bed that night he locked his door from the inside and waited up most of the night. But his father had left the house and stayed away for several days. Finally, when he returned, he acted as though nothing had happened, but Tony knew the miserable bastard was only biding his time, waiting to catch him unawares. That was when he had bought his first knife, a six-inch switchblade finely honed and razor sharp. His street friend had instructed him on its use: stick it hard in the belly and then pull the cutting edge up. He had explained that every vital organ in the human body was only three inches below the skin and a six-inch blade like his was more than enough to cut most of them in half. Now it was just a matter of deciding when and where.

That time came three days later, when his father jimmied open his bedroom door at three a.m. and found Tony sitting in bed waiting for him. The switchblade flashed open and his father stared at it, then turned and ran. Tony never saw him again. Three months later they learned he had been killed in a barroom fight.

His cell phone rang at eleven thirty, driving away his reminiscences.

"I'm sorry to be calling you so late. I hope I didn't wake you." Walsh's voice sounded so calm, as if no danger surrounded them, no threat existed. It was the same as it had been twelve years earlier when Walsh had plucked him off a Los Angeles street only minutes before the police arrived to arrest him. Walsh had opened the doors of the church to him and employed him to help enforce its rules. At Walsh's suggestion he had changed his name to further thwart the police and they had moved him to Florida.

"No, I was awake."

"I understand from Ken Oppenheimer that you're not happy with the support you're getting. Is that true, Tony?"

"It's true," he said, trying to keep his voice neutral.

"What specifically did you find unsupportive?"

"Everything," Tony snapped. "Everything that matters. I was stashed away in that house in Safety Harbor without regular contact with anyone. Just told to sit and wait." He instantly regretted lashing out at Walsh. This was the one person in the church who had always been supportive of him. In fact, he had always viewed himself as essentially Walsh's creation.

"It was my fault," Walsh said. "I was being overly cautious. I gave the police too much credit. But I won't make that mistake again."

Tony thought of how close the police had come. "And maybe I was taking too many chances."

Walsh chuckled on the other end of the phone. "You are a bit cavalier at times. A touch of restraint would be a good habit to cultivate. But I've always felt your occasional lapses were due to an eagerness to do good for the church, and that's a quality I admire." He paused to let his words sink in. "Tony, are you familiar with the word *unmock?*"

"Yes, it means to make someone or something disappear, or stop existing."

"Precisely, either figuratively or literally, and that's your job within the church. But only on a direct order from me."

"I understand."

"Good. And for the time being we're going to forget about this retired police officer. His son is the greater danger."

"Do you want him . . . ?"

"No, not yet, I'd prefer that he be disgraced in some way. But that's going to require some thought. So, for the time being, you just sit tight and stay out of sight." Walsh chuckled again, at the rhyming words. "How poetic I am," he said.

Rolf joined in with a faint laugh.

"I promise you, it won't be long before we can get you out of here."

"That's good to hear," Rolf said, hanging up the phone.

"You're the only one who can handle that psychopath," said Oppenheimer, who'd been listening to the conversation on a muted handset.

"I hope you're right. And I hope he stays handled. Otherwise we may be forced to unmock Mr. Rolf," Walsh responded

Chapter Twelve

Meg Adams saw the older woman surreptitiously making her way down the dock. She recognized her immediately as Harry's birth mother; a woman who had killed her two children, except one of them had lived. She looked at her watch. It was seven a.m., too early for the dock Nazi to be in his office. She debated whether to call Harry or the police. Harry had gotten in so late the night before and had just wanted to sleep. He had turned down a glass of good wine *and* her. This wasn't something that had happened very often in her life. It made her like him even more.

Meg stepped off her boat and approached Harry's mother. "Can I help you?"

Lucy Santos stopped dead in her tracks, almost as though Meg's words were a barrier suddenly placed in her path. "I know you?" she asked as her eyes flitted from side to side.

"I'm a friend of Harry's and I know who you are. You're his mother and you are not supposed to be here. You'll be arrested if you don't leave."

Lucy stared at her for almost half a minute. Her face twisted into a hateful rage. "*Puta*," she said. "Get out of my way."

Lucy's hand slipped into her purse and Meg got scared. Then she heard feet hitting the dock behind her and suddenly Harry was moving past her.

Harry grabbed his mother's wrist and pulled her hand from her purse, then twisted the wrist until the eight-inch carving knife she held fell onto the dock. He spun her around and within seconds had her hands cuffed behind her back.

"Harry, Harry, why you do this to me?" Lucy pleaded.

"You're under arrest. You have the right to remain silent. Anything you say can and will be used against you in a court of law. You have the right to an attorney. If you cannot afford an attorney, one will be appointed for you. Do you understand what I have told you?"

"Oh, Harry, why you do this to me?"

Harry glanced back at Meg. "Call the police—911—and tell them an officer needs assistance. Tell them who I am and that I just made an arrest of an armed woman and give them this location. I don't want to let go of her until they get here."

Harry watched as two uniformed officers led Lucy Santos to a waiting patrol car. With the police officers and his mother headed away, he turned his attention to Meg. "What you did was foolish and dangerous. She could have hurt you . . . badly. And I assure you, she's very, very capable of doing just that."

Meg studied her shoes. "I didn't know what else to do. I saw her coming down the dock, headed for your boat. The marina office wasn't open yet, and I didn't want to call the police. I didn't want you waking up and learning that I'd had your mother arrested."

"She's not my mother. She gave up that right when she murdered my brother and me." Harry watched Meg's cheeks redden. "I don't mean to lecture you. I'm just worried about her hurting you. No matter what the shrinks at the prison hospital say, she's dangerous. She's not carrying that carving knife to open her fan mail. She's still as crazy as a shithouse rat."

Meg looked up at him like a little girl. "I just don't want you to be mad at me."

Harry shook his head and slowly allowed a smile to come to his lips. "I guess you haven't had many male friends whose mothers carried carving knives in their purses."

"Only one or two," Meg replied in kind.

"Come on, I'll buy you breakfast."

After breakfast Harry took Meg back to her boat, then went to the Clearwater police headquarters to sign the paperwork on his mother's arrest. Because she had a knife in her possession and had to be disarmed by a police officer (albeit, her son), Lucy was sent to the Pinellas County women's jail to be held until her arraignment in court.

Harry then caught up with Max Abrams to see if anything had developed in the search for Tony Rolf.

"A big zero," Max said from behind his desk. "And until something does, my captain wants me to concentrate on more immediate stuff." He shook his head in disgust. "I asked him what was more immediate than another attempt on Jocko Doyle's life and he said not to worry, he was increasing the police protection around Jocko."

"I've been expecting that, but since he's agreed to increasing the guard, maybe you could ask him to put M.J. Moore in charge of the detail."

"Yeah, good idea," Max said. "I'll put in for her."

"Okay. And I'll stay on Rolf and keep you posted on anything I find," Harry said.

"Anything comes up on him here, I'll let you know. In the meantime, I got a court order to enter that house we thought he was in. I'm sending in a forensics team to search the house and dust for prints. If he was there we'll know by the end of the day."

* * *

Harry reached out to Vicky to fill her in on where the search for Rolf stood. They met for lunch at Pete & Shorty's Tavern, an old-time Clearwater bar/restaurant on Gulf to Bay Boulevard. On first glance it was a ramshackle place with a long bar complemented by booths and tables that were clearly from another era. There were additional tables on a covered patio as well that substituted fresh air for the feeling of a time gone by, but Harry and Vicky preferred the old Florida ambiance offered indoors. There was an ancient pulley system running above the bar that carried food orders out to the kitchen and a staff of loyal waitresses who greeted everyone like a long-lost relative. The walls were covered with framed newspaper articles and old advertisements calling back to a day before air-conditioning, when Clearwater was just an oversized beach community that catered to winter visitors.

Harry and Vicky declined the offered menus and ordered the restaurant's signature pork tenderloin sandwiches, the pork pounded to a thin sliver and then breaded and fried, each piece big enough to overflow the roll on which it was served. Then they settled in to comfortable cop talk.

"The captain is being his usual prick self about me taking time off," Vicky said, "but there isn't much he can do about it. It's all legitimate vacation time or comp time."

"And he still doesn't know we're after the clown who shot Jocko?"

"He hasn't a clue," Vicky said. "Abrams has done a great job of shielding us from both his own bosses and ours. We've got no business working a Clearwater case in any official capacity. You're working it on your own time as a private citizen, and that's not a problem as long as the Clearwater cops don't object. So far, nobody who could object has caught on to what we're doing. And you know our captain would object. He'd figure this case would be one of the biggest during his time on the job and he wouldn't want to be left out. If he wasn't such a know-nothing political hack, I'd invite him to join us, just to play it safe, but it would just be extra work teaching him what to do."

Harry appreciated her comment; it was a sad truth about the sheriff's office. In Florida, sheriffs were elected officials who were in charge of court officers, the jails, the farms that inmates raised their food on, all in addition to regular policing duties, serving as the law-enforcement arm of every town that didn't have its own police department. In short, it was the greatest source of patronage in each county, where jobs and promotions were often tied to political support rendered during the last election. On the policing end, almost every job above the rank of lieutenant was directly linked to those who had worked to get the sheriff elected.

"It would probably help if I knew how long it's going to take to bring this son of a bitch to book," Harry said. "But I can't even offer a decent guess and it's embarrassing. The way he's got us running in circles while he slips by our guards and tries to kill an ex-cop *for the second time* is maddening—especially when that ex-cop happens to be my father."

"We wouldn't be running in circles if the people in charge of that make-believe church weren't helping him," Vicky said. "There's no question in my mind that they're hiding him out until things quiet down and they can find a safe place to stash him."

"Yeah, I agree. But I can't prove it."

Vicky drummed her fingers on the table. "I just wish I could understand what makes people join this half-assed church, or cult, or whatever the hell it is."

"I've been reading up on them," Harry said, "and I'm starting to get a handle on what they're all about."

"You mean you're not spending *all* your free time with the sailboat lady? Tell me."

"Okay, Ms. Wiseass, let's go back to what Lilly Mikinos told us—that most of the people who join up have a desperate need to belong to something that will exert a positive control over their lives. But from what I've read and seen there's very little that's positive about it. It's all an illusion that the people who run the church keep reinforcing at every turn. When you sign up—and by the way, members of Sea Org sign a billion-year contract because Scientology believes in reincarnation and joining covers all your future lives as well, which is why they sign that contract—anyway, when you do, you're told you're going to change the world. But before you can do that you have to change all the bad things about yourself—things they call *overts*. To do this and to help other people do it, everybody is encouraged to write *knowledge reports* about each other, which basically means that everybody is supposed to rat each other out, everybody is supposed to become that little girl in elementary school who keeps running to the teacher telling on everybody else. Then you go into auditing, where you confess all your fears and failures. And your auditor, or minister, measures your progress using some gadget called an E-meter or Electropsychometer, which the church says can only be used by these specially trained church ministers to help locate areas of spiritual stress.

"So, when you're finally diagnosed you're told you're some piece of shit who needs all kinds of work to become *clear*, or a person whose mind isn't reactive to any outside stimulus. And that's where all the very expensive courses, the Bridge to Total Freedom, starts to come in. And when you finish those initial courses and become *clear*, you're still not finished. Now you graduate to a whole new series of courses that are even more expensive and that will help you be *spiritually free* and become an *Operating Thetan.* And even that has levels—one, two, three, and so on. And by the time you finish you've invested some heavy cash—150 grand and up."

"So where do these people get the money?" Vicky asked. "Everybody isn't a movie star who can afford 150K."

"They cash in or sell everything they own, take out loans that the church helps them secure. And before long, unless they're wealthy, they've sold everything and they're up to their ass in debt. So the money just keeps flowing into the church coffers, and the individual member's life becomes more and more entwined with Scientology. By then they've also broken away from their family and friends who don't belong to the church because they've been told that nonbelievers are *suppressive persons*, who will try to destroy a member's beliefs, and before they know it the church owns them body and soul, and they sit there wondering where the hell their lives went. And if they try to get out they find themselves facing someone like Tony Rolf."

"You make it sound pretty grim, even scary," Vicky said.

"I guess I do," Harry answered. "And it's even worse for the average Joe who joins up, someone who's not a celebrity, or who doesn't already have a successful profession or business. If you're that average Joe and you want to advance in the church, you have to join Sea Org, which is like the church's religious order. If a member of Sea Org breaks any of the rules, he or she must join the Rehabilitation Project Force, where you wear all-black clothing and part of your job is manual labor—like scrubbing out dumpsters and garbage cans and cleaning bathroom floors in the church's motels and dormitories. And you get paid next to nothing; in my mind, that puts you just one step short of being a slave." Harry took a long breath and shook his head. "If someone I loved fell under Scientology's spell, I'd be scared shitless for them."

"From what I've heard, it's even worse for women who join Sea Org," Vicky said. "Forget the fact that you're not allowed to have sex unless you're married, if you are married and get pregnant you get pressured to have an abortion."

"I heard that but I don't understand it. Most religions encourage children in order to build their ranks."

"Not Scientology. They pay their average Sea Org people a pittance—twenty-five or thirty bucks a week plus room and board for working seventy, eighty, ninety hours. They allow them to get married, but if they start letting them have kids they'll lose that slave labor. Their people just won't be able to work those hours, let alone for those wages. So they pressure them to have abortions. It's either abortions or paying everybody a living wage and building day care facilities. Guess what they choose? Of course they deny it, but I bet Rolf and their other goons have taken scores of pregnant women to Planned Parenthood and made sure they had the procedure."

Their food arrived and Harry and Vicky dug in.

After leaving Vicky, Harry touched base with Max and learned that Rolf's fingerprints were all over the house they'd been watching the previous day. The question now was: where had the son of a bitch gone?

Chapter Thirteen

Meg Adams left her Clearwater Beach high-rise and entered the limo that was waiting for her. She gave the driver a Tampa address and settled back for a long ride. She was dressed in a Giorgio Armani ensemble with a black-and-champagne-striped blazer with a notched collar, over a champagne camisole and blue-gray slacks. Her black-leather high-heeled shoes were open at the toe. Altogether she had paid more than $3,500 for the clothing she wore and her closets were filled with a myriad of other designer fashions. There was no boyfriend living in the beachfront condo, he had been as fictitious as the name Adams.

The limo pulled up in front of the original Columbia Restaurant in Ybor City. There was another Columbia in Clearwater Beach less than a mile from Meg's condo, but she preferred the ambience of the original—which started as a pushcart in 1905, grew to a corner tavern selling Cuban sandwiches and a renowned salad, and finally to a full-scale restaurant during the heart of the Depression.

"I'll be at least an hour," Meg told the driver. "You needn't come back sooner unless I call."

Entering the Columbia was like stepping back in time. There were several beautiful dining rooms, each with its own distinct style. Meg chose the balcony overlooking the indoor patio garden, both for its privacy and its feel of being part of a grand old home in the heart of Havana.

After being led to her table by a handsome maître d', Meg slid into her chair and smiled at her guest.

"You look elegant as always," Regis Walsh said. He sent a genuine smile across the table, something that was highly unusual for him. But he truly liked the young woman; admired her talent and her business acumen. He only wished he had more people as dependable as her.

"How is this so-called dead detective? Does he still hold out hope of capturing our Mr. Rolf?"

Meg tapped the side of her nose. "He keeps his own counsel on that one. But I have noticed a bit of frustration."

Meg owned her own security agency and Walsh had employed her services numerous times. When she handled a case herself, rather than assign it to a member of her staff, the cost was tripled. On sensitive cases like this, Walsh felt it was worth every penny.

"Have you found anything we can use against him?" Walsh asked.

"His mother," Meg said. "She's mad as a hatter, but the state prison system has seen fit to release her, although presently she's being held for violating a court order to stay away from her son."

Walsh leaned forward and lowered his voice almost to a whisper. "Is she a real danger to him?"

"I believe she is. I believe she intends to kill him."

"Kill her only child? My lord, I never dreamed of anything . . ." Walsh paused. "Of course she did kill him once already, if all that dead detective nonsense is to be believed."

"He's safe from her for now, and if things go well for him in court he may be rid of her indefinitely," Meg explained.

"What are chances that the court will rule in her favor?"

"Next to nothing," Meg said. "She doesn't have a lawyer or the resources to hire one. That means the court will appoint someone who will just go through the motions. If she had a sharp criminal lawyer she could probably beat the charges against her, or at least have them delayed. After all, she was arrested by the person she was ordered to stay away from. A good criminal lawyer could raise the possibility that she was set up by her son. He did fight her release from prison quite vehemently."

Walsh drummed his fingers on the table, but said nothing.

The waiter arrived to take their orders. Meg started with an extra-dry Grey Goose martini to Walsh's single malt and soda. When the waiter returned with their drinks, Meg ordered the signature "1905" salad and the croquetas de langosta from the tapas menu, while Walsh, who described himself as "famished," ordered the scallops Casimiro and the grilled grouper.

Walsh smiled across the table as Meg sipped her drink. "Again you have proven invaluable," he said.

"It's always a pleasure to work with you, Regis. Do you want me to continue to remain close to Detective Doyle?"

"For the time being, I want you to remain very close to our policeman. I need to know if and when he plans to take any action against us so we can stay one step ahead of him. In the meantime, perhaps we'll also find a way to help his mother with her legal difficulties. I'll need your help with that as well. I know you've helped significantly already, but there's a bit more I'll need from you with regard to Lucy Santos."

"Of course," Meg said.

Walsh's smile was so cold it sent a chill down Meg Adams's spine.

Chapter Fourteen

Tony Rolf paced the salon like a caged animal. He needed to get out, to move around; to have contact with people. He looked about and couldn't deny he was surrounded by luxury he had seldom known in his life. But no matter how luxurious his surroundings, he still felt like a prisoner. It reminded him of how he had once locked himself in his room to keep himself safe from his mother's lover. He had known all those years ago that the son of a bitch would be coming for him. He had beaten the fat bastard so badly that he had gone straight to the emergency room. After that Rolf had begun locking his bedroom door, knowing it was only a matter of time before his adversary would seek revenge. He had begun keeping his knife close so he would be ready for him. If he'd had the wherewithal to obtain a pistol he would have gotten one, but he lacked both the money to buy one and the skill to use it effectively. Walsh had remedied that when he'd made him part of his staff. Now he had both weapons and was equally skilled with each. And he was still trapped behind locked doors. How ironic was that? And he had not heard another word from Regis Walsh, his benefactor and protector. If the man were here right now he would spit in his face.

He allowed that thought to percolate. He knew instinctively that such an act would cost him far too much. Walsh was his only way to escape the police, just as he had been all those years ago.

He took out his cell phone and called Walsh. The call was automatically transferred to Kenneth Oppenheimer.

"I need to speak to him," Rolf said as soon as he recognized Oppenheimer's voice.

"I'm afraid he's at a meeting out of the office," Oppenheimer replied. "I'll leave him a message and I'm sure he'll get back to you as soon as he can."

Rolf picked up on the hint of distain in Oppenheimer's voice. The feeling was mutual and Rolf realized how much he would enjoy doing something that would terrify the fat, sloppy, self-serving son of a bitch.

"You know, Kenneth, there's something about you that truly annoys me, and that is not a wise thing to do."

"What's not a wise thing, Tony?"

"Annoying me, Kenneth, that's what. In fact, it might be considered downright dangerous."

"That sounds like a threat, Tony. I hope it's not."

"Why don't you come over to the boat and we'll discuss it."

Oppenheimer remained silent for almost a minute. "I'm afraid I'm busy right now," he finally said.

Rolf's laughter came over the line as Oppenheimer ended the call.

"The man is simply out of control," Oppenheimer said. "He seems to believe he has the right to terrorize people at will."

"That's his brief," Walsh said. "He puts the fear of God in anyone who strays outside the rules of the church."

"And he did an excellent job. But he doesn't stop there, Regis. Now he terrorizes anyone who crosses his path. He seems to take pleasure in it, and I don't feel I can exert any control over his actions. I don't even learn about the actions he takes until they're over and done with and we're faced with the consequences."

Walsh noticed beads of perspiration on his assistant's upper lip and forehead. The air-conditioning in the office was set at a comfortable seventy-two degrees. Could he really be *that* frightened of the man?

"Kenneth, what is going on? I've never seen you so rattled." Walsh stood and moved to the other side of his desk so he was directly above the seated Oppenheimer.

Oppenheimer stood as well, and turned to face his boss. He was taller and heavier than Walsh so without intending to do so he had reversed the position of dominance.

Walsh put his hand on Oppenheimer's shoulder. "Sit down and relax, Kenneth. I'm going to make arrangements to have someone help you with Tony Rolf."

"Who would that be?" Oppenheimer asked as he slumped back down in his chair.

"Someone you will enjoy working with; someone who is capable of soothing the savage beast."

Meg Avery ended the call and placed her cell phone on the glass-topped side table. Before her lay a panoramic view of the Gulf of Mexico, the very view that had convinced her to invest $1.2 million in the eighth-floor condo she had called home for the past two years. As the head of Avery Security, which had been founded by her late father twenty years earlier, it was an expense she could easily afford; a far cry from the thirty-six-foot Morgan sailboat that she lived aboard as Meg Adams.

She would miss Harry Doyle. He had been a delightful lover and a challenging adversary. But her long-term loyalty always went to the client she was working for—in this case the Church of Scientology. Now Regis Walsh had made an abrupt change in her assignment—from keeping close watch on Harry Doyle to providing security for Tony Rolf until the church could relocate him to a safer place. Walsh had also let it slip that the church would be helping Harry's mother beat the charges that her son had filed against her. To do this they would be hiring Jordan Wells, a well-known Tampa criminal defense lawyer who had worked for them in the past. Wells, as always, would keep the name of Lucy Santos's benefactor strictly confidential, citing attorney-client privilege if necessary.

Meg had actually spoken out against the plan, arguing that Lucy Santos was clearly "mad as a hatter" and a "true physical threat to her son." But that warning had only produced a small self-satisfied smile from Walsh.

"The man is a trained police officer, well qualified to handle a frail middle-aged woman no matter how mad she is, wouldn't you agree?" he had asked. There was no way Meg could fail to agree. "And dealing with her will hopefully keep him occupied and give us the time to take care of our problem."

"You could just feed your problem to the police," she had suggested as a final argument, only to be told that such a move might prove too risky. Meg could only assume he was alluding to the potential dangers that would arise if Tony Rolf decided to talk about the church. But that wasn't her concern. Her firm had been hired to do a job; she would leave it at that.

When Harry Doyle returned to the marina he saw that Meg's boat was not in its slip. He assumed she had gone for a sail. It was a beautiful evening and he wished he had the energy to do the same. Instead he boarded his own boat and, after a light dinner of leftovers and a stiff bourbon, fell into an exhausted and deep sleep.

The next morning Meg's boat was still not back and he walked up to the marina office and asked the dock Nazi if he knew where she had gone. A smirk formed on the man's mouth and with more pleasure than was called for, he informed Harry that a young blond man had come to the marina the previous afternoon and presented him with a note from Meg stating that she had asked the bearer of the note to remove the boat and that she was taking it to the Bahamas for an indefinite period. "I called the phone number she left and she confirmed the note was legit," he said. "She paid for the slip for six months in advance and she doesn't get that money back. I told her that." He shrugged. "That's about two grand. Hey, easy come, easy go for her, I guess."

Harry wanted to reach across his desk and throttle the bastard. But he simply nodded, thanked him, and headed for the parking lot. Once in his car he called Meg's cell phone and received a recorded message that the number was no longer in service. *Usually you don't scare them off so abruptly,* he told himself. He glanced at his watch. He could only hope she would call later and explain. Then he headed off to meet Max Abrams.

When Ken Oppenheimer arrived at the boat that morning with Meg Avery in tow, Tony Rolf decided that the gods were truly smiling on him. The woman was dressed in a proper gray business suit that on her seemed to ooze sex. Tony imagined that anything she wore would do the same. Maybe it was the red hair, maybe that and the look in her green eyes. Whatever it was, it was definitely there. Or maybe it was because he had seen her before—living aboard a sailboat in the marina where he had spied on that cop—living there and clearly bedding that very same cop.

"Ms. Avery is going to help us get you safely out of the area," Oppenheimer explained. "You're to accept anything she asks you to do as if the request came directly from Mr. Walsh."

"You work for the church?" Rolf asked. "When you were with that cop, the one they call the dead detective, were you working for the church then?"

Meg smiled at him. "Yes, I was," she said. "We were both watching him then. But you didn't know who I was or what I was doing."

"Ms. Avery runs a company called Avery Security," Oppenheimer went on. "They provide protection for corporate executives, celebrities, or, as in your case, people who are trying to stay one step ahead of the authorities. They also conduct very thorough investigations."

Rolf smiled. It was something Oppenheimer had never seen before and he stared at Rolf for several moments, thinking how strange he looked with a grin on his face.

"So we'll be working together, trying to keep the authorities at bay?" Rolf asked.

Meg returned his smile. "Mostly I'll be helping you stay out of sight." She sensed he was about to object and raised a hand, stopping him. "It's important, Tony. Think about it. If they can't find you, they can't tie you to anything. I'll help you do that—stay out of sight until you can be safely moved."

"That's one of the problems," Tony said. "I can't stand the confinement. It makes me feel like I'm some little kid locked in his room. My father tried that when I was a teenager and it didn't work."

"What happened?" Meg asked.

Tony stared at her. There was a sly look in his eyes, as if he was trying to decide what, if anything, he should tell her. "Maybe we'll talk about it sometime," he said.

He had glanced at Ken Oppenheimer as he spoke. Meg wondered if he was trying to tell her that he would be more forthcoming when they were alone. "I think Tony and I need some time so we can get to know each other a little better."

Oppenheimer jumped at the suggestion. "That's a great idea. I'm supposed to give a deposition this morning. So I was going to leave anyway. But I'll be available by phone if any problems arise. Call me if there's anything you need."

Tony chuckled as the cabin door closed behind Oppenheimer. He looked at Meg. "Think he was in a hurry to get out of here? That fat bastard is always eager to leave. He's afraid to be in the same room with me."

"I think you may be right," Meg said, then gave Tony a hard look. "But remember this, Tony: I'm not."

When Harry got to the Clearwater police headquarters, he found Max Abrams in a foul mood. "You don't look happy."

"That's because I'm not fucking happy. I'm fucking pissed, is what I am. And I'm pissed because I want to slap the shit out of some Scientologist asshole and I'm not allowed to do that."

"What have they done now?" Harry asked.

"What have they done? Let's see. You no doubt remember that Walsh's staff was supposed to be here for questioning this morning, along with Walsh himself and his assistant Oppenheimer. They were going to bring an attorney with them, right? Well, it seems their attorney has gone to a judge claiming that my insistence that the questioning be done here at police headquarters is going to disrupt church operations. So they asked, and the judge agreed, that all questioning should take place in the church's office so that people not being questioned could get on with their work."

"Does it matter?" Harry said. "Once they decided to bring one of their attorneys into this, the chance that we'd get anything solid went out the window."

"You're right, but that sleazy bastard Walsh is just playing with us, and that's what pisses me off. One of his goons is killing people and *trying* to kill a former member of this department and now *he* starts playing games? And what am I supposed to do? I'm supposed to let him get away with it? Not on the best fucking day of his life will that ever happen."

"So I take it we're going back to Walsh's office."

Max looked at his wristwatch. "According to my cheapo Timex we're due there in half an hour."

Meg went to the galley and brewed a fresh pot of coffee. She had taken off her jacket and moved about in a scoop-necked, sleeveless silk blouse that accented her figure. Tony could tell she wore nothing under the blouse and his eyes fixed on the movement of her ample breasts beneath the shimmering gray fabric. Meg noticed his interest and fought off a smile. He was such a transparent creature it was almost comical and she was certain that transparency led to rejection more often than not.

"The first thing we have to do is change your appearance again," she said. "The blond hair dye needs to be redone. I can help you with that. Next you'll have to get some contact lenses. They'll be plain glass, of course, unless you have a prescription, but their main purpose will be to change the color of your eyes. You can choose the color. Your eyes are a pale blue now, so I would suggest a dark blue or green, but as I said, the choice is yours."

Tony stared at her, mesmerized. No one had taken this much interest in him for as far back as he could remember. Regis Walsh had shown some, but that was limited to getting him a job and a new identity.

"We should also redo your skin tanning," Meg continued, driving his thoughts away. "I know someone who will come here to the boat and treat you. I would suggest that you tan every part of your body that will not be covered by a bathing suit." She studied him even more closely, tilting her head to one side. "Show me your teeth." Tony did as he was told. "No, they're fine, nothing that will draw undo attention to you." She picked up the tray holding the coffee pot, two mugs, milk, and sugar. "Now, let's sit down and relax and you can tell me all about yourself. But remember this: the more you tell me, the better equipped I'll be to help you. Whatever you hold back . . . Well, I can't help you with things I don't know about."

When Max and Harry arrived at the Scientology offices, Kenneth Oppenheimer and a lawyer who identified herself as Melody Ford were waiting for them.

The lawyer, who was a tall, awkward, horse-faced woman somewhere in her thirties, made a show of looking at her wristwatch peevishly. They were five minutes late. Max mimicked the gesture, noting the time with a snort that Harry interpreted as: *Who gives a fuck?*

Melody Ford brushed back a strand of brown hair that that fallen across her forehead and extended a hand toward an unoccupied office. "I thought we could work in there," she said.

"*We?*" Max replied.

"I'll be counseling the people you interview," she said a bit tartly.

"Has everyone in the office asked you to represent them?" Harry asked.

"That's my understanding." She glanced at Ken Oppenheimer.

"We offered legal representation to everyone. No one declined," he said.

Max offered up another derisive snort. "Well, I'll tell you what we'll do. *We* will ask each person if they want an attorney present or not. If they say they do, we will invite you to join us. If they don't, we won't."

The lawyer bristled. "I intend to be there with each of my clients. I have been engaged to represent them and I shall do exactly that." She strode past them into the office and placed a tape recorder on the desk.

Max picked it up and handed it back to her. "Thanks, but I have my own. This is just taking up space that I need." He took a seat behind the desk and moved his arms in a circular gesture as if clearing away unwanted clutter. Then he took out a notebook and pen and placed them on the desk in front of him. Next he removed a tape recorder from his jacket pocket and put it beside the notebook and pen. He looked up and smiled. "All set, Melody. You don't mind if I call you Melody, do you?"

"I'd prefer Ms. Ford," she said.

"Do I detect annoyance, Ms. Ford? That's what I do, you know. I *detect* things."

"Let's get on with this," she snapped.

"Hey, what's the rush? They're paying you by the billable hour, aren't they?" He withdrew a list of names from an inside jacket pocket and extended it toward Ken Oppenheimer, who was standing just outside the doorway. "I believe this is the list of employee names that you provided me with. Can you confirm that it is?"

Oppenheimer stepped forward, took the list, glanced at it, and began nodding his head.

"Speak up, Ken. I want to get everything on tape." Max tapped the top of the recorder.

"Yes, this is the list." He handed it back to Max.

"Okay, it's in alphabetical order, so we'll take it that way. The first person we'll interview is Marylyn Arles." He looked up at Melody Ford and pointed toward the door. "Go get your client, counselor."

Marylyn Arles was in her midthirties, a bit on the plumpish side, with scraggly brown hair, bright blue eyes, and a beautiful smile.

Max told her to sit in one of the office chairs and asked if she had retained Ms. Ford to represent her.

Confusion spread across the woman's face. She looked at Melody Ford, then back at Max, and shrugged. "I really don't know."

"The church hired me to represent you and the other members of the staff," the attorney explained.

"Oh," Marylyn responded.

"Do you feel you need Ms. Ford to help you answer my questions?" Max asked.

Confusion returned to Marylyn Arles's face. "I don't know. I don't think so."

"You have the right to counsel. The church hired me and I'm here to help you with the questioning," Ms. Ford snapped back. "If I tell you not to answer something, you simply say: *On advice of counsel I decline to answer*. I'll tell you if and when to say that, understood?"

Marylyn looked back at the attorney. "Will I get into trouble if I say that?"

A broad smile spread across Max's face. He was enjoying himself thoroughly. "No you won't, hon," he said.

"Do not call my client *hon*," Ms. Ford said. "And please allow *me* to answer when she asks *me* a question."

Max ignored her and asked his first question: "Do you know a church employee named Tony Rolf?"

Marylyn glanced at the attorney, who nodded.

"I know who he is. But I don't *know* him, like, personally."

"What does he do for the church?"

"You mean what's his job?"

"That's right."

"I don't know for sure. I know he deals with people who have gotten themselves into trouble."

"He *deals* with them? What does that mean?" Max had pushed himself to the edge of his seat.

"I want you to decline to answer that question," Ms. Ford said.

Marylyn turned around, looking confused once again.

"Just say, *On advice of counsel I decline to answer.*" Irritation was heavy in Ms. Ford's voice.

Marylyn did so, her confusion only growing.

"Did Tony Rolf work out of this office?" Max asked.

"I think so. I saw him here a lot, anyway."

"Did you ever talk to him?"

"No, he was scary. I was afraid—"

"That's enough. No more on that question, Ms. Arles," the lawyer said.

Max shook his head. "Jesus, let the woman finish."

"I think not," Melody Ford countered. "You've established that Mr. Rolf worked out of this office—though he was seldom here—which is what Mr. Walsh and Mr. Oppenheimer have already told you. He was an employee of the church and until it's shown that he has committed some crime, I don't intend to allow him to be smeared by innuendo."

"You represent him too?" Max asked. "Well, good, please produce him so we can ask him a few questions. Like why he keeps trying to kill one of our retired police officers."

"That's an allegation that is yet to be proven," Ms. Ford shot back.

* * *

Tony Rolf sipped his coffee. He was seated in one of the salon's soft leather chairs, directly opposite the sofa on which Meg Avery sat, her legs tucked up beneath her.

"When did you come to Clearwater, Tony?"

"At the beginning of 2005," he said. "I was living in Los Angeles and had just turned eighteen."

"And you joined the church here or there?"

"There. Mr. Walsh brought me to the church and later he gave me a job here in Clearwater."

"How did you come to meet him?"

"I was living on the streets and a guy who befriended me turned out to be a Scientologist. He brought me to a church office and introduced me to Mr. Walsh. Walsh sort of took me under his wing and brought me to Clearwater, helped me change my name, and gave me my job. He also enrolled me in some church courses."

"Why the name change, Tony?"

He hesitated. "The police were looking for me. He said it would be safer to have a new identity. It has been. He was right."

"Why were the police looking for you, Tony?" *It's like drawing water from a well with a leaky bucket,* she thought to herself.

Again, Tony hesitated. "How do I know I can trust you?"

"Mr. Walsh trusts me. Do you trust Mr. Walsh?"

"Yes, he's the only one I do trust."

"Well, then I think it's clear you can trust me."

"I killed my stepfather," he said after another pause. "It was self-defense, but that might be hard for me to prove."

"And this was back in 2005?"

"December of 2004," Rolf said.

"I'd like you to tell me your stepfather's name."

"Why do you have to know that?"

"I told you, Tony, the more I know, the better I can protect you."

"His name was John Gandolini. He was a wop who had latched onto my mother after my real father was killed back when I was fourteen. My mother met him in some bar they both hung out in and within a couple of weeks he moved in with us. After that he took her money and beat the shit out of her for all the years they were together."

"Did he beat you too?"

"No, but he tried to intimidate me. He was a big asshole. People said he worked as an enforcer for a couple of loan sharks. Then one day, when I was eighteen, I beat the shit out of him. He left then, but I knew he'd be back. And sure enough, back he came, all sorrow and regrets. A few days later, that's when he tried to kill me. He had to, you see, because he knew he couldn't beat on me and he couldn't intimidate me anymore. He was just like my father. He just didn't have the good sense to go away."

Meg digested what she'd been told. She couldn't wait to get to her computer and find out all the facts behind the 2004 death of one John Gandolini.

"I'm glad you're being so open and honest with me," she told him. "Tomorrow we'll get started on changing your appearance."

Tony smiled at her, and it was so chilling that she had to struggle to keep her reaction under control. It would be like walking a tightrope to keep him under control, but she had done it before with people just as dangerous.

"That cop who's trying to nail my ass to a barn door—were you sleeping with him at the marina?"

"That's a very impertinent question," Meg said. "Why do you want to know?"

Tony leaned forward in his chair, elbows on his knees. "I told you about killing my stepfather. Now you can reciprocate, right?"

"Yes, I was. I needed to get close to him fast. He was a danger to the church."

"The church doesn't approve of that, you know: sex outside of marriage. You'd be in for some heavy-duty discipline if they ever found out."

"But I'm not a member of the church."

"You're not?" Tony seemed genuinely surprised by this bit of information.

"No, ours is strictly a business arrangement. I'm just a hired hand doing a job."

Tony sat in his chair nodding his head. He seemed to be having difficulty digesting that idea.

Chapter Fifteen

Meg Avery sat in front of her computer reading about the death of John Gandolini. It had occurred in Los Angeles on December 25, 2004, and had been ruled a homicide by the medical examiner. The murder weapon had been a double-edged knife approximately six inches in length and Mr. Gandolini, who had been forty-five at the time, had been eviscerated in a prolonged and vicious attack. *Eviscerated on Christmas Day*, Meg thought. A shudder went through her body as she read on. The victim had been killed in the residence of Victoria Rawlings, forty-eight, with whom he had lived sporadically for the past ten years. Police had named Ms. Rawlings's son Anthony, eighteen, as a person of interest. A source in the police department, who spoke on condition of anonymity, said Anthony had an extensive and violent juvenile record. His current whereabouts were unknown.

Meg went on to the next article, which identified John Gandolini as a low-level hoodlum with an extensive criminal record. He was reputedly a strong arm for several LA bookies and loan sharks, but his numerous arrests were all dismissed when the victims and witnesses refused to testify. There were also several charges of domestic violence against his girlfriend Vicky Rawlings and several other women. All but two of those charges had been subsequently dropped by the alleged victims.

So that's why the police never ran Tony down, Meg thought. Gandolini had been a thug and a career criminal. For the LA cops, Gandolini's murder had been a simple case of good riddance to bad trash.

But that did not change what Tony Rolf was. He was a dangerous and unstable person. Ken Oppenheimer had analyzed the problem perfectly and it made her wonder about Regis Walsh and the level of judgment he was exerting. Why had he brought him into the fold at all? Had Tony or some third party convinced him that he had acted in self-defense? She thought back to the words used in the first newspaper story—*a prolonged and vicious attack* . . . on Christmas Day.

Meg cautioned herself not to dwell on those unpleasant facts. Tony Rolf was a job, that was all, a job for which she was being very well paid. Tomorrow she would begin gathering the experts who would alter his appearance to the point that his own mother would have trouble recognizing him. When the work was done, she would collect her company's fee and move on. She wondered if she would take a job working for the church again. She supposed only time would tell.

The following morning Harry was at the Clearwater Police Department waiting to join Max for the final interviews at the Scientology offices. The previous day they had gotten through most of the staff and were left only with Regis Walsh's secretary, Walsh himself, and Kenneth Oppenheimer. The first round of interviews had been mostly uneventful—much as they had expected them to be. The various members of the staff were totally uninformed, or completely intimidated by Regis Walsh and Kenneth Oppenheimer. Harry had concluded that it was a combination of both. Even the staff member who had slipped Max the note about Rolf being hidden away in Safety Harbor had suddenly gone blank.

Just as Max announced that he was ready to go, Harry's cell phone rang. It was the clerk for Judge Walter McCoy of the Pinellas County criminal court. The clerk informed Harry that his mother's attorney had requested an emergency hearing asking that the charges against her be dismissed.

"Her attorney? I didn't know she had one," Harry said.

"She's got a humdinger," the clerk said. "None other than Jordan Wells, who, as I'm sure you know, is considered one the best criminal defense attorneys in the state. The hearing will be at three o'clock today. Be on time. The judge is very insistent on punctuality."

"Who's been assigned to prosecute?" Harry asked.

"No one; there hasn't been time. But they'll need to have someone here by three sharp."

"Who hired Wells? My mother sure as hell doesn't have that kind of money."

"I have no idea," the clerk said. "It's not pertinent to the proceedings."

It's pertinent to me, Harry thought as he ended the call. *And I have a pretty good idea who's behind it.*

Harry hung up and filled Max in, reminding him that the criminal court building was a good half an hour away from the Scientology offices.

"We'll be finished in plenty of time," Max said. "Now who the hell do you think hired a slick son of a bitch like Wells?"

"Do you have any ideas?"

"Oh . . . yeah," Max said.

"Me too," Harry said. "One very sleazy bastard named Regis Walsh."

"It would fit in with their history," Max said. "From what I've read, whenever someone is designated as an enemy of the church, they're known to spare no expense at laying a little misery on their doorstep. A few celebrities who fell out of their good graces have written books about it."

"Well, let's go take on Mr. Walsh and Mr. Oppenheimer," Harry said. "If I'm such an enemy of the church, I have a reputation to live up to."

Melody Ford was her old cheerful self when they resumed their questioning, this time of Mavis Quincy, Regis Walsh's personal secretary.

"I'm sure you understand that as Mr. Walsh's secretary, Ms. Quincy has access to some very sensitive church information," Melody Ford said. "Consequently, she has already been instructed not to answer any questions that touch on those areas."

"Can you give me a hint about what areas don't touch on sensitive church information?" Max asked.

"Very few," the lawyer replied.

Mavis Quincy looked calm, cool, and collected as she took a chair in front of the desk Max was using. She was in her midforties, with clear blue eyes, short brown hair, and a soft, pleasant smile.

"How long have you worked for Mr. Walsh?" Max asked.

"A little over ten years," Mavis said.

"Is he a good boss?"

"Is that question really pertinent?" Melody Ford interjected.

"It is to me," Max said. "If she doesn't like him, it could color her answers."

"Okay, go ahead," the attorney said, her voice heavy with exasperation. "Answer his question."

"He's an excellent boss."

"I'm sincerely glad to hear it," Max said. "I wish mine was."

Harry held back a smile. It was the first time he'd seen the charming side of Max Abrams on the job.

"Do you know a man named Tony Rolf?"

"Yes, he works for the church."

"Is that the only way you know him?"

"Yes, I don't know him personally at all."

"Who does he work for?"

"Well, he works in the office of church discipline and everyone who works there works under Mr. Oppenheimer and Mr. Walsh."

"Which one of them did he work for specifically, if you know: Mr. Oppenheimer or Mr. Walsh?" Max asked.

"I believe he reported day to day to Mr. Oppenheimer, but everyone is ultimately under Mr. Walsh. I believe Mr. Walsh took a special interest in Tony."

"Why is that?"

"I was told he had a particularly difficult life. Mr. Walsh, I believe, wanted to help him."

Saint Regis, Harry thought, *protector of homeless young killers*.

"Do you know where Tony Rolf is now?" Max asked.

"I do not."

"Do you know if Tony Rolf has been in touch with Mr. Walsh or Mr. Oppenheimer?"

At that point Ms. Ford once again asserted herself: "You are to answer that on advice of counsel, you decline to answer."

Mavis began to repeat the lawyer's words but Max cut her off: "It's okay, I get the drift. Thank you, Ms. Quincy." He looked up into the attorney's sneering countenance. "Can we have Mr. Oppenheimer now."

Ken Oppenheimer was visibly nervous when he took a seat in front of Max Abrams.

"Mr. Oppenheimer, do you know Tony Rolf?" Max began.

Oppenheimer twisted in his chair. "On advice of counsel I decline to answer that question."

"Wait a minute," Max said, throwing his hands in the air. "The guy works for you, reports to you regularly, and you can't tell me if you know him or not?"

"On advice of counsel I decline to answer that question," Oppenheimer said.

Max pushed his chair back and rotated his shoulders as if trying to work out a cramp.

"I object to your physical machinations," Melody Ford said. "They are clearly intended to intimidate my client."

Max stared at her. "I'm stretching. I've got a crick in my neck. If I wanted to intimidate him I'd take out my rubber hose."

"That wouldn't surprise me at all," the attorney snapped.

Max shook his head and turned back to Oppenheimer. "Do you work here?" he asked.

Oppenheimer stared at him as if uncertain what to say.

"Do you work for the Church of Scientology and is your office in this building?"

"Yes," Oppenheimer said.

"See, now we're communicating," Max said. "Isn't that nice?" He paused. "No answer?"

Oppenheimer looked at Melody Ford for guidance. The lawyer only rolled her eyes.

"I have a daughter who used to roll her eyes just like that when she was a teenager," Max said. "Then she grew up and stopped doing it."

Melody Ford glared at him. Max offered up a smile in return.

"Are we finished with Mr. Oppenheimer?" Ms. Ford asked.

"Is he going to answer any more questions?"

"It's possible," she said. "But I doubt it."

Max slapped his hands together. "Then let's have Mr. Walsh."

Walsh kept them waiting for fifteen minutes before he entered the room with a broad smile spread across his face. He was dressed in a gray suit that was clearly tailor-made, a pale blue fitted shirt with a striped tie, and black Bally loafers.

"Sorry, gentlemen, I was on a call to our offices on the West Coast."

"Early for the West Coast, isn't it?" Max said.

"The longer you're around us you'll find we work long hours, usually starting before dawn and going well into the evening," Walsh replied.

"Well, that's interesting," Max said. "But I'd like to get on with this interview. Detective Doyle has to get over to the criminal court building."

"Whatever you wish," Walsh said.

"Okay," Max began, "your name is Regis Walsh and you run the office of church discipline for the Church of Scientology?"

"Yes."

"Do you have an employee named Tony Rolf?"

"I do."

"How did Mr. Rolf come to work for you?"

"Mr. Rolf was working for the church in Los Angeles. He had a maintenance job, doing repairs, cleaning, that sort of thing. I met him there and took note of his work ethic and came to believe that he had potential for more demanding work. So I offered him an opportunity to work in our office in Clearwater. He accepted. That was eleven years ago."

"I take it you have found his work here satisfactory?"

"I have."

"Sort of a model employee, would you say?"

"I never use terms like that, sergeant. I've found they have a way of coming back to haunt you."

Max jotted something down in his notebook and went on: "Did you ever have to discipline Mr. Rolf for overzealousness?"

"I've had to correct him from time to time—suggest that he try a different approach. Not often, but occasionally."

"Were you surprised when you discovered that he had been named a person of interest in the murder of a young woman who was a member of your church and the attempted murder of a retired Clearwater police officer?"

"I was, indeed. I also firmly believe you will ultimately find him innocent of those crimes."

"Do you know where Tony Rolf is now?"

"On advice of counsel I decline to answer that question," he said.

"To the best of your knowledge, did Tony Rolf ever physically harm anyone?"

"Again, on advice of counsel I decline to answer that question."

Max turned to Harry. "Do you have any questions for Mr. Walsh?"

"Yes, I do," Harry said. "Mr. Walsh, do you know a Tampa attorney named Jordan Wells?"

"I'm sorry, detective, but on the advice of counsel I decline to answer that question."

And fuck you too, Harry thought.

The Pinellas County criminal court, also known as the Justice Center, was located next to the county jail, which was convenient for both the jailers and the jailed since it reduced the need to transport prisoners and the inevitable loss of court time that produced. It was a modern building and lacked the gravitas of dark wood paneling, heavy, oversized furniture, and a high bench that allowed judges to tower over the courtroom. Instead, each courtroom had clean walls painted in pale colors and blond furniture. The overall affect was intense sterility.

Harry arrived fifteen minutes early and went immediately to the prosecution table. He introduced himself to the young assistant state attorney who had been assigned to his mother's case. The young lawyer identified himself as Jeremy Peters and told Harry he had only gotten the case file that morning and would appreciate any information he could provide. Harry gave him a quick summary of his mother's crimes, her subsequent release on parole, and the condition imposed on her that she remain at least one hundred yards away from her son at all times. He explained that he had detained her next to the boat he lived on, after relieving her of a large carving knife she had taken out of her purse.

"Wow, that sounds cut-and-dry," Peters said. "We have only one problem, as far as I can see, and that's the person who's representing her."

"Yeah, Jordan Wells," Harry said.

"Is she wealthy?" Peters asked.

"Poor as a church mouse."

"Then how the hell can she afford him? Scuttlebutt is that he gets a grand an hour while he's in court and five hundred an hour when he's in his office or anywhere else. He doesn't work pro bono unless there's a slam-dunk lawsuit. The guy's a bleeping shark in a three-piece suit. The people in my office call him the Prince of Darkness—and that has nothing to do with the fact that he's black."

"I think my mother has a benefactor."

"Do you know who it is?" Peters asked.

"The Church of Scientology or one of their executives, I'm not certain which."

"Is your mother a Scientologist?"

"No. And it has nothing to do with her. I'm involved in an investigation of one of their goons. This is just an attempt to slow me up—put my mother back out on the street so I have to deal with her."

Peters looked at him skeptically and shook his head. "This case gets crazier by the minute. Do me a favor, will you? Go live in a different county." A sudden flurry of activity drew Peters's attention to the rear of courtroom. "Well here he is, the Prince of Darkness."

Harry turned and watched Jordan Wells make his way down the center aisle. His arrival was filled with dramatic flair, replete with a perfectly tailored blue silk suit and flamboyant yellow silk tie, and two equally well-dressed young women trailing behind, carrying briefcases. The three of them went directly to the defense table and began setting up; then Wells turned and offered a curt nod to Peters, followed by a smile that said, *Prepare to be eaten alive, little boy*.

There was movement at a side door and Harry turned and saw his mother entering the courtroom between two corrections officers. She was wearing an orange prison jumpsuit and her hands were cuffed. She looked haggard and her eyes darted around the room, settling first on her attorney, then on Harry.

Wells made a fuss about having her handcuffs removed, then guided her to a seat next to him at the defense table. Harry rose to go to the spectator seats, but Peters placed a hand on his arm. "We have a few minutes before court is called to order," he said. "Give me another rundown of what happened at the marina."

Judge Walter McCoy entered the courtroom ten minutes later and the proceedings were called to order. McCoy was a short, plump man in his early fifties and his black robes did nothing to mask his girth. Harry knew him from previous criminal cases and had testified before him on numerous occasions. Unlike some judges who were openly arrogant about their power, McCoy had a reputation of living with constant dread that one of his decisions would be overturned or, even worse, criticized by the media. This often led him to decisions that boggled the mind. The judge had the red face of a heavy drinker and as Harry looked up into it now he felt reasonably certain that McCoy would not risk turning a child murderer loose on the streets. Of course, that precluded any tricks Jordan Wells had up his sleeve. Court cases were always a crapshoot, he reminded himself.

The judge asked the court clerk to read the charges against Lucy Santos. Once that was done, he turned to the attorneys and asked Peters to summarize the state's position. Peters made it short and sweet: Lucy Santos had trespassed onto the marina property where her son, Detective Harry Santos Doyle, kept the boat on which he lived. All this, Peters said with a bit of dramatic flourish, despite a parole board directive that she remain at least one hundred yards away from him at all times. When Detective Doyle confronted her, he added, she was holding a six-inch carving knife. Peters removed a plastic bag containing the knife from his briefcase and held it up for the judge to see.

Harry watched the young prosecutor and wondered if his dramatic performance was intended as much for Jordan Wells as for the judge. He might well be auditioning for a future job in Wells's office.

Peters continued by reminding the judge of the charges that had originally brought Lucy Santos before the court—"The murder of her own child," he said with all the flair he could muster. He concluded that the state attorney's office intended to prosecute Ms. Santos for the trespassing charge and to present the grand jury with evidence that she possessed a deadly weapon and used it to menace her son, a duly sworn police officer, causing him to disarm and detain her and call in backup officers from the Clearwater Police Department, who placed her under arrest.

Wells rose to his feet like a thundercloud, his voice reverberating with outrage. "Your Honor, the defense is prepared to present witnesses that will prove beyond any reasonable doubt that Ms. Santos was lured to the marina by a call stating that her son wanted to meet with her, and that she was *not* armed with any weapon, let alone the carving knife in question, when she arrived there. We shall prove that instead she was confronted by her son and illegally handcuffed and detained until two Clearwater police officers arrived to place her under arrest. We will further prove that her son, Detective Harry Santos Doyle, vigorously opposed her release from prison and made repeated complaints about her after state authorities pronounced her no danger to society or herself and released her in her own custody."

"Then you are requesting a hearing," the judge said.

"We are," Wells responded. He picked up a sheet of paper and held it out toward the bench. "Your Honor, I have a list of witnesses with a summary of what their testimony will be. I take this unusual step to support my contention that a preponderance of reasonable doubt exists in this matter and that this reasonable doubt fully supports my client's claim of complete innocence to these charges. The defense does this so that our client, Lucy Santos, might be released without bail to help prepare her defense."

Peters jumped to his feet, claiming that the seriousness of the charges required that the defendant be held without bail.

The judge called the attorneys up to the bench for a sidebar conference. When Peters returned he had a copy of the list Wells had prepared. He looked at Harry and then down at the paper, slowly shaking his head.

From the bench, Judge McCoy stated that a hearing on Ms. Santos's arrest had been scheduled for two weeks hence and that bail for her release had been set at one hundred thousand dollars.

Wells rose to his feet, thanked the court, and said that bail would be posted within the hour.

Lucy Santos was led away, this time without handcuffs, followed by her attorney.

Harry followed Peters out into the hallway. "What the hell happened? And who are the witnesses he's going to present?"

"Boy, he really blindsided us." Peters handed Harry the list of witnesses.

Lucy Santos would testify that she received a call from a man who identified himself as her son, asking her to come to the marina the following day to discuss "family matters."

There was a man who was a technical representative for AT&T who would testify that Lucy Santos received a call from a pay phone in the marina one day before she appeared there and was arrested.

Megan Avery, a.k.a. Meg Adams, who kept her sailboat in a slip across from Harry Doyle's boat, would testify that she witnessed the entire confrontation between Harry and Lucy Santos and at no time did she see a knife in the woman's hand.

Tyler Tully, the dockmaster at the marina, would testify that Harry Doyle made repeated requests for the police to be called if a woman named Lucy Santos was discovered on the marina docks.

And Harry himself would be asked to explain his repeated attempts to keep his mother imprisoned and, when that failed, why he invited his mother to the marina to discuss so-called "family matters" when he knew she was under a parole board and court order to remain one hundred yards away from him at all times.

"Do we know who is posting the bail?" Harry asked.

"Wells said the full amount would be posted in cash."

"Who do we know who has that kind of money?" Harry asked, his words heavy with sarcasm.

"Who is this Meg Avery, a.k.a. Meg Adams?" Peters asked.

"I knew her as Meg Adams, and she did have a sailboat docked in the slip directly opposite mine. I promise you I'll know more by the time of the hearing, but I fully expect to find that she was employed by the Church of Scientology."

"Well, I hope you can find out something. I don't like being sandbagged."

"Don't feel alone," Harry said. "Wells sandbagged me too, and so did she." He offered up a cold smile. "That doesn't happen very often, and when it does, it's something I don't forget."

When Harry left the courthouse he ran into Vicky in the parking lot.

"I was just coming to give you some moral support," she said. Vicky was dressed in form-fitting jeans, jogging shoes, and a man-tailored blue shirt. Her Glock was on her right hip and her badge was on her belt.

"You look ready to wrestle with bad guys," Harry said.

"Not glamorous enough for you, eh?"

"Believe me, I've seen all the glamour I ever want to see." Harry filled her in on what Wells had pulled off in court, his belief that Regis Walsh was behind it, and how Walsh and the church had used Meg Adams against him and were now possibly financing his birth mother's bail. He watched Vicky's eyes darken and he could tell she was struggling to control her anger.

"Before this is all over, I'm going to find a way to knock that redheaded bitch on her ass."

"Thanks, partner. And I'll be right there so I can testify that you never touched her. I can play that game as well as Ms. Adams or Avery or whatever the hell her name is."

"Look," Vicky said, "you stay on Rolf's ass. That's what Walsh is trying to keep you from doing. I'll find out who Adams/Avery is. Before I finish we'll know everything about her, right down to the number of pimples on her ass."

Chapter Sixteen

Meg Avery thought about Harry Doyle sitting in the criminal court building only now learning that his lover had been a wolf in Victoria's Secret panties. Poor Harry, he actually deserved better, she thought. But the world was what it was, and as her late father had taught her long ago, there was only one bottom line—money in the bank.

She watched Abu LeBouf, a makeup artist she had used many times when disguises were required, spread body-tanning lotion on every part of Tony Rolf's body not covered by underwear. It had been a battle at first. Abu was a flamboyant gay man and Tony had resisted the idea that the guy would be rubbing lotion all over his body. Meg had been forced to take Tony aside and lay down the law. The carrot that went along with the stick was that he would be able to safely go out in public—within limits—when his disguise was in place, and tanning was the first step.

She smiled thinking back on the battle. Abu LeBouf—and that completely made-up name did not help—had feigned exasperation, then outrage, then hurt feelings, until she thought Tony was about to grab him by the throat. Finally everyone surrendered to common sense and Tony disrobed down to his boxer shorts. An hour later he had tanned skin that looked completely natural.

Next, a hair stylist who Meg had used before arrived at the boat to dye Tony's hair a natural blond and teach him how to touch it up when necessary. This time the stylist was an attractive female who Tony flirted with outrageously.

When the young woman was finished, Meg fitted him with dark blue contact lenses. Finished, she led Tony into one of the staterooms that had a full-length mirror. The transition was shocking.

"I'll teach you how to use stage putty for your cheeks. You'll do that each time before you go out. It will change your face so completely your own mother wouldn't recognize you," Meg told him.

"Yeah, it's great even the way it is now," he said. "When can I go out?"

"I'll get in touch with Mr. Walsh. As soon as he sees you and gives you the thumbs-up, we'll be good to go. I've never seen anyone so anxious to leave such luxurious accommodations," she teased.

"Even luxurious accommodations can be a prison," Tony said. "Once I know I can leave, I'm sure I'll enjoy them much more."

I doubt it, Meg thought. *You are a person born to dislike everything.*

Regis Walsh arrived at eight o'clock that evening. At Meg's direction, Tony stripped down to his boxer shorts. She applied the stage putty, altering his facial features, and took him into the salon. Walsh appraised him for several minutes, at one point walking a full circle around him.

"Astonishing," he said. "I would never suspect that he had any abnormal skin condition, and even his hair and eyes look completely normal." He broke into a wide smile. "The only problem, Tony, is that Meg has made you too bloody handsome. People, especially women, won't be able to take their eyes off you."

"So I can go out?" Tony asked, remaining oblivious to the compliment.

"Yes, with Meg accompanying you." He turned his eyes on Meg, appraising her now. "I suggest you wear a blond or brunette wig. Your red hair is too striking. After what happened in court today, I think the police may be keeping an eye out for gorgeous redheads."

Meg inclined her head acknowledging the compliment. "I have several wigs that I've used in the past. I'll alternate them each time we go out."

"Splendid," Walsh said. "Now let me tell you both what happened in court today."

Vicky started with the police computer. She typed in the name *Meg Avery* and immediately got a hit. The screen came up with several documents, each containing a photograph of the woman who had lived on a sailboat across from Harry's boat.

Meg Avery was listed as president and CEO of Avery Security. The firm was licensed to provide investigative services, personal executive and celebrity security—armed or unarmed. The company offered trained security personnel to work in private industry, stores, shopping centers, banks, etc. It employed 208 people.

Vicky let out a low whistle. This woman was worth megabucks all by her little self. She read on: Avery Security had been founded by Meg's father, William Avery, who had served as president and CEO until his death in 2007. Meg Avery was licensed to carry a weapon, held a license as a private detective—separate from the firm's license—and was trained in martial arts. *Harry's lucky she didn't kick his butt*, Vicky thought.

The company had offices in downtown Tampa in a high-rise building that held several large law firms. Meg's personal residence was not listed but Vicky knew several ways to uncover that as well. *I'm on your tail, Meg. It's only a matter of time before your sweet little ass is mine. And then, martial arts or not, I'm going to knock you on your butt.*

Next Vicky pulled up Meg's original application for a concealed-weapons license. As a professional, she and every licensed member of her staff had to list all the places where their weapons would be secured when not being carried. And there it was, Meg's private residence: *The Ultimar Beachfront Condominium, 1560 Gulf Boulevard, Sand Key, Clearwater, Florida.*

Vicky had been there once on another case. The complex comprised three high-rise buildings, all with balconies offering views of the Gulf of Mexico, two pools, a spa, three professional-quality tennis courts, and a private beach. The individual units varied in size but all were luxurious by anyone's standards. The person she had interviewed on that old case lived in one of the two-story penthouses. The level of luxury was sinful, she had decided then. She also knew that she wanted one all for herself.

So now you're hunting down someone who may very well have one, she thought. *One more reason to hate the bitch.*

Vicky met Harry for a drink at six o'clock. They chose the original Crabby Bill's at Indian Rocks Beach. Harry was already there when she arrived, seated at the bar with a tall draft and a dozen raw oysters set out before him. He looked haggard and she suddenly realized how hurt he was at being so completely taken in by that sultry redhead.

She slipped a copy of the notes she had compiled on Meg Avery in front of him. "This includes her home address, her business address, and a very brief history of her life so far. I say *so far* because I hope we're going to lay some hurt on her that will dramatically alter her résumé."

"I think I'll pay her a little visit," Harry said.

"Not alone, you won't. I wouldn't put it past her to take one look at you and start screaming rape, and have a dozen witnesses to confirm it. You've got to be careful dealing with this bitch, partner. She and her friend Walsh are out to destroy you. By now I'm sure they're pressing the sheriff to start an internal affairs investigation on the whole thing. It's time to play cover-your-ass on everything we do."

"Maybe you should step away from it. I don't want you risking your career. I can afford to lose my job. The sale of my house made that possible. You're not in the same financial position."

"I'm not going anywhere, Harry Doyle, so let's put that BS to bed right now."

Harry slept fitfully and awoke a half hour before dawn. It was cloudy and overcast, killing any chance of the beautiful sunrise he had been looking forward to—something that might drive away or at least obscure the insanity that had taken place in court the previous day.

This woman, his birth mother, had killed both of her children. He had been brought back to life after his heart had stopped beating. His six-year-old brother Jimmy had not been so lucky. He was now six feet underground, decayed in his small coffin. And his mother, the woman who had killed them both, was playing the victim with the help of a well-heeled lawyer and a corrupt executive for a church that Harry felt was little more than a money-making scam created by a demented science-fiction writer who supposedly once told an interviewer that if someone wanted to become rich, they just had to start their own religion.

Harry shook his head. *Stop it*, he told himself. No matter how you looked at it, he was feeling sorry for himself—pure and simple—and that would get him nowhere.

Meg took Tony to dinner at Mystic Fish in Palm Harbor, a restaurant she loved. She was dressed in a pale blue Armani cocktail dress, a white silk Gucci scarf, and light blue St. Laurent studded leather sandals, topped off with a blond wig. Tony wore a summer-weight Todd Snyder sports jacket that Meg had bought for him over a white linen shirt and jeans. They drove to the restaurant in Meg's red Mercedes Cabriolet with the top up. "No sense pushing our luck," she told Tony.

"Right now I feel invincible," he said.

"Better to feel invisible," she told him. "We don't want to take a chance that Harry Doyle might get lucky."

Tony laughed. It was a strange high-pitched sound that set Meg's teeth on edge.

"According to what I've heard, he only gets lucky when dead people talk to him. So I just won't leave any corpses around for him to yak it up with," he said.

He is one scary character, she thought. But it explained why Walsh had used him with difficult church members. One visit from Tony Rolf would scare you right back on the path of church righteousness. Either that or it might get you killed.

Dinner was excellent, as always. Meg had started with a mojito followed by a Caesar salad and a selection of small plates—escargot, seared scallops, and grilled octopus—and a glass of Maso Canali pinot grigio. Tony's choices were more pedestrian: rum and tonic, then a New York strip steak, rare, and a large draft of domestic beer.

Equally as satisfying to each of them was the fact that no one gave Tony a second look.

Throughout dinner Meg noticed Tony's attention drawn to one particular waitress. She was tall, tan, young, and lovely, as the song goes, with pouty lips and a blond ponytail that swung back and forth like a pendulum. The final time he ogled her, Meg leaned across the table and whispered, "If this was a real date I'd be insulted."

"Why?" he asked, all innocence.

At that moment the blond waitress walked by and Meg looked at her then back at Tony. "Need I say more?" she asked.

He smiled sheepishly. "Are you jealous?"

"I would be if you were my lover."

"I'd like that—being your lover." He grinned at her and it sent another shiver down her spine.

"I'm afraid that's not possible," she said, forcing another smile. She regretted the slightly flirtatious tone she had been assuming. She was dressed up as if on a date, but now she recognized the confusion her disguise had inadvertently spawned in Tony's feeble mind.

"Why?" There was a sudden demanding note in his voice.

"I never mix business with pleasure."

"What about the cop?"

"He wasn't a client, he was an adversary. I was playing him."

"He must know that now and I bet he's really pissed."

This guy takes real pleasure in other people's pain, whether it's real or simply perceived, Meg told herself. Her next thought hit with a sudden and unexpected certainty: *Tony Rolf is a sociopath and a rotten son of a bitch. And that's who you're working to help—a rotten, sociopathic son of a bitch who is unquestionably a killer as well.*

Meg paid the bill with a corporate credit card and shepherded Tony out to her car. As soon as they started north, Tony began suggesting places they could stop for a nightcap.

"Not tonight," Meg said, trying to soften the rejection with a smile. "I'm exhausted and we have a busy day scheduled for tomorrow."

"What's up for tomorrow?"

"Mr. Walsh is coming to the boat at eight, and the three of us will go over places you might be sent."

"Walsh told me I'd have a voice in that." His voice was filled with suspicion.

"And this is it," Meg said. "This will be your chance to reject any of our ideas . . . within reason, of course."

"Why do you say that? What does *within reason* mean?"

"It means we have to get you out of here, at least for a period of time. The police are trying to tie you to at least two murders and two counts of attempted murder of a retired cop, who also is Detective Doyle's father, by the way. A great many things are stacked against you right now and the best solution is to get you out of here until things cool down. Then we can change your name again, and within a year you can be back working for the church. I doubt it will be here in Florida, but it will be someplace where you'll be safe and secure. Mr. Walsh wants that very much," she concluded, not knowing if that were true or not.

Tony stared out through the windshield and she could see the muscles dancing along his jaw. Walsh would have to do some solid selling, she told herself. If Tony went off on his own he'd be a danger to everyone. She wondered if Walsh would order him *put down* if it came to that. She knew one thing: she would refuse that assignment if it were offered.

Meg dropped him off without difficulty—no demands that she come inside; no wrestling matches in the front seat of her car. Tony was consumed now with the prospect of a move to a new place far away from Florida. *He can only handle one problem at a time*, she told herself. He would undoubtedly spend the night working himself up to the meeting with Walsh. If she were asked, she would recommend someplace very far away.

Chapter Seventeen

Vicky Stanopolis pulled up to the security gate at the Ultimar condo complex at seven a.m., flashed her tin at the guard who sat inside a fully enclosed security booth.

"I want to see Meg Avery," she said.

"Who shall I say is calling?" the guard asked.

"Pinellas County Sheriff's Detective Stanopolis."

The guard reached for a phone and punched in a number. As he did so, Vicky noted the patch on his right sleeve. It read: *Avery Security*.

The guard spoke to someone and replaced the receiver. He keyed the microphone and told Vicky that "the maid said she's out of town."

"Have you seen her?" Vicky asked.

"No, I haven't."

"And you'd know her if you did, right, because she's your boss?" Vicky patted her upper arm to indicate his shoulder patch.

The guard looked like a little kid who just got caught doing something wrong.

"And you'd know her. Right?" Vicky repeated.

"Yeah, that's right," the guard answered.

Vicky slid her business card into a slot in the guard's booth. "When you *do* see her, tell her I want to hear from her."

The guard nodded but the look in his eye told her she had just wasted a business card.

* * *

At eight a.m. Harry received a telephone call from Detective John Otis from the sherriff's office of internal affairs.

"I need you to come in and meet with me, forthwith," Otis said.

"I'm on leave," Harry told him.

"I'm aware of that but this can't wait. The word came directly from the sheriff."

"What's it about?" Harry asked.

Otis hesitated. "Look, it's got something to do with the court case against your mother. Her attorney is claiming you used your authority to set your mother up on some trumped-up charges. Sheriff says we have no choice but to investigate. When can I expect you here?"

"Give me an hour," Harry said. "But I can tell you right now, it's all bullshit."

"See you at nine," Otis said.

Harry called Max and Vicky, informing each of them that he'd be tied up that morning.

Max, being an old New York City cop, told him to bring a lawyer with him, while Vicky said she knew Otis from a civilian complaint filed against her when she had worked patrol. "He's hard to read and sometimes he comes across as a hard-ass, but he's fair," she said.

Meg and Walsh arrived at the marina at the same time, and Meg quickly briefed him about the visit she had from a member of the sheriff's office that morning, a Detective Stanopolis.

"Do you know the officer?" Walsh asked.

"She's Doyle's partner. He told me she's taking time off to help him with his investigation. I gather they're close."

"Close?" Walsh said with raised eyebrows.

"I don't know the degree of closeness, at least at the level I believe you're referring to. But I got the impression Doyle trusts her completely."

"Then, of course, we cannot trust her at all."

They found Tony Rolf standing in the middle of the salon when they entered the yacht. He had been pacing, Meg figured.

Walsh looked him up and down. "I still marvel at the difference in your appearance. Now let's sit down and discuss some possibilities of places we can send you that will get the police off your tail."

"I still get a say about where, right? That's what you told me."

"That's what I said, and that's the way it will be," Walsh said. "It's why I'm here—to discuss some ideas I have with you."

Detective John Otis extended a hand toward an empty chair in front of his desk. "Take a load off," he said. "There are some questions I have to ask you. Understand, this is informal, for now. If it goes beyond that we'll be recording everything you say and you'll probably want to have an attorney with you."

Otis was a large, soft-looking man, typical of a cop who paid too many visits to donut shops. Vicky had said he was considered one of the better investigators in internal affairs. He was African American, about forty, Harry guessed, with a fast-receding hairline and a waistline that overlapped his belt. His necktie was loosened, exposing a double chin. His square jaw was set firmly and his dark brown eyes offered no hint of what he was thinking. A good poker face, Harry thought.

Harry had a typical cop's view of internal affairs and the people who worked there. It was known to be a fast route to a detective's shield, and was thought to harbor cops who were willing to sell out their own to make a case. In the sheriff's office they were considered highly political animals, and while Harry acknowledged that they were a necessary evil to keep corruption at a minimum, like most cops he didn't trust the men and women who worked there—their motives or their tactics.

Otis leaned forward. "Tell me about your mother," he said.

"What do you want to know? I haven't had much contact with her for the past seventeen or so years. She's been in prison for murdering my brother and me."

"She murdered you?"

"She drugged my six-year-old brother and me. I was ten at the time. Then she dragged us into the attached garage at our home in Tampa and started the car before heading off to her church. My heart had stopped and I was clinically dead when two Tampa cops responded to a call from a neighbor. They broke into the garage, hauled us out, and started CPR. They brought me back. But Jimmy, my kid brother, was smaller and they couldn't save him.

"My mother was convicted and sent to prison, where she was supposedly treated by prison psychiatrists, and ultimately declared sane. They paroled her over my objections, with one provision: that she stay at least a hundred yards away from me and my home."

"Did you feel bitter toward her?" Otis asked.

"Of course I did. I loved my little brother and I wanted her locked up for the rest of her life. Each year, she sent me a letter. She made sure I received it on the anniversary of Jimmy's death. The letter always said the same thing: how she wanted me to be with my brother and with Jesus. Each year she reminded me she was sorry I had lived and was still crazy as all hell, no matter what those prison shrinks said."

Otis nodded as he mulled this over. "Her lawyer, Jordan Wells, is making noises that you set her up, that you invited her to the marina to discuss your problems with her, and that you planted a carving knife on her and had her arrested."

"That's bullshit. None of it ever happened."

"He's also claiming that he has a witness who saw the altercation between you and your mother who will testify that your mother did not have any weapon in her possession when you confronted her."

"Jordan is being paid by either the Church of Scientology or one of its executives. And the woman was a Scientology plant at the marina. They're coming after me because I'm involved in the investigation the Clearwater cops have going into a church employee who is believed to be the man who twice tried to kill my father, a retired Clearwater cop, and who did murder two women, one in Clearwater and one in Tarpon Springs."

Otis took a long, deep breath. "Can you prove all of that?" he asked at length.

"Most of it; with a little effort, probably all of it."

"I hope so," Otis said. "Because if you can't, and Jordan Wells keeps pushing, your tit's gonna be in the proverbial wringer. I'll report back to the sheriff. If he wants me to go further I'll be in touch. My guess is he'll tell me to wait until we see what happens in court."

"And if the media start asking questions, he can say an investigation is already ongoing."

"That's about the size of it," Otis said.

Tony sat in a plush swivel chair and glared at both of them. Meg had just told Walsh her recommendation would be that Tony be sent as far away as possible for at least six months. "We need to let things settle down. Out of sight, out of mind—that's the first order of business. Step two: no more attacks on Jocko Doyle, no more bodies turning up."

"That old cop can identify me," Tony snapped.

"You think he could pick you out of a lineup now?" Regis Walsh asked. "After all the changes Meg has made in your appearance? I doubt even your own mother could do that."

"Then why send me anyplace at all?"

"We have to let this all die down," Meg said. "There are people here who know your voice, your demeanor, people who might see through the changes we've made in your appearance. But over time . . ." She let the sentence die with a rise of her eyebrows.

"Where specifically do you have in mind?" he asked.

Walsh made a face and rubbed his forehead. "Right now, and this is just a thought, right now one of the places I'm thinking about is Alaska."

"Alaska," Tony said. "I'll freeze my fucking nuts off."

Walsh raised a cautioning hand. "Please, Tony, there's a lady present. And actually, Alaska is not as cold as you would think. This would be southern Alaska and the temperatures are more like you'd find in Ohio or New Jersey. We're not talking the North Pole."

"Tell me what's there," Tony said. His voice sounded pouty, put-upon.

"The church has a friend there who owns a successful commercial fishing operation. It's in a small town called Homer at the bottom of the Kenai Peninsula, which is about 220 miles south of Anchorage, where the church has a very active mission."

"I don't know," Tony said.

"Don't make any snap judgments," Walsh urged. "I'll have some books delivered to you and you can learn a little about Alaska, and in the meantime there are a few other places we need to take a hard look at. We have a very active church in Australia and another in North Yorkshire in the UK; we have people in South America and Europe, even Northern Africa. But I'm trying to find a location where you would more easily blend in—not stand out, so to speak. I want to avoid places where language would be a problem. Remember, we are not talking about a permanent relocation. I want you back in the United States working for the church in six months to a year, tops."

"Here?" Tony asked.

"That's quite possible. I certainly want you to continue the very effective work you did for us, but at first it will more likely be LA or Phoenix." He shrugged his shoulders. "There are dozens of possibilities once we shake this current problem. But first things first. Think of it as going clear of the authorities. Once we're past that, many doors will open for us."

Harry called Vicky and asked her to meet him at his boat. When he got there he found her already aboard, sitting on the upper deck, taking in the sun.

"You look relaxed and comfortable," he said.

"I'm on vacation," she joked. "How did everything go with Otis?"

"Good, I suppose. At least as good as I could have expected. He was up front with me, said everything would depend on what Jordan Wells did next. In the meantime, the sheriff is going to cover his ass. Without saying so directly, Otis let me know that if he can prove any of the crap he alleged in court, I better get myself a lawyer."

"So Wells will be pulling the strings," Vicky said.

"That's right, and Regis Walsh is most likely the only one who can tell Wells to back off."

"I love the way these Scientology big shots always have somebody else doing the dirty work."

"They have a knack for sensing where you're vulnerable and going straight at it," Harry said. "In my case it's my mother. If they can keep me bogged down with her crazy shit, the less time I'll have running down Tony Rolf. And if they're threatening my job, maybe I'll give up altogether."

"They don't know you very well, do they? Stubborn, to a fault . . . occasionally pigheaded . . . known to leap tall buildings in a single bound."

"That's me, a pigheaded superman."

Vicky got up and went to the starboard rail. It held a clear view of Meg's former slip. "I found your lady friend's apartment."

"Former lady friend," Harry corrected.

"Anyway, it's in the Ultimar condo complex on Sand Key. Guess who runs security there." She turned back to look at him. "Avery Security, her own little company. They decide who goes in or out. When I asked to see her, the security officer on duty made a show of calling up to her apartment. Told me the maid said she was out; had no idea when she'd be back."

"I don't want to go there. But it would be good if we could sit on the apartment, try and spot her going out and follow her. Who knows, she might lead us straight to Tony Rolf."

"I'm already on it," Vicky said. "I'm running DMV checks for cars registered to Meg Avery, Meg Adams, or Avery Security, in Pinellas and Hillsborough counties. I should have a list by late this afternoon. I'm scheduled to work four to midnight for the next week so I can sit on her condo a few mornings. If I'm lucky, one of the cars will show up with her behind the wheel."

"Fax Max a copy of the list so his guys can keep an eye out for her too," Harry said. "Once we pin down the car she's using, it'll be easier to run a regular tail."

"And you think she'll lead us to Rolf?"

"I'm betting on it," Harry said.

"Then we better be sure we have good people following her. She spots the tail, she'll never go near him."

"I'm thinking we limit it to you, Max, and me for now. If Max has some guys he wants to use, that'll work for me. It's his case after all."

Tony Rolf was slightly shell-shocked. The idea that he might be sent as far away as Alaska had never occurred to him. It was like being sent into exile; like that French general . . . Napoleon, yeah, just like Napoleon. He remembered reading about it in high school. Napoleon was sent into exile by the British, sent to some island. He never got off that island, like he died there. Tony gave that some thought. Did this mean that Walsh was abandoning him? No, there was too much Tony could tell the cops, too many things that would implicate Walsh and through him the church. If the man wanted to get rid of him, he could send some goon to take him out to the *Freewinds* and have him dumped somewhere. He had seen a documentary about L. Ron Hubbard, the church's founder. How he used to have crew members thrown overboard when they displeased him. The documentary said he'd eventually haul them up half-drowned. *No, no, you're letting your imagination run wild.*

Tony looked at the cell phone sitting on the table next to his plush swivel chair. Meg had brought it to him, told him to use it to call her . . . but only in an emergency. He picked it up and punched in her number. He needed some reassurances. Meg liked him, he could tell, so he'd ask her straight out if she thought Walsh was on the up and up on this. He hesitated, then disconnected the call. He wasn't going to make a fool of himself.

Five minutes later Meg called back. "Did you call me, Tony?"

"Yeah, I guess I was having a panic attack. All this talk about Alaska, it just got to me. Who the fuck does he think I am, some fucking Eskimo?"

"I was in the shower when you called. There's nothing to get worked up about. I'll bring you some literature about Alaska tomorrow and we'll go over it together. Okay?"

"Yeah, that'll be great."

"I'll see you around ten. I want to sleep in a little."

"Okay, ten it is."

They better get him out of here fast, Meg told herself. *Otherwise he's going to freak out and do something crazy. Then they'll all be screwed.*

She picked up the phone and called Regis Walsh's private line. There was no answer at his office. So Walsh did have a home to go to. All he had ever given her was his office number and whenever she had called he was always there. Tonight he wasn't. Would wonders never cease?

Meg took a cab to the marina at ten. Her car had been picked up by the Mercedes dealership at nine and taken in for service. It would be delivered to her at the marina by noon.

Tony was up when Meg arrived at the boat shortly after ten. He looked as though he had been up for hours and had already worked himself into a lather. She placed the books she had brought on a cocktail table, took a seat on the sofa, and patted the place next to her indicating that Tony should join her.

She picked up the first book and opened it.

"You're late," he said.

"Yes, I'm twenty minutes late. I'm sorry."

"Are you saying that I'm being picky?"

Meg could tell he was spoiling for a fight. She intended to scotch any opportunity to have one. "No, I said I was sorry for being late. It couldn't be helped, but I'm still sorry."

He seemed to grudgingly accept this.

"Okay, let's look at the area Mr. Walsh was talking about. It's near the end of the Kenai Peninsula, a town called Homer. The town was founded by a gold miner named Homer Pennock in 1896. It now has 5,400 residents. It's located on Kachenak Bay and surrounded by the Kenai Mountains and has both active volcanoes and several glaciers. There are a number of fjords that run off the bay. In summer it's a sports-fishing center, mostly for haddock and king salmon. There are nineteen hours of sunlight in summer and in winter the Aurora Borealis dominates the skies." Meg stopped reading. "It sounds beautiful, although I think nineteen hours of daylight would be hard to get used to."

"I think the whole place sounds scarier than shit," Tony groused. "And you haven't even gotten to the 2,000-pound brown bears prowling through the area, or the 1,500-pound moose. Big enough to kill my sorry ass if I got too close."

Meg smiled. He was exaggerating the weights but not by much. She decided to defuse the issue, not challenge it. "It's like the old Groucho Marks joke. The patient says: *Doctor, it hurts when I do that.* The doctor replies: *Don't do that.*"

"So what the hell does that mean?"

"It means, as far as big brown bears are concerned, don't get too close."

"You're a big help," Tony said.

Vicky had been sitting on the Ultimar condo since seven a.m. She had spotted the red Mercedes at nine; saw that the license plate matched one on the list she had gotten from the DMV the previous afternoon. The car was registered to Avery Security and there was a man driving. Vicky debated whether to follow it and decided against it. She reasoned it was probably a boyfriend, another Avery employee who also lived in the building, or someone who had dropped something off for Meg Avery before she'd set up the stakeout. She decided to let the car go on and not risk missing Meg leaving later. Had she followed the car she would have ended up at the dealership and gotten the address the car was to be delivered to, and eventually to Meg and Tony Rolf.

Vicky called Harry at noon and told him she'd be leaving the stakeout but would be back the following morning. Harry thanked her and said that he or Max would take a turn the next afternoon. He promised to stop by and bring her breakfast in the morning.

Jocko Doyle was released from the hospital at four. Harry was there to drive him home, where Maria was preparing a lavish dinner. Harry always liked visiting the house where he had grown up. It was a welcoming place for him, a place where he had healed as a young boy, a place where he had always felt safe and secure despite the horrors he had endured at the hands of his birth mother. Harry led Jocko to his favorite chair as Maria buzzed around them, offering food and drink to tide them over until dinner.

When Maria went back to the kitchen, Jocko beckoned Harry to come closer. "She's gonna drive me nuts, you know," he whispered.

"It'll be okay," Harry said, keeping his voice low. "A little pampering will be good for you. She'll give you plenty of good Cuban food. I bet you put on five pounds in the first week. She's probably got your favorite beer in the fridge—in fact, I'm going to grab a couple. So just sit back, relax, and enjoy yourself. Later we can watch the Rays on the tube."

Jocko waved him off. "Go get the beer. Just stop all the *relax and be well* bullshit. Sitting here waiting to heal is gonna drive me nuts."

"What do you want to do instead?" Harry asked.

"I wanna do what you're doing; I want to get out and look for that albino bastard."

Harry just shook his head and headed to the kitchen. "You're married to a crazy man," he told his adoptive mother.

"What's he wanna do now?" she asked.

"He wants to go out looking for the guy who shot him."

Maria made a disapproving noise. "Over my dead body is the only way he'll do that." She made the sign of the cross to ward off any evil spirit who might have been listening.

Harry kissed her on the cheek, then went to the fridge and grabbed two bottles of Modelo Especial. He noticed he had been right—there were at least a dozen bottles chilling there. "What's for dinner?" he asked as he reached for the lid of a simmering pot.

"Arroz con pollo," Maria said, ushering him away from the stove.

Harry took a deep breath, inhaling all the savory flavors of the Cuban recipe. "My mouth is already watering," he said, bringing a broad smile to Maria's face.

"Arroz con pollo," he announced as he returned to the living room and handed Jocko a beer.

Jocko made a low, satisfied sound in the back of his throat. "Well, maybe being home won't be so bad after all."

"What time does the Rays game go on?" Harry asked.

"Seven. They're playing the Yankees, going up against Tanaka. It should be a good game." Jocko paused a beat, then asked: "You think that albino bastard knows where I live?"

"Officer Moore has been assigned to this sector. She'll be cruising by on a regular basis."

"I'm just wondering if that police artist who turned out to be a Scientologist gave up my home address."

"If I find out he did, I'll personally break both his legs," Harry said.

"No you won't. I didn't raise a stupid son. But these bastards we're up against, I worry about them. They always seem to have people in just the right spot when they need them. How the hell can they do that?"

"I wish I knew." Harry thought about Meg Adams, or Avery, or whatever her real name was. She had played him for a chump and he had walked right into it with a big shit-eating grin on his face. He wondered if it was just a case of the little head overruling the big head. He had never even suspected anything. Maybe she was just that good, he told himself. But even if she was, it didn't matter. He had still been played and this burned inside him. It made him feel like a fool.

Meg worked from home the following morning. After tending to some problems at the agency she turned her attention back to Tony Rolf. She started with Regis Walsh by issuing her unsolicited advice that they move ahead with plans to get him out of the area as quickly as possible.

"I talked up a move to Alaska, but the idea seemed to make him nervous. He was even talking about 2,000-pound bears."

"That's a bit of an exaggeration."

"Of course it is, but do you think 1,500 pounds is going to make him feel better? He thinks he's going to be living in subzero weather. I told him the climate was much milder than he thinks. I put together some weather charts from the Internet and I'll give those to him this afternoon. But frankly, he'll just think up something else, some other reason to reject it. The idea of going to Alaska clearly has him rattled.

In the end you're just going to have to lay down the law."

"So, you think it's a good place for him?" Walsh asked.

"I do. I'd prefer Australia, only because it's even farther away, but international travel with the cops looking for him will be hard."

"I agree. And Alaska Airlines has a flight out of Tampa every day. Doyle and Abrams will be watching for the *Freewinds*, figuring we'll get aboard in international waters. In fact, I'm going to play that card to the hilt; wait until the *Freewinds* is in international waters off the Florida coast before we move him."

"What then?" Meg asked.

"Then we'll send boats out to the ship, drawing the attention of the Coast Guard and the police, while we take Tony to the airport and put him aboard a flight to Alaska."

"And the police will be left chasing a boat while their quarry flies away to the frozen north. I love it. How long before we can put the plan in motion?"

"I expect the *Freewinds* to be within range in about a week," Walsh said. "I've already ordered new identity documents for Tony from a source we've used before. When the ship is just outside US territorial waters, we'll move."

A slow smile spread across Meg's face. *Poor Harry*, she thought. *He's going to find himself snookered again.* She wondered how his very male cop ego would deal with it. *Rather badly would be my guess.*

Harry took over the surveillance of Meg's condo at three p.m. Vicky had told him about the red Mercedes Cabriolet she had seen yesterday, explaining that it was on the list of cars registered to Avery Security, but since a man had been driving she had let it go rather than break off the surveillance. Meg had never shown herself, although she could have been in one of several taxis that had left the condo complex.

At four thirty he saw the red Mercedes pull up to the gate, preparing to leave the complex. Harry was parked directly across the street and he pulled across two lanes of traffic, cutting the Mercedes off before it could enter Gulf Boulevard.

Harry exited the car, holding out his badge as he approached the driver's side. He rapped the badge against the window. Meg lowered the glass and smiled up at him. The first thing he noticed was that she was now a blonde—a wig, he guessed.

"Hello, Harry," she said. "This is a rather dramatic way to meet."

"I guess you're not out of town, no matter what your flunky in the booth says."

"It's nice to see you. I've missed you."

"Stop the crap," Harry said. "You played me and you did a good job of it. But the game's over now. Where's Tony Rolf?"

"I haven't the faintest idea."

"Be careful, Meg. He's dangerous. And he's wanted. I'd hate to have to bust you for harboring a fugitive."

"I'm not harboring anyone, Harry, least of all Tony Rolf."

Harry smiled at her. It was a cold, hard smile. "You're beautiful, Meg. You're a beautiful little liar. Be careful. It might cost you more than you bargained for. If you cross me you could end up behind bars. If you cross Tony Rolf you could end up on a slab in the morgue."

Harry turned on his heel, got back in his car, and pulled it forward to allow Meg to enter traffic. Then he pulled in behind her three cars back. He knew she would see him following her, but it didn't matter. He wanted her to know he was on her tail and that he would remain there, whether she saw him or not, until she made a fatal mistake.

* * *

Meg drove her Mercedes to the Countryside Mall. She parked outside the entrance to Dillard's department store. She made two phone calls before she exited the car: one to Tony Rolf to tell him she'd be late for their scheduled meeting, the second to a member of the Avery Security staff asking him to meet her outside the Macy's entrance to the mall. From just inside Dillard's she watched Harry circle the row she had parked in until a space opened up close to the Mercedes. Before he had even left his car, she was on her way to the Macy's entrance on the other side of the mall. Twenty minutes later she was entering the yacht where Tony Rolf was hiding.

"You're late again." Tony's voice was peevish. "What's the reason this time?"

"Harry Doyle was following me," she said.

That stopped him cold. She hoped it would be sobering for him, let him truly understand that he was being hunted. He went to the salon window and peeked out into the marina. "Do you think he followed you here?"

"No, I made sure he didn't. But I had to abandon the Mercedes in the Countryside Mall parking lot. I'll have somebody pick it up tonight, stash it someplace, and then bring me a rental car."

"They're really hot on my tail, aren't they?"

"Yes they are." Meg paused for effect and gave him a long, hard look. "All the more reason to get you relocated as soon as possible." She reached into her large purse and pulled out the weather sheets she had prepared. She handed them to Rolf. "These will give you a clearer picture of what the weather will be like on the Kenai Peninsula. Tony, I really think you're going to love it there, and if you don't, remember, it will only be for a year, tops."

"Are you going to visit me there?" he asked.

"I'd love to. Perhaps Mr. Walsh will have me take you up there."

He stared at her. She could tell he didn't believe a word of it; there was a hard glint in his eye. *Don't play with him*, she warned herself. *He's too unstable.*

Harry thought about how easily Meg had lost him. She was good. He watched a man come and pick up the Mercedes in the parking lot. He wouldn't be seeing that car again. He guessed she'd be using a car not registered to her company or herself, perhaps a rental that she could change every few days.

Harry called Max and filled him in on what had happened.

"She's a cutie," Max said. "Let's see how she does with a three-man stakeout. I'm gonna put three of my best guys on her tomorrow. One will be outside her building and his only job will be to spot her. When he does, he radios the two other cars, one north of the condo and one south of it. Those two cars will follow her, switching positions regularly. The original car will remain far back and join the rotation only if he's needed."

"Should work," Harry said, "but warn your guys that she's good, she's *very* good. And don't forget to tell them she might be wearing a wig."

"A wig."

"Yeah, today she was a blonde. I liked her better as a redhead," Harry said.

"As a redhead she took us to the cleaners."

"Yeah, there is that."

Harry dropped in to see his father before heading to the boat. Jocko was snoozing in his favorite chair.

"Everything okay?" he asked his mother.

Maria smiled. "Everything is good. That nice police officer, M.J. Moore, she stopped by to check on everything. She said she'd be ten minutes away if we needed her. She even gave us her private cell phone number. Such a nice woman."

Yes, Harry thought, *she is a good woman and a good cop. Just like Vicky. So who do you latch onto? A beautiful redhead who took you to the cleaners.*

The three-car tail was set up and ready to go at seven a.m. Harry had taken the shotgun seat in the lead observation car. A second car north of the condo entrance held Max Abrams with Clearwater Detective Jimmy Walker behind the wheel. The third car, with Detective Joe Falcone driving, was parked south of the condo.

At ten a.m., Meg exited the condo in a white Chrysler Sebring convertible, top down, her red hair flashing in the sun.

It was a beautiful Florida day—the sun was warm, the skies cloudless and a deep crystal blue, the temperature eighty degrees with a gentle wind blowing in off the Gulf of Mexico. This was why people flocked to Florida each year, Meg thought. She drove along the coast watching young men and women in bathing suits and flip-flops entering various shops or making their way to the beaches for a day of surf and sunshine and the chance to meet someone new. At the Clearwater Beach traffic circle she turned onto the Memorial Causeway. To the right was the marina where Harry kept his boat. She glanced in the rearview mirror and smiled. She had spotted the three-car tail as it had formed behind her. She had assumed Harry would be in the car that had been parked across from the condo entrance. He was the best choice to pick her out as she left the condo and set the tail in motion. Now, if they were running their tail as it was designed, he would be the third car back. They hadn't expected her to be in an open car, her windblown red hair displayed like a cape to a bull. She intended to drive to her office in Tampa, where she would put on the brunette wig that was in her briefcase, switch cars, and drive back to the marina where Tony was hiding. It was a long, tedious drive, but it was necessary to keep the wolves at bay. She tried to imagine Harry's face when he realized she had eluded them again. It would not be the ruggedly handsome face she had almost fallen for. No, indeed, it would be like the gloomy Indian who had been in the Sunday funnies when she was a child—a raincloud fully formed above his head.

By the time Meg got back to the marina, Tony Rolf was on the aft deck sitting in the sportfisherman's fighting chair, soaking up some sun.

"I wish we could take the boat out," he said, "but I've never handled one this size."

"I have," Meg responded. "Before you leave we'll go out and I'll teach you."

"When can we do it?" Tony asked, jumping at the suggestion.

"Pick a day when the weather is like this and they're predicting calm seas." At times such as these he was like a small puppy eager for a scratch behind the ears. "Now, let's go into the salon and go over some more information about Alaska."

This time he didn't object and Meg hoped his silence meant a growing acceptance of the idea. With Tony, of course, you never knew.

When they were seated in the salon, Meg took some papers out of her briefcase. "As we've told you, the man who will be helping you in Alaska is a very wealthy businessman who also happens to be a member of the church. His name is Malcolm Vandermere. His friends call him

Dutch, and he's a bit of an eccentric. He lives in Gustavus, a small bush town on Glacier Bay, population somewhere around 450 people.

"He owns a fishing fleet that sails out of Homer in the summer, and a fish-packing plant, and he also owns a big game–hunting camp about twenty-five miles inland. He has a twin-engine plane that he flies from Gustavus to Homer, or into Juneau to pick up whatever provisions he needs, or to treat himself to a fancy meal."

"How does Mr. Walsh know him?"

"They went to college together, Yale, and they belonged to the same 'secret society,' Skull and Bones. A number of presidents have belonged to that society, including both Bushes. It's said that members watch over each other throughout their lives and no member is ever allowed to fail. If he hits a rough patch in business, others will bail him out."

Tony stared at her, wide-eyed. "Is that true?" he asked.

"I'm told it is, although its members are sworn to secrecy, so who knows? That's why it's called a secret society. I've heard that for a time Skull and Bones was the wealthiest corporation in Connecticut. Legend has it that its building on the Yale campus holds the bones of the Apache chief Geronimo."

"How did they get those?" Tony asked.

"They were supposedly stolen from his grave by George H.W. Bush's father, Prescott Bush, when he was a student at Yale and a member of Skull and Bones. Prescott later became a US senator for Connecticut."

"Jesus!" Tony exclaimed. "I can't wait to meet this guy Vandermere and see what he'll tell me about Skull and Bones. I wanna hear how they play fairy godmother to all these rich guys."

"I wouldn't count on him telling you much," Meg said. "The fact that people know so little about their society is what makes it so powerful."

"Yeah, but—"

"Just look at it as another example of the rich helping the rich."

Tony looked up at her as though he'd just experienced an epiphany. "Yeah, I guess that's the way it's always been."

"And always will be," Meg added.

Harry and Max sat in the same car. They had come to the realization that Meg had taken them to the cleaners yet again. After sitting outside her office for two hours, Max had gone up and had asked to see her. A fresh-faced receptionist told him that she had been there briefly earlier, but had left over an hour ago. Max had smiled, marched past her, and entered the main part of the office, where he found dozens of eager people working away. After flashing his tin he was directed to Meg's office, where he found the door open and Meg nowhere in sight. Her secretary was huffy at first, but when Max again flashed his badge, she repeated the same story the receptionist had given him.

"Can I have your name, sergeant? I'll tell her you called."

"Tell her that her old friend Max Abrams was here and that I'll be seeing her soon."

When he returned to the car he looked at Harry and shook his head. "She did it again," he said. "She's gone but not forgotten."

"She must have had another car waiting for her here."

"You know, Harry, I'm starting to not like that woman."

"Maybe we should form a club."

"Who's in it so far?"

"You, Vicky, and me, but it's growing fast," Harry said.

Chapter Eighteen

"So you really are going to cook," Tony said. Meg had picked up two steaks and some premade mashed potatoes, along with tomatoes, cucumbers, and balsamic dressing for a salad. She also had two bottles of a good Malbec from Argentina.

"It's a simple meal, I think I can manage it," Meg said. "Besides, Mr. Walsh said I was to take good care of you."

"He really said that?"

There it was again, she thought. Disbelief that anyone was looking out for him, that anyone cared if he was happy or sad, whether he continued to exist or simply stopped walking this earth. She had never seen such self-loathing, had never met someone who thought others questioned if he was worthy of life itself.

"I thought you were just being nice," Tony said.

"Well, I am. But Mr. Walsh is also concerned about you. He considers you a valued member of the church and he's asked me to look out for you."

Tony seemed to mull that over, then walked to the salon window and watched a sailboat head out into the gulf. His hands were at his side and his fingers twitched nervously. She knew his childhood had been one incident of brutality after another, mostly due to his mother's penchant for falling in love with brutal men. She also knew he had killed his so-called stepfather. And his mother had also disappeared by the time Walsh found him. She wondered if he had killed her as well.

He was certainly capable of it, she told herself. And it would explain the self-loathing that seemed to permeate every facet of his being. All that and being born an albino, an oddity of nature, something he could see every time he looked in a mirror, every time he saw someone glance at him and make a distasteful expression. So many things to turn him into the hate-filled monster he had become.

"You want your steak rare, right?" she asked.

"Yes. I want to hear it moo when I cut into it." He grinned at his own joke and watched to see if she would do the same.

Meg instinctively sensed what he wanted and gave it to him. "Moo," she said, offering up her best foolish grin. She turned back to the stove and lit the broiler. "I'd rather cook this on the grill that's out on deck but I don't want to attract the attention of other boat owners. The less curiosity we attract, the better our chances of remaining unnoticed until you're ready to leave."

"Yeah, I guess that's the way it has to be." He paused. "Don't you think my disguise is good enough that I could move about a bit?"

"Move about how?"

"Just take a walk; maybe stop at a bar for a beer, anything, just to have some contact with people. I mean contact with you and Mr. Walsh, even that idiot Oppenheimer, is good. But especially with you—I mean, that's really good. When nobody's here I start to get a little stir crazy. I just want to get out, see people, you know? Sometimes I open one of the curtains on the salon windows and sit far back with binoculars and just stare out."

Lonely, Meg thought. At those times he becomes the lonely little boy he has always been. It could be a recipe for disaster if they let it go too far.

"I'll talk to Mr. Walsh. We're so close to getting out of here, I just don't want to blow it all by becoming too cavalier about what we can safely do and what we can't. Do you understand?"

"I . . . I . . . think so."

"I just don't want to do too much and blow it all."

"Yeah, okay, I get it."

Meg went back to the steaks, and started preparing the salad. "After dinner maybe we can take a drive, even stop for a nightcap somewhere. Would you like that?"

Tony grinned at her. "Oh yeah, that'd be great."

They drove south on Alternate 19 in Meg's latest rental, a black Cadillac ATS with heavily tinted windows. It was comparable to being sealed in a vault that no one could see into, thus providing all the anonymity anyone would want.

"The only danger is being pulled over, and that won't happen unless I break some law. The most common is driving with a taillight or headlight out. Otherwise cops are reluctant to pull over high-priced cars—unless there's an African American or Latino driving. If the driver is white, the pricier the car the greater the likelihood a complaint will be filed if the driver feels harassed."

"Really? Is that a statistic or something?" Tony asked.

"Cops will tell you that themselves. I have several retired cops working for me who swear it's true. The one factor that will change it is out-of-state license plates. In some places, especially small towns in the South, that almost guarantees a traffic stop."

Meg turned onto Main Street and parked in front of Casa Tina, a Mexican restaurant with excellent food and an even better bar. "I feel like a mojito," she said. "And they serve Modelo Especial on draft."

"Sounds great to me," Tony said.

They entered the restaurant and Tony was immediately taken with the décor. Mexican artifacts lined the walls, many relating to Day of the Dead festivities.

There was a square bar with almost every seat taken. A smile from Meg got two young men to move down a seat, opening up two spots for them. She sat facing Tony to avoid any conflicts and they ordered her a mojito and a beer for Tony.

"You know some really cool places," Tony said.

"What kind of places did you usually go to?"

"Places downtown, around the church offices. Sometimes I'd go to O'Keefe's down near the hospital. A lot of nurses hang out there and occasionally I'd see someone I recognized from the church. When I did I'd make sure to get their names and turn them in to Oppenheimer."

"Why?" Meg asked.

"The church doesn't want its members spending money in bars. It wants them to spend money on courses. When I spotted them and turned their names in to Oppenheimer, they'd get a letter questioning their life choices. Then, if I saw them in a bar again, I'd go right up to them and ask why they were ignoring the message they had gotten."

"Did they ever argue with you?"

"A few tried, but when I explained that this was a friendly warning, that my next visit would be to their homes, they usually packed it in and left." There was an especially nasty smile on Tony Rolf's face as he explained this.

"You enjoyed scaring them, didn't you?" Meg suggested, regretting the words as she saw how they registered with Tony.

He seemed surprised at first; then his features settled into a glaring anger.

"I didn't mean that as a criticism," she said, laying a hand on his arm.

He looked down at her hand, then allowed his eyes to rise slowly to her face. "What else could it be taken as? You people who aren't part of it have no idea how hard it is to keep some of these members in line. You stay off them for a minute and they're doing stuff they know is wrong. Drinking, meeting up with non–church members, little homosexual or heterosexual trysts—there was no end to it. We have to stay on them all the time."

Tony's jaw was set like the true believer he was. There were no excuses for violating the code of conduct the church set. He would make sure the rules were followed, and God help anyone who did not conform. No wonder Walsh valued him—he was the perfect enforcer. And if Tony lost control every so often . . . well, that was a risk one had to take. Meg shook her head and let the thought die. She wondered if Walsh ever felt concern about what he had created in Tony Rolf. It certainly didn't seem so, though she was sure that sooner or later he and his church would pay a heavy price for it. In the meantime, well, others would pay that price. And the church, in choosing to look the other way, seemed very much to condone the abuse inflicted on its members.

And what's your part in it? she wondered. She knew that she fully intended to complete her current contract with the church. She was a good businesswoman and she always fulfilled her end of a deal. Would she accept a new contract? That was another question.

Tony was still brooding and Meg decided to ignore it and let him stew if he wanted to. She felt certain she could handle any violent outburst directed her way. She held a black belt in tae kwon do and if it came down to weapons, there was a .380-caliber Walther she was licensed to carry always close at hand.

"Well let's get going, I have a busy day tomorrow," she said.

"I want another beer."

"What you want to do is sit and brood because you don't think you're appreciated. I don't have time for that, Tony. You're going to have to do that brooding all by yourself. So if you insist on having another beer, you'll have to get a cab back to the marina." *Look in my eyes*, she thought to herself. *Know that you don't intimidate me.*

"You like to live dangerously, don't you?" he hissed.

"If that's some kind of half-assed threat, you know what you can do with it." Meg spoke the words with a smile on her lips, but her eyes were cold and hard and she could tell he was uncertain, perhaps even shaken by her defiance. *You're not used to it, are you, Mr. Rolf? You're used to frightening people, especially women.*

Tony picked up his beer and downed what was left of it in one swallow. If it had been served in a can rather than a glass, he undoubtedly would have crushed it in his hand. *You're such a predictable jerk*, she thought.

"Let's go," he said.

Without a word Meg took a twenty from her purse and laid it on the bar. Then she swung herself off the stool and started for the door. Tony followed, his face black with rage.

They drove back to the marina in silence. When they arrived Meg turned to face him. "We'll try to go out for a nightcap some other time, Tony. Whether it works or not depends on you. If you continue trying to intimidate me, I'll simply stop helping you. I don't find it pleasant to be threatened." She stopped and offered him another cold smile. *I hope you're getting the message.*

"You come because Mr. Walsh tells you to."

"You're right; it's part of the contract my agency signed. But I am not a member of the church, and if I or my agency decides we can no longer fulfill our part of the contract, all it means is that the church stops paying us."

"I'll see you tomorrow?"

"You will."

Tony watched her go, his anger brewing into a smoldering storm. So she had no fear of him. *We'll see about that, see just how brave you are. But not now, not while I still need you. But you will pay. Yes indeed, you will.* He turned away from the boat and headed for a downtown bar where he knew he could find a woman to talk to. Maybe he would even find someone from the church breaking the rules. That would be sweet. He could hand out some punishment. It had been too long since he'd been able to do that. He only wished it could be Meg on the receiving end. *In time*, he told himself, *all in good time. Then she'll wish she never tested me*.

The bar he chose was on Cleveland Avenue in downtown Clearwater, only a short walk from the marina. Members of Sea Org were still there in nearby church buildings, scurrying about as they always did, making a show of how busy they were; how hard they were working. *Always move quickly, always look busy and overworked*, members were warned. Church officials wanted everyone busy and seemingly productive, even when they weren't. He had been taught that early on: question the guy, challenge whether he's working as hard as he can. Everyone can work harder. Don't accept their excuses; make them feel guilty for even making an excuse.

Tony entered the bar and was immediately overcome by the fierce sound being offered up by a local four-piece band. There was a woman seated at the bar who was bouncing and shaking her upper body to the beat. He slid in next to her and ordered a Tampa-Style Lager, a product of the Cigar City Brewery.

When the music came to a stop the woman took the time to give him a once-over, then drained her glass and smiled at him. "Wanna buy me another?" she asked, as if it were the most natural thing in the world.

"Sure," Tony said. "What are you drinking?"

"Jai Alai," she said. "My name is Cindy Lewis, what's yours?"

He could tell she was slightly drunk. "Tony Rawlings," he answered, choosing his name from back in his LA days.

"You from here?" she asked. She was slightly overweight, no more than eighteen or nineteen. She had blond hair that looked as though it had just been washed, blue eyes, and a small mouth that seemed to form a pucker when she spoke. *Not at all bad*, he told himself.

"I said, are you from here?" she repeated.

"California. Actually, I'm from Los Angeles."

"What brought you here?"

He gestured with a movement of his head that indicated life going on over his shoulder. "I work for the Church of Scientology. I came here to take a special course."

"Oooh," she said, making her voice sound spooky. "Are you clear?" It was a taunt sometimes used to try to rattle church members.

"As a matter of fact, I am." There was an edge to his voice that Cindy picked up on.

"Oh, I'm only teasing you," she said. "We get a big kick out of some of the Sea Org people who come in here, or sit outside at the sandwich shop next door all dressed up in their sailor suits, all the time talking about going clear."

She continued to prattle on. Tony turned her off, not listening anymore. Her voice became white noise to him, just a dull humming sound. He smiled, letting her think he was enjoying her nonsensical jabbering. "Do you live nearby?" he asked.

"I've got an apartment just a few blocks north of here. How about you? Where are you staying?"

"I'm staying on a friend's boat. It's in a marina not far from here. I like waking up to the gentle rolling waves that other boats create when they move in and out of their slips."

"Sounds romantic." She was playing with a strand of hair, twirling it around her fingers.

"You go to school or work somewhere nearby?" Tony asked, although he couldn't care less.

"I was in St. Pete's for a semester, but I didn't like it. Right now I'm waitressing at the Island Way, just off the causeway. It's an upscale place so it's good money. But if you work dinners—that's where the good tips are—it really cuts into your social life."

Yak, yak, yak, Tony thought. *Does this stupid woman think any of it matters?* More white noise, filling his ears until he wanted to reach out and clamp a hand over her mouth, or grab her by the hair she kept playing with and smash her face into the top of the bar.

He bought her another Jai Alai and got another lager for himself. The beer seemed to make her even more talkative but he kept buying them until it was past midnight.

"I have to get up early," he said. "Would you like me to walk you home?" Either way, he knew he would wait for her outside.

"Sure, that would be cool. A girl can't be too safe these days. I hate walking home alone. The streets around here are so creepy when they're dark."

They left the bar and headed east on Cleveland, then north on Fort

Harrison Boulevard, and turned onto Jones Street. It was his old neighborhood and Tony could walk it blindfolded. Just past North Garden Avenue there was an empty lot where they would "stop and talk." She was still prattling on when they reached it, something about getting herself a dog, and Tony took her arm and guided her into the lot.

"It's a shortcut," he said.

"A shortcut to where? I live straight ahead."

There was the first hint of fear in her voice now and Tony reached into his pocket, came out with his switchblade, and snapped it open. He raised the blade to her throat. "Shut up and go where I tell you," he hissed. He had his left hand on her shoulder, the blade of the knife pressed against her throat with his right. "Give me any trouble and you're going to bleed like the pig you are."

She started to blubber and the sound sickened him. "Don't hurt me. I'll do anything you want. Just tell me what to do and I'll do it."

He pressed the blade harder against her throat. "Just . . . shut . . . up," he growled as he pushed her deeper into the empty lot.

She stumbled and fell forward and the blade nicked her throat. Her hand flew up to the wound and when she pulled it away there was a smear of blood. "Oh God, oh God," she sobbed.

"Shut up. It's just a scratch and you did it to yourself."

The sight of blood panicked her and she tried to pull away. Tony grabbed her hair and jerked her back. But Cindy was terrified now and she continued to struggle. He pulled her back again, up against him. He could smell her sweat and almost taste her fear as he thrust the knife into her abdomen and pulled up. He stepped back when blood began to rush from her body, and for a moment she just stood there staring at the gaping wound in her belly. When her intestines started to ooze out of her body she looked up at Tony, eyes wide. She gasped, "Why did you do that to me?" Then her eyes rolled up and she fell forward.

Tony stared at her for almost a minute. Then he reached down and placed two fingers against her carotid artery. There was nothing, not even a weak flutter.

Chapter Nineteen

Harry's cell phone awakened him at six.

"You dressed?" Max Abrams asked.

"No, what's up?"

"We've got a murder, a young woman, seventeen or eighteen, MO fits our boy. You wanna have a look?"

"Definitely," Harry said.

Max gave him the location of the body.

"I'll be there in twenty minutes."

Harry put down the phone and called Vicky. When she answered he gave her the location. "I'm going to follow it all the way through the autopsy. I'm also going to ask them to compare the DNA samples taken off Lilly Mikinos and Mary Kate O'Connell."

"You think it's him, don't you?"

"Let's wait and see." Harry paused. "Yeah, I do. It has to be him."

Harry reached the location twenty minutes later. Crime scene techs were searching the area leading from the sidewalk to the body.

Max met Harry on the sidewalk and led him around the techs, giving them a wide berth, then on to the patch of ground that a living Cindy Lewis had claimed as her final place on this earth.

Harry looked down at her eviscerated body. She was a young woman, still in her teens; her eyes stared blindly, the pupils already beginning to cloud, the skin pale. She was slightly overweight, but in a pleasant, attractive way, definitely a young woman who should be looking forward to a long, joyous life. His eyes dropped to the gaping wound in her abdomen, entrails out, already beginning to shrivel and dry in the morning sun. "Who kills people like this, gutting them like slaughtered animals?" he asked no one in particular. "It's primitive, something from the dark ages, when monstrous crimes were commonplace."

Harry continued to stare at the body when a name flashed into his mind—*Tony Rawlings*. It came again and again. He turned to Max. "Does the name Tony Rawlings mean anything to you?"

"No, why do you ask?"

"It just keeps coming to me." He lowered his voice. "Sometimes that happens to me at a crime scene."

"Like the victim is communicating with you? I've heard the stories about you. They're true, huh?"

Harry nodded. "I try to downplay it, but it happens."

"I'll run the name through the computer," Max said.

"I'd also like to cross-check any DNA we pick up here with Lilly Mikinos and Mary Kate O'Connell."

"Good idea. When she goes in for the post I'll make a request for a comparison."

Vicky arrived just as they were completing their plans. "Anything I can do to help?" she asked.

"We're going to canvass the area bars and restaurants. According to the driver's license in her jeans, her name is Cindy Lewis, age nineteen, with an address farther up on Jones Street." Max shook his head. "She almost made it home."

They left the body to the crime scene investigators and morgue attendants and headed back to the Clearwater police headquarters. Back in Max's office they waited while he fed the name Tony Rawlings into the computer. Five minutes later they had a hit from the Los Angeles

PD—a warrant issued over a decade ago for a teenager named Tony Rawlings, who was wanted for questioning in the murder of his stepfather, John Gandolini, on Christmas Day 2004, and the subsequent disappearance of his mother, Victoria Rawlings, forty-eight. Gandolini had died from stab wounds from a double-edged knife. He had been eviscerated. Rawlings was an albino.

"The Church of Scientology has a big operation in LA. It's where their celebrity center is," Harry said.

"So you think maybe Tony Rawlings joined up with the Scientologists in LA and was eventually brought to Clearwater to work in Walsh's operation?"

"With a little name change to Tony Rolf," Vicky said.

"You think Regis Walsh knew he had killed this Gandolini guy and maybe his mother too?" Max asked.

"I think these Scientologists know everything there is to know about every member of their church," Harry said.

"So you believe Regis Walsh knowingly harbored a fugitive."

"I do," Harry said. "Whether I can prove it or not, well, that's still up for grabs."

"We'll see what happens after we name Tony Rolf as a person of interest in this murder," Max said.

"Let's pull out all the stops," Vicky said. "Name him a person of interest in all three killings—Cindy Lewis, Lilly Mikinos, and Mary Kate O'Connell. Label the son of a bitch what he is: a serial killer."

"And identify him as an employee of the Church of Scientology," Harry said. "Light a little fire under Regis Walsh."

"See where that jerk runs off to," Max added.

"He won't run anywhere," Harry said. "But he'll get rid of his boy Rolf as fast as he can."

* * *

A canvass of area restaurants and bars came up with a description of the man with whom Cindy Lewis had spent the last hours of her life. He was described as twenty-five to thirty years of age, blond, blue eyes, approximately five feet ten inches, 175 pounds, clean shaven with a well-tanned complexion. The description fit about one hundred thousand men in the general vicinity of Tampa Bay. It could, with some cosmetic help, also fit Tony Rolf.

Harry and Max attended the autopsy of Cindy Lewis—Vicky declined, saying she had met her quota of autopsies for the year. Max had requested George Rios, the same lab tech who had searched the body of Lilly Mikinos for DNA and Assistant Medical Examiner Dr. Angela Sugarman, who had performed the post.

When they finished with the body they all gathered in Sugarman's office to review the preliminary findings. Sugarman went first, saying the cause of death was straightforward—a massive wound to the abdomen by a double-edged blade, a stiletto, which caused a partial evisceration of the victim's intestines, accompanied by massive blood loss. "The victim would have died within a few minutes," Sugarman concluded. "But it would have been a painful, terrifying death."

Max turned to Rios. "Any luck with DNA?"

"Nothing under the fingernails," Rios said. "It appears the victim did not fight her killer. There was hair on her clothing that was not hers. It was dyed blond, white beneath the dye. We're running the tests now, but I'd bet they're going to match the hairs we found on Lilly Mikinos."

"With the same DNA?" Harry asked.

"I'd be very surprised if it wasn't a perfect match. I'll let you know in twenty-four hours."

"I guess we'll be checking in with you tomorrow," Max said.

"*You* will," Harry said. "I'll be in court to watch Jordan Wells try to spring my mother."

Chapter Twenty

Harry arrived at court at nine a.m. and immediately huddled with Assistant State Attorney Jeremy Peters. He gave Peters a small briefcase that held all the letters his mother had sent him on the anniversary of his brother's death, each one saying how she wanted her sons to be together again "in the heavenly kingdom of Jesus Christ."

"You'll notice that they are all postmarked one day before the anniversary of Jimmy's death. She was always very precise about mailing them so they would arrive exactly on that date."

"And *every* letter was a wish for your death?" Peters said.

"I always took it that way."

"Okay, I'll bring this up when you testify."

"Who have they got?" Harry asked.

"Megan Avery, Tyler Tully, William Harvey, an employee of AT&T, and your mother, of course," Peters said. "I'll call you first, and since you'll already have testified you can remain in the courtroom to listen to the other testimonies. I may need to call you again in rebuttal. We'll just have to wait and see what his witnesses say."

"Who else are you going to call?" Harry asked.

"You're it. I didn't want to bring in anyone from the prison, especially the shrinks who said she was well. I'm going to base our case on her violation of the parole order that she remain one hundred yards away from you at all times."

"How is Wells going to explain that away?"

Peters shrugged. "He claims she was lured there. He's got to prove that you did the luring. That's going to be his biggest hurdle. We'll just have to wait and see what rabbits he's got in his hat."

Lucy Santos was gently guided into the courtroom by Jordan Wells, who again looked like an advertisement from GQ. Harry looked him over and decided that his gray silk suit, red silk tie, and Gucci loafers probably set him back more than Harry made in a month. He leaned over to Peters and whispered: "He sure is a fashion plate. How come he looks so much better than you?"

"Just hope he's not better when he opens his mouth."

But he will be, Harry thought. *That's why he can afford to look so good.*

Harry refused to acknowledge or even glance at his birth mother. To do so would only produce one of her pathetic looks and he did not want to encourage any of her acts; he had seen all of those he ever wanted to see.

The court was called to order as Judge Walter McCoy entered the courtroom and ascended the bench. He dispensed with all formalities and immediately asked both lawyers if they were ready to proceed. Each acknowledged that he was.

"Well in that case, gentlemen, let's skip the opening statements—I've read your briefs and fully understand the arguments you plan to make. If you agree, let's go directly to witnesses."

Peters rose and told the court he had only one witness, Detective Harry Santos Doyle, but he reserved the right to call rebuttal witnesses if that proved necessary.

McCoy nodded and told him to proceed.

Harry moved to the witness chair, placed his hand on a Bible held by the court clerk, and swore to tell the truth.

"Please state your name, rank, and badge number," Peters began.

Harry did so.

"What is your relationship to Lucy Santos?" Peters asked.

"She is my birth mother."

"Why do you describe her as such?"

"Because after Lucy Santos was sent to prison for the murder of my brother James, and the attempted murder of myself, I was adopted by John and Maria Doyle of Clearwater, who raised me from the age of ten. They provided me with all the love and nurturing I ever received and I consider them to be my parents."

Lucy gasped and Wells promptly handed her a box of tissues and placed a comforting arm around her shoulders.

McCoy looked down from the bench and spoke directly to Wells: "Counselor, I'll expect you to keep all histrionics to a minimum. Please advise your client that such activities will not be looked upon with favor by this court."

"Yes, Your Honor," Wells said. "But please understand this is a trying time for Ms. Santos."

"It is a trying time for all of us, Mr. Wells," McCoy said.

Well, that's one for us, Harry thought. McCoy had just overruled any histrionic bullshit.

"Detective Doyle, did you oppose your mother's release from prison?"

"I did."

"Why did you do so?"

"I considered her a danger to me."

"What made you reach that conclusion?"

"Each year, on the anniversary of my brother Jimmy's murder and my attempted murder, my birth mother, Lucy Santos, would send me a letter telling me that she wanted me to join Jimmy in heaven so we could be there when she arrived and we could all be with Jesus."

Wells jumped to his feet. "Objection!" he shouted. "There is no supporting evidence for this horrible allegation, at least none that I have been shown, Your Honor. Unless counsel is prepared to offer corroborating physical evidence, I ask that this line of questioning be overruled."

Peters opened the briefcase Harry had given him and asked to approach the bench. "Here, Your Honor, are the letters Detective Doyle referred to, each and every one of them. The court will see that all but the last letter are postmarked from the women's prison where Ms. Santos was incarcerated. In each letter Ms. Santos makes reference to Detective Doyle joining his dead brother James in heaven. Each one is clearly a threat."

"Since when, Your Honor, is a mother's wish that her child goes to heaven a threat?" Wells bellowed. "My mother prays regularly that heaven will be in my future and I wouldn't be surprised if Judge McCoy's mother wishes the same for him."

"Let's leave my mother out of this discussion," McCoy snapped. "Objection overruled. The court will place the letters into evidence."

"May I be provided with copies, Your Honor?" Wells asked.

McCoy ordered the assistant clerk to make copies for both attorneys. "Proceed, Mr. Peters."

"Detective Doyle, do you live aboard your boat at the Clearwater marina?"

"I do."

"Why did you choose to live there?"

"I owned a house off Mandalay Avenue. After her release from prison, my birth mother kept appearing in the neighborhood. I thought living in a secure marina would make this less possible. Living aboard a boat would also offer the opportunity to move quickly to another location if and when she did find out where I was living. So I sold my house and purchased the boat."

"It's a large boat?"

"Yes, it's fairly large; forty-eight feet, to be exact, with three staterooms, three heads, and a large salon and galley."

Wells rose to his feet. "Your Honor, we are all pleased that Detective Doyle lives in such comfort and splendor, but can we return to the issue at hand?"

"Yes, let us proceed, Mr. Peters," the judge said.

"Yes, Your Honor. Detective Doyle, on the day in question, when your birth mother appeared at the marina where you live, how did you become aware of her presence?"

"I overheard her arguing with another boat owner, a woman I knew as Meg Adams, and when I went outside I saw that my birth mother was holding a six-inch carving knife in her hand, and that Ms. Adams was backing away, clearly alarmed."

"What did you do then?"

"I jumped onto the dock and confronted Ms. Santos and disarmed her. Then I asked Ms. Adams to call the Clearwater Police Department with an 'officer needs assistance' call. She did so and two Clearwater police officers arrived and arrested Ms. Santos."

Peters looked up at the bench. "No further questions at this time, Your Honor."

"Does the defense have any questions for this witness, Mr. Wells?" the judge asked.

Wells rose slowly. "Indeed we do, Your Honor." He walked in front of the defense table, then slowly returned to his place behind it. "Do you love your mother, Detective Doyle?"

Peters jumped to his feet. "Objection. Whether Detective Doyle loves his mother has no bearing on this case."

"Your Honor, it does indeed," Wells said. "The defense intends to show that Detective Doyle's feelings toward his mother"—his voice rose to a roar—"in fact, his *hatred* for his mother led to this entire incident!"

"I'll allow this line of questioning to continue for now," the judge said.

"Again, Detective Doyle, do you love your mother, Lucy Santos?"

"I do not," Harry answered.

Wells studied his well-polished Gucci loafers. "In your experience that is unusual, is it not? I mean, is it not unusual for a man not to love the woman who brought him into this world?"

Harry looked him coldly in the eyes. "I stopped loving her when she tried to take me *out* of this world."

"Do you hate her?" Wells asked.

"I don't know," Harry said. "I hope not. I wish I could pity her for her illness. But I'm not sure I can."

"And why is that?"

"She killed my little brother. He was only six and he *did* love her. He loved her with all his heart."

"He told you that?"

"He did."

"Did he love his father?" Wells asked.

"We didn't know our father. He left right after Jimmy was born."

"And you were what, four?"

"Yes. I only vaguely remember him. Jocko Doyle, my adoptive father, is the only father I ever knew."

"Jocko Doyle was a sergeant with the Clearwater Police Department, is that so?"

"Yes, he's retired now."

"And you've been investigating a recent crime in which he was shot, have you not?"

"I have."

"And all this was going on when you had this confrontation with Ms. Santos, is that also true?"

"It is."

"So you had a great many emotional things going on, did you not? I mean, your adoptive father being shot, the normal stress of your very stressful job, the crimes you were investigating, and on top of it all, your birth mother being recently released from prison and wanting to meet with you? That is a great deal of stress, is it not?"

"If you say so."

"Oh, come now, detective, with all you had going on in your life, isn't it fair to say that the last thing you needed was further conflict with the birth mother who, when mentally ill in the past, tried to take your life?"

"I was doing my best to avoid her."

"You were? Let's look into that statement just a bit." Wells made a show of picking up a sheet of paper. He raised his eyes to Harry. "Does the marina where you live have a public phone?"

"Yes."

"How many times have you used that phone?"

"I've never had occasion to use it," Harry replied.

"Are you sure, detective?"

"I'm sure."

"Do you have a land line on your boat?" Wells was slowly pacing behind the defense table.

"No, I do not."

"No land line."

"That's correct."

"Do you have a cell phone?"

"Yes."

"Do you use that phone for police business *and* personal use?"

"I have two cell phones: one issued by the sheriff's office for business use and a second one that I pay for myself for personal use."

"Are they both issued by Verizon?" Wells asked.

"Yes."

"Would either of them show any calls to your birth mother, Lucy Santos?"

Harry sat and thought. "I cannot recall ever making a call to her on either phone," he finally said.

"Never?" Wells elevated his voice to emphasize his incredulity.

"I cannot recall ever making a call to her on either phone."

"Did you ever call the prison where she was incarcerated?"

"Yes."

"Did you call to speak to her?"

"No."

"If not to speak to her, for what reasons did you call?"

"Whenever she had a parole hearing I would call to make sure I had the time and date right. The prison system is notorious for not keeping victims or their families informed about changes in the hearing schedules."

"And you wanted to be certain you would be there to oppose her release?"

"That's correct."

"Why?"

"I considered her a danger to me and to others."

"You are a trained police officer, are you not?"

"I am."

"Trained in defending yourself against attacks from a . . . 110-pound, middle-aged woman?" He extended his hand toward Lucy Santos at the defense table. She blinked.

A ripple of laughter went through the courtroom. The judge used his gavel to command quiet.

"May I have your answer, detective?" Wells pushed.

"Yes sir, I am trained to defend myself."

"And yet you were *afraid?*"

"I was concerned."

"Oh, I see, you were concerned, not afraid."

Peters jumped to his feet. "Your Honor, I object to the defense counsel's continued use of sarcasm to belittle this highly decorated officer."

"Let's ease up on the sarcasm, Mr. Wells," Judge McCoy said, then turned to Harry. "You may answer the question."

"Yes, I was concerned."

"Why, because of some harmless letters she sent you hoping that you would one day arrive in heaven?" There was a wide grin on Wells's face.

Harry held the man's eyes with a level gaze. "I was concerned because she had already killed me once when I was ten years old. I didn't want her to have a second chance."

"The truth is that you wanted to set her up for a parole violation, isn't that so? The truth is that you used the pay phone in the marina to call your mother and set up a meeting to discuss your personal difficulties, isn't that so? And the truth is that you planted the six-inch carving knife on your mother after you asked Meg Avery to call the police. That is also the truth, is it not, Detective Doyle?"

"Your Honor," Peters shouted over Wells's thundering words, "certainly defense counsel cannot be allowed to ask *and* answer his own questions!"

Judge McCoy leaned forward. "The state's attorney makes a valid point, Mr. Wells. Ask your questions one at a time and wait for Detective Doyle's answers."

"At this time I have no further questions of this witness, Your Honor."

"I have one additional question, Your Honor," Peters said.

"Proceed," the judge responded.

Peters stood and stared long and hard into Harry's eyes. "Detective Doyle, in response to Mr. Wells's earlier question, you said that you were concerned about Ms. Santos's release from prison because she had already killed you once and you didn't want to give her another chance. Can you please elaborate?"

"Objection!" Wells shouted.

"Overruled, counsel," McCoy said. "You opened this door. You may answer the question, Detective Doyle."

"According to reports filed with the Tampa Police Department, Ms. Santos drugged my six-year-old brother Jimmy and me." Harry spoke slowly, his voice suddenly filled with sadness and regret. "When we were unconscious she dragged us into the garage of our Tampa home and started her car. She then left us there to die and went to her church. Fortunately, a neighbor heard the car running inside the closed garage and telephoned the police. Two patrol officers arrived, broke into the garage, and found us. Neither Jimmy nor I had a heartbeat and we weren't breathing. The officers dragged us out of the garage and started CPR and were able to bring me back. Jimmy, who was younger and smaller, did not respond. He was pronounced dead at the scene."

"Thank you, detective," Peters said. He turned to Wells and added: "Your witness, counselor."

Wells stood and peered at Harry. Then he extended a hand toward Lucy Santos once again. "This woman was judged mentally ill when she killed your brother Jimmy, isn't that true?"

"Yes," Harry said.

"And after years of psychiatric treatment she was declared well, was she not?"

"Yes, she was," Harry answered.

"But you never forgave her, did you?"

"No," Harry said. "She—"

"No further questions."

"Your Honor," Peters said, rising to his feet, "I would like to hear *all* of Detective Doyle's answer."

"You may finish your answer, detective," McCoy said.

"She showed no remorse in the letters she sent me year after year. I interpreted them to mean that she still wanted to 'send me to Jesus,' which was the reason she gave to the Tampa police when they arrested her for Jimmy's murder and my attempted murder."

"No further questions, Your Honor," Peters said.

McCoy shifted his gaze to Wells and asked: "Anything further, Mr. Wells?"

"I have no further use of this witness, Your Honor," Wells said.

"Mr. Peters, do you have another witness?" McCoy asked.

"No, Your Honor, the prosecution rests."

"Call your first witness, Mr. Wells," McCoy said.

"The defense calls Tyler Tully."

Harry had taken a seat directly behind the prosecution table and he now watched Tyler Tully, a.k.a. the dock Nazi, being led to the witness stand by a court officer. It was a transformation he had not expected. He had only seen Tully dressed in a white T-shirt bearing the name of the marina, tan khaki cargo shorts, flip-flops, and a pith helmet. Today he was dressed in sharply creased tan slacks, a dark blue polo shirt under a light blue seersucker sports coat, and penny loafers. His short blond hair was slicked back with gel.

Wells stood and favored him with a broad smile. "Mr. Tully, what is your job at the marina?"

"I'm the dockmaster." He seemed to inflate slightly with self-importance.

"And what does that entail?"

"I'm responsible for the safety of seventy-eight boats worth many millions of dollars, the safety of all persons who come onto the docks, and the protection of those docks from damage by weather, other boats, and vandalism. I'm also responsible for all fees owed by boat owners, and compliance to all rules and regulations of the marina."

"Is Detective Doyle, who is seated in this courtroom directly behind the prosecution table, a tenant at your marina?"

"He is."

"Is he a good tenant?"

"Yes, he is." Tully gave Harry an insipid smile.

"Mr. Tully, is there a pay phone on the marina's property?"

"Yes."

"Have you ever seen Detective Doyle use that pay phone?"

"Yes, I believe I have."

"Did you see him use it on more than one occasion?" Wells asked.

"Yes, I believe so."

"No further questions." Wells walked back to the defense table.

Peters stood. "Mr. Tully, would it surprise you to learn that Detective Doyle has testified that he has never used that pay phone?"

Tully looked at him blankly, then turned his gaze to Wells as if searching for some help. "Well, I thought he had," he said.

"Could you have been mistaken?" Peters asked.

"Well, anything's possible," he said, adding a silly smile. He caught a sharp look from Wells, and quickly added: "But I'm pretty certain I saw him use it."

"No further questions," Peters said.

"Your next witness, Mr. Wells," the judge said.

"The defense calls William Harvey."

Harry watched a tall, slender man, about fifty years of age, with a long nose, thinning hair, and heavy bags under his eyes, walk to the witness stand to be sworn in.

Wells remained behind the defense table. "Only a few questions, Mr. Harvey. Did you, pursuant to a request from my office, check the calls made from a pay phone at the Clearwater marina?"

"I did," Harvey said.

"Did you find any calls made to a cell phone owned by Lucy Santos?"

"I did. There were four such calls."

Wells handed him a sheet of paper. "Does this list, signed by you, note the times and dates those calls were made?"

"It does," Harvey said.

Wells handed a copy to the judge. "Your Honor, please accept this as defense exhibit one." He passed a copy to Peters as well. "No further questions."

"Mr. Peters?" the judge said.

"No questions, Your Honor."

"I think this would be a good time to break for lunch," the judge said. "Court will reconvene at one o'clock."

* * *

When Harry returned from a quick sandwich at a nearby restaurant, he found Meg Avery standing outside the courtroom.

"Hi, sailor," she said as he walked past her.

Harry stopped and moved toward her. Peters was standing farther down the hallway and Harry beckoned him over.

"Making sure you have a witness?" Meg asked in a teasing voice.

"It seems to be the wise thing to do," he said.

"Yes, I suppose it is. I'm sorry. But it was business, not personal, as they said in *The Godfather*."

Peters arrived and Harry introduced Meg as someone he had known as Meg Adams, a fellow dock mate when the incident occurred with Lucy Santos. "Her real name is Meg Avery and she's the president and CEO of Avery Security," he added.

Meg, as always, looked beautiful. Now, unlike her days at the marina, she also looked glamorous. She was dressed to the nines in a dark blue Armani suit over a pale blue silk top, with dark blue Christian Louboutin pumps, all of it set off by her coifed red hair. Harry could tell Peters was already smitten.

"I just wanted to tell you something," Harry said. "If you're still working for the same people, and you have any contact with Tony Rolf, please be careful. We believe he just killed another woman last night." With that, he turned and entered the courtroom, with Jeremy Peters reluctantly following in his wake.

When court resumed Jordan Wells called Meg Avery to the witness chair, where she swore to tell the truth. She looked at Harry and gave him a small, regretful smile, and he knew without question she was prepared to lie through her teeth. Her words—*It was business, not personal*—rang in his ears.

Wells came around to the front of the defense table and faced her. To Harry, they looked like models ready to head down the runway, each impeccably dressed in several thousand dollars' worth of clothing.

"Ms. Avery," Wells began, "did there come a time earlier this year when you were living aboard a sailboat in the Clearwater marina under the name of Meg Adams?"

"Yes, there was."

"What can you tell us about that?"

"Very little, really," Meg said, softening her words with a smile.

"Why is that?"

"I am president and CEO of Avery Security and I was there working for a client who has asked my firm to provide it with anonymity. I can tell you that my work had nothing to do with Lucy Santos or the case now before this court."

"I accept your client's request for anonymity and your need to respect it," Wells said. "On the day in question, in the matter that is now before this court, were you present when an incident occurred between Lucy Santos, the defendant in this matter, and Sheriff's Detective Harry Doyle?"

"Yes, I was."

"What did you observe?"

"I was on deck when I saw Ms. Santos walking down the dock."

"How did she appear to you?"

"She appeared to be looking for someone and she appeared confused."

"Confused in what way?"

"She seemed confused in the way someone seems when they are not sure if they are in the right place."

"Did you speak to Ms. Santos?"

"Yes, I did."

"What did you say?"

"I climbed down off my boat and asked her who she was looking for."

"What happened then?"

"Harry Doyle, who kept his boat in the slip across from mine, suddenly appeared on deck and jumped down to the dock and grabbed Ms. Santos. He put her in handcuffs and asked me to call the police with an 'officer needs assistance' message."

"And did you do what the detective asked?"

"I did."

"You and Harry Doyle were dock mates and friends, were you not?"

"Yes."

"And you knew he was a law-enforcement officer, correct?"

"Yes, I did."

"And after you made the call, did two Clearwater police officers subsequently arrive and place Ms. Santos under arrest?"

"Yes, they did."

"Now, Ms. Avery, are you a trained observer?"

"Yes, I am."

Wells turned to the judge. "Your Honor, I have a list of training courses that Ms. Avery has completed. The corporation that she heads is a multimillion-dollar enterprise that employs several hundred people, including former police officers, FBI, and other federal agents. These people can be called to testify as to her expertise."

Peters rose to his feet. "That will not be necessary, Your Honor. The prosecution is familiar with Avery Security and we understand that Ms. Avery is a trained observer."

"You may proceed, Mr. Wells," the judge said.

"Ms. Avery, at any time did you see a six-inch carving knife in Ms. Santos's hand?" Wells asked.

"No, I did not."

"Did you subsequently see a six-inch carving knife?"

"Yes, I saw Detective Doyle hand a knife matching that description to one of the police officers."

"Did you overhear anything that was said by Detective Doyle?"

"Yes. Harry, Detective Doyle, said he had taken the knife away from the woman who had been arrested."

"But you didn't see her with that knife."

"No."

"Were you surprised when he said she had been holding the knife?"

"Yes, but I assumed he meant that he had found it on her person."

"The arrest report says she had menaced him with it."

"I didn't see that."

"Thank you, Ms. Avery." Wells turned to Peters, but his eyes remained on Harry. "Your witness, Mr. Prosecutor," he said.

Peters turned to Harry, who leaned in and whispered in his ear: "She's lying, but I can't prove it."

Peters rose slowly to his feet. "Ms. Avery, is it possible that you simply failed to see the knife, either because of your position on the dock or because you were preoccupied with telephoning the police?"

"Of course it is, but I have to say that it would be highly unusual for me to miss such a blatant detail. And, of course, at that time Ms. Santos was handcuffed and her hands were behind her back and there was no knife on the dock or in Detective Doyle's hands."

"Thank you. No further questions at this time." Peters slowly returned to his seat. He purposefully avoided Harry's eyes.

Wells rose to his feet. "Your Honor, I debated whether or not to call the two arresting officers, but after reading their reports it was clear their testimony would add nothing to what they had written. I will therefore submit the reports to the court, and if the prosecutor chooses to call them as rebuttal witnesses, I will certainly not object. I now call the defendant, Lucy Santos, and if it pleases the court I would like to have fifteen minutes to speak with her before she testifies."

"You may have fifteen minutes," McCoy said.

As Wells led Lucy Santos out of the courtroom, Harry asked Peters: "How badly did Avery's testimony hurt us?"

"It set new levels for reasonable doubt," Peters replied. "In fact, it would not surprise me if the judge asked my office to investigate possible perjury charges."

"I told you the truth, Jeremy. I testified to exactly what happened."

"I believe you, Harry, and I don't think a perjury investigation would come up with anything. But it adds one more area of doubt in your mother's case."

"What about proving Meg Avery lied through her beautiful teeth?"

"Bring me one witness who will testify that she told them she saw a knife in your mother's hand and I'll charge her. Otherwise I don't see any way of challenging her statement. How do I prove that someone saw something they say they didn't?" Peters paused. "What can I expect from your mother?"

"She doesn't want to go back to prison. She wants to stay close to me. She'll say anything he tells her to say."

Lucy Santos took the witness stand, keeping her eyes fixed on her attorney.

"Please state your name," Wells began.

"Lucy Santos."

"How old are you?"

"I am fifty-two."

"Where have you spent the last twenty years of your life?"

"I was in prison."

"What were you convicted of doing?"

Tears began to flow down Lucy Santos's cheeks. "I killed my little boy Jimmy, and I tried to kill my other boy, Harry."

"Why did you do these things?"

"I was sick."

Wells paused to let her words have full impact. "Are you still sick?"

"No, I'm better now."

"Do you have any intention of hurting your son Harry?"

"No sir, no, never. I would never hurt my Harry." Lucy turned her head and stared directly at her son. "I would never hurt him."

"Did there come a time within the last month that you went to the marina where your son Harry lives?"

"Yes, I went there."

"Did you know that there was a parole board order and a court order that you were to have no contact with him?"

"Yes, I know," Lucy said. She lowered her eyes.

"Why then did you go there?"

"He ask me to come. He said we need to talk about the problems we have. So I go. What could I do? I'm his mother. I have no choice."

"When did he ask you to do this?"

"The day before I went there or maybe two days, I'm not sure. I had to get the day off from work."

"Where do you work?"

"I work in the laundry at a hotel on the beach."

"A hotel on Clearwater Beach—you work in their laundry room?" Wells asked.

"Yes. I work five days every week."

"And you were given the day off on the day you went to the marina?"

"Yes."

"What happened when you got to the marina?"

"I followed a man through a special gate they have there and I went to slip number fifty-five, where my son told me he keeps his boat." She dabbed her eyes with a handkerchief. "But I don't see him."

"Did a woman ask you who you were looking for?"

"Yes, a nice young lady, she ask me that, but before I can answer Harry runs up to me and grabs me and puts handcuffs on me."

"Did you have a knife in your hand at that time?"

"No."

"Did you bring a knife to the marina that day?"

"No."

"I have no further questions, Your Honor," Wells said.

Peters rose to his feet. "Ms. Santos, is it possible you had a knife in your purse?"

"No."

"Have you ever carried a knife in your purse?"

Lucy Santos looked confused, uncertain how to answer. She stared at Wells; he raised a hand to his chin.

"No, I never had a knife in my purse."

"When Mr. Wells touches his chin, is that a signal to you to answer *no* to the question you've been asked?"

"Objection, Your Honor!" Wells thundered as he jumped to his feet.

"I withdraw the question, Your Honor," Peters said. "No further questions at this time."

When Harry left the courthouse he felt bruised and battered by Wells's summation. He had been painted as a man who would do anything to have his mother sent back to prison. The judge had not made any immediate ruling, but he had also left Lucy Santos free on bail. Jeremy Peters said it was a clear signal that Jordan Wells would likely prevail and that charges against his mother would be dismissed.

"Come up with another witness who saw the knife and I'll try to reopen the case," Peters had said.

Fat chance, Harry thought. Regis Walsh and his minions had cleaned his clock. He'd be lucky not to be accused of perjury.

CHAPTER TWENTY-ONE

A party was held in Regis Walsh's office to celebrate what he considered a major victory. Wells had assured him that charges would be dropped against Lucy Santos and that he planned to press the sheriff's office to proceed with an internal affairs investigation into Harry Doyle's actions.

"I don't think the sheriff will have any choice once the judge rules in our favor. Our lovely Ms. Avery's testimony alone is very damning evidence that Detective Doyle misused the powers of his office."

"I wish we weren't taking that route," Meg said. "Harry Doyle's a good cop and a decent guy. We beat him and I understood the need for that. Do we have to destroy his career as well?"

"Detective Doyle is an enemy of my church, a dangerous enemy, an enemy who must be stopped," Walsh replied bluntly.

"But you *have* stopped him," Meg said.

Walsh pointed to the food and drinks set out on the conference table of his office, then turned to Ken Oppenheimer. "Please, Ken, make sure everyone has enough food and drink. This is a celebration, after all." He took Meg's elbow gently in one hand and led her away from the others. "I have a bonus check for you, to express our appreciation of a job well done. I have one more assignment for you and then your work for us will be finished."

"What is the assignment?" Meg asked.

"I want you to take Mr. Rolf under your wing for one more night.

Then I want you to escort him to the private air terminal at Tampa Airport where he will catch a flight to Miami aboard a private jet. Once in Miami he'll board a commercial flight to Alaska." Walsh patted the breast pocket of his suit coat. "I have his tickets and some cash here. It will keep him comfortable for quite some time. And so it will be goodbye to Tony Rolf until the world forgets his past transgressions." He laughed heartily. "Then, my dear, Tony will get a new name and a new location and he'll be back in the fold."

"And what will you do to find a replacement for him here?"

"My dear girl, certainly you know that Tony Rolfs exist by the dozens. You only have to find one who you have a reasonable chance of controlling."

"At court today Harry Doyle warned me that Rolf has killed another woman. That's four now, isn't it?"

"I'm afraid the police are going to try to hang every murdered woman around Tony Rolf's neck. It makes life easier for them. Thank God for serial killers."

"Thank God he'll be gone."

"Will it make you sleep better at night, Meg? Even though you know there are others waiting to take his place?"

"Yes, it will, Regis," she said, making no effort to take the edge off her voice. "And please don't ask me to deal with your next monster."

Meg took the envelope holding the tickets and the cash for Rolf and used her cell to call him. "Tony, I want you to pack for a long journey. I'll pick you up at eight. You'll be staying at my condo tonight and leaving for the airport early tomorrow." She listened, closed her eyes in exasperation, and then continued: "Let's put all that aside for now, shall we? You have to move, and move quickly." She paused again, listening. "I'll see you at eight."

Meg went to the table that held the food and drinks and poured herself some Old Grand-Dad. Jordan Wells sauntered up. There was a smug smile on his face that Meg wished she could wipe away.

"In need of strong spirits?" he asked.

"And a shower," she said. "How about you, Jordan?"

"I learned long ago to separate the guilt my clients might feel from my view of my own actions on their behalf."

"Do you find it that easy?"

"Usually. Not always, but usually," he said.

"I think I'm having one of those *not always* moments." She winked at him. "Usually I smile all the way to the bank. Sometimes it's just harder than others."

Jordan nodded sagely. "Sometimes the Church of Scientology can be a difficult client. That's why I charge them so much. Triple what I charge other clients." He put his arm around Meg's shoulders and walked her away from the others. "But they do come up with some challenging cases."

"Like mentally ill mothers who want to murder their sons?"

"A case in point," Wells said. "I hope we have a chance to work together again soon."

"I hope so too, Jordan. But with a different client."

He raised his glass and walked off.

Meg picked Tony Rolf up at eight. He had one large suitcase and a carry-on. He would undoubtedly have to buy clothing in Alaska, but at least it was late June and truly heavy clothing wouldn't be needed until the Alaskan summer had passed. She popped the trunk and waited while he loaded his bags. When he got into the passenger seat she handed him the envelope Walsh had provided.

"Your tickets and cash for living expenses." She watched out of the corner of her eye as Tony counted the money and perused the airline tickets.

"Miami to Seattle; Seattle to Juneau; Juneau to Glacier Bay/Gustavus," he said. "Two full days of travel, what a treat. But it looks like some pretty decent hotel reservations. Sure you don't wanna come?"

"Mr. Walsh said there was enough money to cover your expenses for a considerable time."

"Five grand," Tony said. "You can never accuse Regis Walsh of being cheap. Oppenheimer, now that's a different matter. He would have given me a one-way bus ticket and a peanut butter sandwich to eat along the way." He paused. "I bet Regis pays you well."

"He pays my company," Meg said. "And everyone pays my company well."

"Or he doesn't get to see your smiling face, huh?" Tony was grinning.

Happiness was impossible to read on Tony's face. Everything seemed to come through a veil of anger, filtered through the hostility that never left his eyes. Except . . . she thought, except when a near-miraculous innocence took hold of him. Meg had marveled at that innocence the few times she had observed it. And yet she still wondered if it was real.

She opened the latch on her purse, which lay on the console that separated their seats. Her Walther was now just a short reach away. "Did you kill a woman the other night?" she asked.

"What the hell makes you ask that?" Tony snarled.

"Harry Doyle told me you did. He told me to be careful if I planned to help you."

"That fucking cop, he pins everything on me. In case you forgot, the last time I was out, I was out with you."

Meg pulled her car onto the Memorial Causeway and saw the broad expanse of Clearwater Beach and the Gulf of Mexico spread out before her. "It's very beautiful. Did you enjoy your time here?"

"You make it sound like I won't be coming back," Tony said. "You know something I don't?"

"Not at all. I have no idea what plans Mr. Walsh has for you. Did you look at your tickets?"

"Yeah, sort of," Tony said with a shrug.

"Look again, Tony. They're first class tickets," she said. "You don't buy first class tickets for people you don't value."

Tony opened the envelope again and studied the tickets. "Like I said, you can't accuse Regis Walsh of being cheap. I've never flown first class. Is it really different?" The look of innocence was back on his face now and he was smiling again.

"Very much so," Meg said. "When you get to Miami International, make sure you get there early, then check in and go directly to the VIP lounge and let the pampering begin."

Meg pulled up to the entry of her condo. "John, there will be a limo calling for my guest at seven," she said to the security guard on duty. "Please leave a note for the man working that shift. I don't want to deal with any confusion. I'll be working from home tomorrow and I don't want to be disturbed."

"I'll make sure it's done, Ms. Avery." The guard raised his fingers to his forehead in a casual salute.

"It's nice to be boss, isn't it?" Tony said.

"Yes. I always liked it." Meg glanced at him out of the corner of her eye. He seemed calm. *Just stay that way*, she thought. *Let's have a nice quiet night and then it's goodbye, Tony Rolf.*

Meg parked in the garage under her building. Most units in the complex were limited to two reserved parking places. As the occupant of a two-story penthouse, she had four. She exited the car with Tony trailing behind and waved to a camera hidden in the ceiling. The glass door that shielded the garage from the building buzzed open and the two of them entered. Meg used a key to operate the elevator and the door slid quietly open. She used the key again to send the elevator to her penthouse. They rode silently up until the elevator door opened directly into the foyer of her unit.

"Some joint," Tony said. "How big is it?"

"Four bedrooms, four and a half baths, 4,500 square feet in all."

Tony walked into the living room where a wall of windows climbed two stories to a glass-domed roof. When skies were clear it would offer a gorgeous view of the gulf by day and at night a breathtaking look at star-filled skies.

"Are you hungry?" Meg asked.

"I'm always hungry."

"Come out to the kitchen and we'll see what we can put together."

Tony watched her walk toward the kitchen and felt delight at the sway of her hips. He had always believed there was a sexual tension between them and now there was not much time left to exploit it.

Meg rumbled around in the fridge and came up with half a chicken and various cheeses and spreads, then pulled half a loaf of French bread and flatbread crackers from a cupboard. "I have beer or wine—some fairly good wine, actually—and, of course, milk, coffee, and juice."

"What you have here is fine. Are you going to join me?"

"Regis put out a spread at his office, actually. So I've eaten more than enough. Please go right ahead." She set a plate and silverware on the counter.

"Are you going to miss me?"

"It's always difficult when someone with whom you've spent a great deal of time suddenly leaves. Even though I knew that was the plan, it still seems to have happened much more quickly than I expected." She tried to turn the question back on him: "Are you excited about leaving? It should be quite an adventure."

He laughed. "That sounds like one of those nonanswer answers. Don't be afraid, you can say you'll miss me. It won't hurt."

"I'm anxious to know how things turn out for you. I know people who have visited Alaska and never wanted to leave. Others . . ." she shrugged, "they couldn't get away fast enough."

"How do you think it will be for me?" he asked.

"I don't know you well enough to answer that. But I think you're going to like it."

"Why?"

"Why . . . ? Because it's primitive in many ways, but it's also very, very beautiful. When you check out the mountains and the interior beyond, it all looks incredibly challenging. It's as though the land itself is saying, *I'm big and sprawling and rugged and powerful. No one who is less so should cross over into my heartland.*"

"You sound like you were very tempted to stay."

"I think the idea frightened me a bit."

"Frightened you *a bit?*"

"Well, maybe more than a bit. I like the way I live." Meg waved an arm, taking in the room, the gulf, everything. "When you're tempted to give it up, that's a scary concept. Plus, I really don't think I'm cut out to be Nanook of the North."

Rolf gave her a sideward glance. She was so sexy it almost hurt him to look at her. She opened a bottle of Modello and poured it into a glass.

"Eat as much as you want and help yourself to anything else you can find. I'm going to shower and change into something loose and relaxing. Make yourself at home, turn on the television, whatever. I'll be back soon." She headed to an open staircase that led up to the next level.

Tony watched her go, a slow, easy smile spreading across his face. *Now was that an invitation or what? Yes indeed.*

Meg climbed out of the shower feeling relaxed and refreshed. She had laid out one of her favorites—black lounging pajamas. She slipped into them, enjoying the feel of silk sliding against her skin. She sat down at her makeup table and began brushing her hair with long, slow strokes, enjoying the contrast of her red hair against the black silk.

She decided she would call the office tomorrow and tell them she was taking a few days off. To hell with her plan to work at home; she needed more than that—a few days on a quiet, stress-free island, that was what she needed. Call a travel agent and see what was available on the spur of the moment. Perhaps even a short cruise, or a quick flight to Key West. She just wanted to celebrate her freedom from the insanity she had endured for the past few weeks.

She got up slowly, stretched, and opened the door that connected to her bedroom and walked slowly across the large room. She went to a closet and opened a gun safe. There she withdrew a .25-caliber automatic in an ankle holster and strapped it on, then went to the door that opened onto a hallway. There was a keypad set up next to the door. Her bedroom was also a safe room and she intended to use it as such while Tony Rolf was in her home. She punched in a code and listened as a series of deep dead bolt locks released, allowing the door to be opened. As the door swung inward, Tony Rolf stepped out from the side and she jumped involuntarily. He still held the glass of Modello she had poured for him.

"Hi," he said. "Love your pajamas." Tony's eyes were wild, gleefully so.

"What are you doing in here? This is my *bedroom!*" Meg shouted.

Tony Rolf's face slowly turned into a snarl; like a cornered animal, he abruptly changed from passive to aggressive. "What's the matter? I'm not good enough to be here? How many times did you have that fucking cop in here?"

"What I do or don't do in my bedroom is none of your business. This is part of my goddamn home. What happens here is part of my life, not yours, not anyone's—and it is no one's concern but mine."

"You fucking cunt."

Meg stood silent, staring at him. "Get your things together. I will call a hotel and reserve you a room. I will call you a cab to get you there and I will notify the limo driver that his pickup location has changed. You can wait downstairs for the cab. I'll call security and tell them your plans have changed." They both stood there for several moments, before Meg said: "Now get the hell out of my home."

Tony took a step toward her. Meg shifted her body position, prepared now to strike out with a kick to his solar plexus. He feinted forward and pulled back. She had fallen for the feint and kicked too soon. He grabbed her heel and pulled her leg up and away. Her back slammed into the hardwood floor, driving the breath from her lungs. He straddled her chest and before she could move again, his knife was out. He slid his body lower, moving down on her body so the point of his blade was pressing just below her left breast. Any additional pressure would now move the blade up and into her heart.

"It's different than the shit you play at in a gym, isn't it?"

Meg's mind raced, trying to think of what move might free her, allow her to gain a physical advantage over him and get to the pistol strapped to her ankle.

"This reminds me of an old joke," Tony hissed. "There are two fighters facing each other. One fighter shouts, *Karate!* and strikes a fighting pose. His opponent shouts, *Smith & Wesson!* and takes out a .38 and shoots the first asshole between the eyes."

"Very funny." Meg's mouth was dry, so dry she could barely speak. She forced the next words out: "Alright, let's go back to square one. Everything stays as it was. You go to your room and get some sleep. The limo comes at seven. There's an alarm clock by your bed. Set the alarm so you can be up and ready."

The laugh started slowly at the back of Tony's throat, rising to a crescendo that filled the bedroom. "Is there a fucking sign on my forehead that says, *Put a quarter in the slot and speak to the idiot?* Is there? Huh? Sure, I'll just lie down in my bed; you can even come and tuck me in, and I'll go night-night like a good little boy. And you can call the cops, or even worse, you can come back with a knife like mine and you can slide it into my heart." Tony stared into Meg's eyes as he pushed the blade slowly, watching the shock and horror as it entered her heart.

Her body bucked once; then again. It shuddered as her eyes grew wider and her mouth opened in a failed attempt to scream.

He leaned in close and whispered: "Die, you fucking cunt." Then he smiled as he saw all the life slowly fade from her eyes. "Yes, my beautiful Meg, that's perfect. See how much I like it when you do as you're told?"

Chapter Twenty-Two

Jeremy Peters called Harry at ten the following morning. "I just heard from the judge. He's ordering that all charges be dropped against Lucy Santos. He says my office failed to prove that she was not lured to the marina and that the court will give her the benefit of presumptive innocence. He is not asking for any charges against the arresting officer—that's you—since the defense failed to show that you played any part in luring her to the marina. So it's a wash, except for the fact that she's free. He does order her to stay away from you, or anywhere you live."

"Wells will still push it with internal affairs," Harry said.

"Yeah, I expect they'll call you in, they may even suspend you until we submit a report stating that we find you guiltless and do not intend to prosecute. As soon as I get a request from them I'll write up a report stating exactly that and messenger it over to them. It should be a slam dunk unless you have someone out for your ass within the sheriff's office."

"You never know," Harry said.

"It's the joy of government service," Peters said. "Take care, Harry. It was good meeting you."

Harry called Max and filled him in.

"So you have a crazy mother who is still an albatross around your neck," Max said. "Hey, I could make you an honorary Jew."

"No thanks," Harry replied. "I've got enough problems."

"Hey, the food's good," Max said. "We have great corned beef. Anyway, what are you up to today?"

"I'm looking for Tony Rolf. I think he may still be hanging around one of the marinas, one that was close enough to walk to after he killed Cindy Lewis."

"You may be right," Max said. "If you get anything that even hints he's around, give me a call and I'll bring an army of cops down on him."

"You got it," Harry said.

An hour later Detective John Otis of the sheriff's office of internal affairs called. "I heard the court is coming out with a ruling on your mother's case today," he said.

"I heard the same thing. Jeremy Peters called me. Who called you, Jordan Wells?"

"That's right."

"What does that tell you?"

"It tells me that Wells, or whoever he works for, wants your ass," Otis said. "Why is somebody so pissed off at you, Harry Doyle?"

"It's like I told you, they want me shot, stuffed, and hanging over the mantle because Wells is working for the Church of Scientology and I just happen to be trying to arrest an employee of theirs, a little prick who likes to carve up women with a knife."

"How many has he killed so far?" Otis asked.

"Four and counting. It's like I told you, his name is Tony Rolf and he's our own little Jack the Ripper. A Scientology executive named Regis Walsh is trying to get him out of the area before we nail him and embarrass the church."

"That's a pretty heavy allegation. Did Peters say he was charging you with anything?"

"He said I was free and clear as far as his office was concerned. He said he'd give you a report saying so if you asked him for it."

"I'm gonna need that. Wells also called the sheriff; said he thinks you should be suspended."

"I think Wells should be disbarred."

"Fat chance," Otis said with a low chuckle. "He's covered in Teflon like all those rat bastards. I'll call Peters and get him to send his report."

"I appreciate it, John."

"Hey, I know it's hard for you guys in the field to believe, but I love it when our people come up clean."

The phone signaled another call as Harry was finishing up with Otis. It was Max Abrams.

"Are you sitting down?" Max asked.

"No," Harry said.

"Well brace yourself, buddy. Meg Avery's cleaning lady just found her body. The murder weapon was a knife. MO makes it likely that our boy was the perp."

Harry stared straight ahead. "Damn it, I warned her. Just yesterday, outside the courtroom, I warned her to watch out for herself."

"I'm on my way to the crime scene now. I'll pick you up on the way."

Max had three detectives with him when he picked Harry up. He introduced them quickly. "We're going to hit this crime scene with everything we've got," Max said. "I called Vicky and she's on her way. We have to determine if Rolf did this and we have to do it fast. I'm worried his buddy inside the church is gonna pull out all the stops now to get him the hell out of here."

"I'll be very surprised if he isn't already gone," Harry said.

"Why?"

"If he was at Meg's condo, she was doing it as a special favor to

Regis Walsh. She was trying to get him out of the area. It's the only thing that makes sense. It's the only reason she'd let him get that close to her."

Max pulled up to the security gate, flashed his tin, and got directions to Meg's condo. "We'll be impounding her car as soon as we've dusted it for prints."

"I'll show you her parking places," the security guard said. "She had a visitor last night. A limo picked him up at seven this morning." He handed Max a slip of paper. "This is the name of the limo company."

"What did the guy look like?" Harry asked.

"No one would have seen him except the driver. He was picked up inside. That's the procedure here. A driver pulls in, double parks by whichever of the three buildings the passenger is in, then goes to the elevator and brings the luggage out. It's all on film. Everything that happens on the grounds is. I can have a copy for you in a couple of hours."

"That's great," Max said. "Also, get me the film that shows him arriving last night. Let me know when it's ready."

Max sent his three detectives to various assignments—one to search and dust any cars in Meg Avery's four parking spaces, two more to begin canvassing the occupants of her building—while he and Harry went to her apartment to view the crime scene. As the elevator rose Max placed a call to the limo company but got a busy signal. "Wouldn't you know it," he said to Harry. "This fuck lives a charmed life."

When the elevator doors opened they entered directly into Meg's apartment. Two uniforms guarded the entry while crime scene technicians moved about various rooms dusting the furniture, appliances, and walls, as others checked rugs and furniture for any hair or fiber evidence.

A tech immediately came to them and handed them cloth covers for their shoes. "Turn these in when you leave," he said.

It was regular crime scene procedure. The shoe covers made sure nothing new was brought into the crime scene and nothing was carried out.

"How's it going?" Max asked the tech.

"The perp tried to clean up. He did a pretty good job too. But just like always, he didn't get it all."

Max nodded his approval and led Harry up a long spiral staircase that opened onto the second floor. "Some joint, eh?"

"Yeah, some joint," Harry said. "It's a side of her I never knew."

They reached the bedroom, which had another uniform standing guard outside.

Harry had been to hundreds of crime scenes in his years as a cop. But this was the first where he had known the victim intimately. Meg's body lay on the floor, her red hair fanned out around her head, her once-beautiful green eyes dull and lifeless, and her mouth twisted in fear, the last emotion she had known. He put on a pair of latex gloves and opened the front of her black silk pajamas. *Love your pajamas*—the words rolled out at him, telling him they were among the last she had heard. He looked at the wound that had ended her life. It was a narrow slit, clearly made by a knife, just under her left breast.

He ran his gloved hand up to her jaw and traced her lips with his fingers. *Die, you fucking cunt,* came back at him.

Where is he going, Meg? If you know, tell me where he's going. The word *airport* floated back at him. *But to where? Where? Please tell me where.* Harry placed his hands on the sides of her face. *Tell me.* It came like a rush of air, filling his mind, allowing nothing else to enter. He turned to Max.

"He's going to Alaska. Don't ask me how I know, because I couldn't begin to explain it."

Max got on the phone to the limo company that had picked up Meg's overnight guest. This time the phone was answered on the third ring.

"This is Dmitri."

"Dmitri, this is Sergeant Max Abrams of the Clearwater Police Department. Did any of your drivers pick up a fare at the Ultimar condos on Sand Key?"

"Yes sir, I pick up a man myself at seven a.m. I took him to Tampa Airport. Is there a problem?"

"Not for you," Max said. "But for him there's a very big problem. We believe he killed a woman at the Ultimar."

"You are sure?" Dmitri asked. "He seems like a really nice guy. He gave me a hundred bucks for tip."

"Where at the airport did you take him? Which airline?"

"I take him to private terminal. Plane was waiting for him."

"It was a private jet?" Max asked.

"Yes, I pull limo right up to it and he went right on board. One of the pilots even loads up his bags. It's easy job for me."

"What name did he give you?"

"He said his name was Tony. But limo reservation and all charges go to Ms. Meg Avery. She's a regular customer."

"Did this Tony say where he was going?"

"No."

"Did you get a name of the plane's owner, or a company?"

"No. I was told a Gulfstream would be waiting at the terminal and when I pull in there it was. I got out and asked if they were waiting for Ms. Avery's friend and they said yes."

"Did you see the plane taxi out?"

"Yes."

"What time was that?" Max asked.

"It was about eight," Dmitri said.

"Okay, I need you to come into Clearwater PD and ask for me, Sergeant Max Abrams. I'll need a full, signed statement."

Max looked at Harry. "The bastard flew out at eight." He glanced at his wristwatch. "Shit, it's two o'clock already. The son of a bitch could be anywhere in the country. How long does it take to fly to Alaska?"

"I haven't a clue," Harry said. "Let's check all private planes leaving Tampa at eight. They have to have filed a flight plan."

Tony Rolf sat comfortably in his first class seat as his Alaska Airlines flight made its final approach into LAX Airport. His connecting flight was due to start boarding in twenty minutes for the short hop to Seattle. From there he would fly to Juneau and then on to Gustavus/Glacier Bay.

Meg had been right, he thought. First class was the only way to fly. He had been sipping champagne since noon. Even lunch had been good—a choice between broiled haddock or a corned beef on rye sandwich. He got the sandwich because of his passion for kosher pickles. Now he found he was looking forward to dinner.

A flight attendant stopped by his seat to ask if he needed more champagne. She was tall and slender with dark brown hair that fell to her shoulders and light brown eyes that he enjoyed looking at.

He said he did and she asked where in Alaska he was headed to.

"Gustavus is the first stop."

"Oh, it's the bush for you."

"Why do they call it that?"

"It just means you can only get there by boat or plane. You can't get there by car or truck. There are roads when you get there but nothing that goes in or out. Most of Alaska is like that."

"And you don't feel trapped?" Tony asked.

"I never did," she said, "and I grew up in the bush."

"What about big bears and moose and stuff like that?"

"Oh, they're there, alright. You'll see them just about anywhere. But you learn how to avoid any dangerous confrontations." She held out her arms. "See, I was never eaten." She laughed. "I'll go get your champagne."

Tony thought about her light brown eyes. Meg's eyes had been beautiful as she died. Vibrant and green, they had almost sparkled as he slid his knife into her heart. The flight attendant had worn a name tag that said, *Sheila*. He wondered how her eyes would look as she died. Perhaps, with a little luck, he'd find out.

Vicky arrived at the condo at three. Harry was on the phone with Miami International Airport flight control. When he finished the call he turned to her. "Miami says the flight Rolf took made a brief stop and then flew on to Dallas. We don't know if they picked up someone who flew on with Rolf or if he got off and caught a shuttle to the main airport. I left a message for the crew to call me when they land."

"What did you get from the body?" Vicky asked.

"He's going to Alaska."

"That's it then. I've worked with you long enough to know we can't ignore what comes to you."

"Is the stuff he gets always accurate?" It was Max, who had come up behind them.

"It's so accurate it's scary," Vicky said.

* * *

Regis Walsh sat in his office and watched Kenneth Oppenheimer move toward his desk. When he came into the circle of light from the desk lamp, Walsh could see his face was ashen and his eyes were shrouded in fear. He was so tired of it, the stupidity, the absence of self-control. When would he see some pure and simple courage?

"Have you heard?" Oppenheimer asked.

"Heard what?"

"Meg Avery is dead. She was found murdered in her condo. It has to have been Tony Rolf. It's a disaster for us, Regis. Once they catch him, he'll point a finger at both of us."

Walsh noticed the perspiration on Oppenheimer's upper lip. That manifestation of the man's fear disgusted him. It was the very thing that could bring them down.

"So you've already tried and convicted poor Tony, I see. And you already have him turning on the only people who have ever protected him. I happen to know that he was on his way out of town when she was killed. I know that because I provided him with the airline tickets and the cash to escape his persecutors. Right now he's—"

"Don't tell me," Oppenheimer said. "I don't want to know where he is now, who he's with, and especially where he's going. Leave me out of this whole damn thing."

Walsh stared at him without speaking for nearly a minute. "Get out of my office, Ken. And don't come back unless I send for you."

Tony's flight landed at LAX and he headed straight for his connecting flight to Seattle. It was a pity he didn't have an hour or so in Los Angeles. It would have been nice to have a drink with the lovely Sheila, to hear her views about the world, to watch the beautiful light in her brown eyes. Watch it glimmer and then go out.

As always, first class passengers were the first to board the aircraft. They were already comfortably seated and sipping cocktails when the unwashed masses filed in with their carry-on bags—and in some cases their ill-tempered children—trailing behind them. Tony noticed that most first class passengers declined to look at them. These people did not exist and they would never exist for them. In the great scheme of things, they simply did not matter.

Tony had a new flight attendant to care for him now. Her name was Rose and she had already brought him his first small bottle of champagne. He watched her attentively as she performed the mortality play with the demonstration seat belt and the inflatable vest, and when she finished he beckoned her over. She arrived with a smile. She was shorter than Sheila but her curves were far more voluptuous and her eyes were a bright blue, almost startlingly so.

"What time are we scheduled to arrive in Seattle and how much longer until we get to Juneau?" His own smile seemed to dazzle her. He could tell by the way she looked back into his eyes.

She rattled off the times. "Is Juneau your final destination?" she asked.

"No, I have a layover until tomorrow morning, then I grab a flight to Gustavus/Glacier Bay."

"Oh, that'll be a little puddle jumper," she said. "Just up and down; no first class, no service at all. Make sure you bring coffee on board with you."

"That's so disappointing."

"Don't worry, we'll take good care of you on this flight."

Harry got off the phone and turned to Vicky and Max. "Rolf got off in

Miami and took a cab to the main airport. There were several Alaska Airlines flights out of Miami and Fort Lauderdale that Rolf could have made easily. They had stops in Houston, Denver, and LAX, then connecting flights to Seattle and on to Alaska."

"Do you think Meg Avery knew his final destination?" Vicky asked.

Harry nodded and turned toward the stairs that led to Meg's bedroom. An assistant medical examiner was still conducting a superficial examination of her body. Harry introduced himself and learned that the man's name was Igor Vaselevich. What a moniker to go with his occupation, Harry thought.

Igor raised an eyebrow as Harry began putting on latex gloves. "I just want to check something for my report," Harry explained.

"It's very straightforward," Igor said. "Also quick and I believe quite painless."

Harry nodded and reached down and cupped her head in his hands. Her neck had stiffened with rigor mortis and would remain so for several more hours. All the color had drained from her face, and contrasted with her bright red hair, it made her look pasty and unnatural.

Where in Alaska, Meg? he asked silently. *What's his final destination?*

The flash came to his mind again but it was very weak and hard to understand.

"What are you doing?" Igor asked.

Harry looked up at him and gave a slight shake of his head. "Just saying goodbye."

"You knew the victim?"

"Yes," Harry said. "Not well, but I knew her and I liked what I knew."

When he left the bedroom, Vicky was waiting for him. "Anything?" she asked.

"It was very weak," Harry said. "The only thing that came through clearly was the name *Glacier Bay.* I'm going there. Can you come with me? I'll cover all our expenses."

"You bet I can."

"Thank you, Vicky. We better pick up some warmer clothes. It gets cold up there at night."

Tony boarded his plane at nine a.m. carrying a cup of Starbucks coffee.

"Welcome aboard, sir," a plump, middle-aged flight attendant said with a smile.

Rose, his previous flight attendant, had been right. There were no first class accommodations, not even a shapely young thing to welcome him aboard. He didn't bother to take note of this one's name.

When the plane landed an hour later, Tony found himself in one of the smallest airports he had ever seen. The plane taxied to a terminal that was little more than a large room with two check-in counters. Bags on incoming flights were simply unloaded onto the tarmac to allow the passengers to pick them up. There was an effort at security—one TA agent waving a wand over passengers who were waiting to board the flight Tony had just left.

Tony looked around for someone holding a sign with the name *Rawlings* on it. Instead, a short, portly man with a two-day growth of beard approached him and extended his hand.

"Tony," he said, "I'm Malcolm Vandermere. Friends call me Dutch. I went to school with Regis Walsh and I'm your protector here in big, bad Alaska." He released Tony's hand from a bearlike grip.

Tony looked around at the dozen or so passengers who had been on the flight with him. "How'd you know who I was?" he asked.

"Easy, you were the only person on board I didn't recognize." He let out a rolling laugh. "That's the joy of living in a town of four hundred people."

Dutch grabbed Tony's bag and led him to a spanking-new Range Rover Sport. Within a minute they were speeding down a dirt road. Suddenly, Dutch hit the brakes as a female moose ambled across the road. He hit the horn and she jumped and picked up her gait.

"Damn fool moose," Dutch said. "They're okay during the daylight hours—and right now we've got a lot of those, with the sun rising around four a.m. and setting at about eleven p.m. But in the dark they're deadly."

"Why is that?" Tony asked.

"'Cause their eyes don't glow at night like most animals. And their coat is so damn dark; they're just suddenly there in front of you, all 700 to 1,200 pounds of them. And you see how tall they are. Well, you hit those legs and that enormous body just comes right in through your windshield. Then it's good night, Irene, believe you me." Dutch's cherubic face seemed to glow as he spoke.

"What about grizzly bears?"

"We don't have grizzlies. Some call 'em that, but we've got a different variety. What we've got is the brown bear. They're bigger and meaner. A brown bear only knows two kinds of animal: there's other bears like him, and there's food. And if you're not one, you're definitely the other."

"I'd like to see one," Tony said.

"Easy enough. I was going to fly you over the area tomorrow, give you sort of the grand tour of Glacier Bay. You'll see everything from bear to mountain goats to breaching whales."

Tony's face was like that of a little boy who had just been told he was going to Disney World for the first time. "Hey, how cool is that?" he said.

CHAPTER TWENTY-THREE

Harry telephoned the Alaska State Police headquarters in Anchorage and explained his situation. He was told there were no police officers of any kind in Gustavus and that officers were only sent there when a crime had been committed. In cases of fugitives, they required reasonable proof that the criminal in question was actually there.

"We've got the Fourth of July coming up the day after tomorrow," the state cop told him. "It's a big day for parades and for arrests. We won't have anybody in any of the bush towns until the fifth. And those will be cops sent to investigate specific crimes. If you're coming up here, check in again when you land and we'll do all we can to help you find your guy, okay?"

Harry thanked him and explained the situation to Vicky.

"Wow, I've heard about the boonies. I've even seen a few boonies. But these are the *real* boonies. No cops unless a crime is committed. Is it like the Canadian Mounties? You have one murderer, they send one Mountie?"

"We're about to find out," Harry said. He handed her a folder of airline tickets. "Did you pack a jacket and boots, gloves, all that warm stuff?"

"I did."

"It's going to be a long ride with a layover in Seattle. When Regis Walsh hides somebody, he really hides them."

* * *

The next morning Dutch and Tony boarded Dutch's twin-engine Cessna and taxied onto the runway. "We'll go up and circle until I spot a whale, and move around it so you can see it breach."

"What kind of whales will we see?" Tony asked.

"Big whales. You could see almost anything—grays, blues, anything—but this time of year it's mostly humpbacks. When they breach they rise up out of the water and then crash back down, it's pretty spectacular, and their song is the most beautiful of them all. It's haunting is what it is, and once you hear it you never forget."

Once they were in the air, Dutch circled, then pointed through the windscreen. "There's one now."

Tony followed his hand and below he saw a massive dark shape in the water. Then the animal dove, flipping its fluted tail as it disappeared into deeper water.

"Where . . ." Tony began, but Dutch cut him off.

"Wait."

Within a few seconds the giant mammal rose up out of the water, its massive fins extended; then it seemed to roll in the air onto its side and float back down to the surface where its weight sent a plume of water thirty feet into the air.

"Jesus," Tony said.

"They're big. Females get to be fifty feet long, about the same size as a gray whale. They weigh up to forty tons. But they're nothing compared to a blue whale. Those babies grow up to a hundred feet and are twice as heavy. They're the largest animal to ever live on this earth. They're bigger than the biggest dinosaur."

Dutch leveled the aircraft and headed farther up the bay. Ahead Tony could see nothing but snowcapped mountains and wilderness beyond the shoreline. They hugged the shore and Dutch pointed to moose walking along the water's edge. Farther up the steeper slopes, mountain goats moved in small herds; closer to the water, a massive brown bear waddled along looking for an easy meal.

"Jesus, those bears are big too," Tony said.

"If you were down there on the ground and he reared up on his hind legs, he'd be ten to twelve feet tall," Dutch explained. "And he could run thirty miles an hour in short spurts. What I'm gettin' at: if he wanted to have you for lunch, he'd have you for lunch, unless you had a mighty big gun and were a damn fine shot. But there's another problem too. Because of all the hunting up here, the brown bears have learned that the sound of a rifle shot is like a dinner bell. They follow that sound, they know they're likely to find a deer or moose carcass just waiting to be eaten."

Dutch brought the plane down to about one hundred feet. Ahead of them lay the Muir Glacier, a massive ice floe that cut through the mountains until it reached the water's edge. It stood some forty feet above the water, and as they approached a massive piece broke away and slid into the bay.

"Welcome to America's last wilderness," Dutch said. "It's like it talks to you. It says, *I'm big enough if you are*. Now, let's head back and get ourselves cleaned up. We can have us a big steak and arrange for a flight to Homer in the morning." He turned his head and smiled at Tony. "Homer is where I'm gonna hide you out until Regis calls and tells me it's safe for you to leave."

"Why Homer?"

"Because I've got businesses there that nobody messes with," Dutch said. "I've got a halibut fishing fleet and a fish-packing plant, and back in the mountains I've got a big game–hunting operation. Nobody gets into either of them unless I say so."

"Which am I going to?" Tony asked.

"To start out with, I'm thinking the hunting camp. If it looks like nobody's followed you here, maybe we can switch to the fishing fleet or maybe the packing plant, if you don't like being out on the water."

"I don't know . . ."

"We'll give you a look at both of them and let you choose. I want you to be safe, but I don't want you to be miserable. So we'll have a look at each and let you decide."

"Sounds good," Tony said.

Harry and Vicky checked into the Seattle Airport Marriott Hotel for their layover to await morning flights to Juneau and Gustavus. After freshening up they took a cab to Cutters Crabhouse Restaurant, which had been recommended by the hotel concierge. The restaurant sat on the waterfront across from Pike Place Market and offered water views from nearly every table.

After treating themselves to steamed whole Dungeness crab, they settled in for some quiet talk of how they would proceed in Alaska.

"I don't know how much help we can expect," Harry said. "It's a different kind of policing than I've seen."

"It's a different kind of place," Vicky said. "From the reading I've been able to do, it seems that people are spread out in some pretty wild and hard-to-reach places. A crime happens out in the bush, as they call it, and state troopers are sent in to find out what happened, locate the perp, and bring him or her in. And if the perp doesn't wait around to be collared, they have a chase through the wilderness. Doesn't sound like much fun."

"Not with all the animals out there just waiting to pounce."

"I guess some of these backwoods characters are pretty rugged.

Probably like some of the swamp rats you hear about who roam the Everglades."

"Thank God our boy's a city kid. I don't think he'd last very long in the wilderness."

"No," Vicky said. "But neither would we. Let's hope we get some help."

"I'll call when we reach Juneau. Our best guess is that he's in Gustavus. But if they ask how I know that, what the hell do I say—a dead woman told me?"

"I don't think we'd get a very positive reaction if you told them that."

"Yeah, they'd probably lock me up and order some tests by the house shrink."

Vicky raised her coffee cup to her lips to hide the grin on her face.

"Go ahead, say it," Harry pressed.

"I wasn't going to say anything."

"If you're not careful, I'll feed you to the first bear we come across."

"Now what would a big old bear want with a sweet young thing like me?"

"Dessert."

Dutch let out a roar of laughter that filled his massive log home on Strawberry Point. The remnants of the steaks his Tlingit Indian housekeeper had prepared lay on their plates, as they sipped the fine pinot noir brought up from his private wine cellar.

"So you heard that wild-ass story about Prescott Bush, old George H.W.'s daddy, stealing Geronimo's bones when he was a member of Skull and Bones at Yale?" Dutch said. "Now if it was true, I couldn't tell you, because you're not a Bonesman yourself. Only members of the society can know society secrets. And if it was a bald-faced lie I wouldn't say so, either. It's just too damn good a story. It shouldn't be dismissed, it should be perpetuated."

"So that's where you met Regis Walsh," Tony said, "in Skull and Bones?"

"No, we just happened to be roommates in our freshman year. We were both legacy students, meaning our parents or grandparents attended Yale. I wouldn't have gotten in if I wasn't a legacy. George W. Bush was a legacy too, and like him I was a fuck-up in prep school. Like W., I was also a legacy in Skull and Bones." Dutch's round cheeks seemed to swell to even greater size as he warmed to his tale.

"So anyway, Regis and I were roommates as freshmen, and remained close friends throughout our years at college. Now, I was 'tapped' for membership in Skull and Bones at the end of my junior year, which is when you're picked, and I lobbied for Regis to be tapped as well. Years later, when Regis became involved in Scientology and rose in its ranks, he urged me to join and I did. It's been very helpful to me. I have many investors in my various enterprises who are members of the church."

Tony looked the man over. He was a short, plump, red-faced man who had been handed things all his life. A privileged person, as they said, somebody who'd never had to worry about making the rent, or affording a restaurant meal, or maybe putting off buying new shoes until next month because the money wasn't there this month. He was exactly the type of person Tony had always resented. And now here he was, dependant on that very same kind of privileged jerk for his survival.

"It must be nice growing up rich," Tony said, fighting to keep the sarcasm from his voice.

Dutch stared at him, as if momentarily stunned by his words. Then he gathered himself. "It is," he said. "It damn well is. I just never think about it because I've always been rich. My daddy handed it to me, just as his daddy handed it to him, and so on for generations of Vandermeres. It all began in Amsterdam in the 1600s when some ancient Dutch relative started a bank. All I've ever seen is paintings of the old sob."

Tony thought about his own history. It didn't go beyond his drunken mother and her series of abusive boyfriends. Imagine having a relative who had started a bank centuries ago and whose portrait hung in your family's home. That was some heavy shit. And it filled him with rage that someone should have so much and he should have so little. Why? Why had he been handed the shitty end of the stick?

Dutch's house phone rang and he excused himself to answer it. He was back within a few minutes and announced that they were set to fly out of Gustavus at nine the next morning.

"It's a little over five hundred miles to Homer so I like to use a bigger aircraft than my Cessna. A few years back my company picked up an old twin-engine DC-3 that had been completely refurbished inside and out. It can land just about anywhere in Alaska or Canada and it's a big, sturdy old thing that'll get us anywhere we want to go. For long hops, like back to the original forty-eight, we have a Gulfstream jet. But that baby requires a runway a helluva lot longer than they've got in Homer. We keep her in Juneau."

"Have you heard anything about anybody following me?" Tony asked.

"Nothing, but I'll check with Regis before we decide where to start you off—the fishing fleet or the hunting camp. Do you have a preference?"

"I assume the fishing fleet headquarters is still in civilization and the hunting camp is out in the . . . well, out in the woods, right?"

"You got it," Dutch said. "Although this is a pretty ritzy hunting camp. That's why we can charge our guests an arm and a leg to stay there. You wouldn't exactly be living in a dirt-floor cabin."

"Well, I guess I'd prefer the place that has more civilization to it."

"Okay, then we'll start you out in the fishing office in Homer, and if word comes down the pike that the police are heading that way, we'll move you out to the hunting camp." Dutch tapped the side of his nose. "And I assure you, nobody gets out there without my say so."

"Sounds good to me," Tony said.

Harry and Vicky landed in Juneau at nine a.m. just as Dutch's DC-3 was heading down the runway in Gustavus. It was July 3 and Dutch and Tony would be several hundred miles over the Gulf of Alaska by the time Harry and Vicky landed in Gustavus—a day late and a dollar short, as Jocko would have said.

The interior of the DC-3 had a four-seat grouping of lounge chairs facing each other in its forward section and two sofas that converted into beds in the aft. Dutch and Tony occupied two of the lounge chairs, each with a drink on a side table. Tony looked out a starboard window at the snow-covered mountain range spread out as far as he could see. July, and there was all that snow, he thought. The lower ranges were clear and green and thick with heavy growth in pines and cedar. This was where the brown bear and moose and deer would roam free. Dutch had told him that there were areas so remote that the animals there had probably never seen a human being. Ahead of them, to the south of Homer, lay Kodiak Island, home to the largest brown bears in all of Alaska. Dutch had told him that the largest on record weighed 2,400 pounds and stood nine feet eight inches tall on its hind legs. It had a nine-inch layer of fat covering its body. And they were only slightly smaller than polar bears.

"What are you thinking about?" Dutch asked.

"I was just looking out at the wilderness and remembering what you told me about the animals that live there," Tony said.

"Awesome, isn't it?"

"Scary awesome."

"A little realistic fear is what keeps you alive out there. You find yourself getting a touch cavalier, you might as well just go ahead and call the undertaker."

"You ever been out there alone? I mean really alone, where you have to find your way back on foot?"

"Do you see me sittin' here before you?"

"I do," Tony said.

"Well, given the scenario you just proposed, you wouldn't see me, because I'd be mixed in with a big load of bear shit and deposited out in those woods."

Tony laughed at the image. "Renewable energy, Alaska style."

Dutch slapped his knee. "Exactly."

They flew on for another hour, each dozing occasionally. When they both awoke at the same time, Dutch leaned forward and tapped Tony on the arm. "I never asked Regis much about you, but what exactly did you do for him?"

Tony wondered how much he should offer. "You know that Regis is responsible for maintaining discipline in the church?" He waited while Dutch nodded. "We have the usual problems of all large organizations. We have people who bad mouth the church and its leaders as a way of self-aggrandizement; we have others who simply cannot obey church rules. We have homosexuals, for example, who we have to either help change their lifestyle or banish them. We have people who choose to be promiscuous. I have to convince them to stop or drive them out.

We have outsiders, usually family members, who try to drive a wedge between the member and the church."

"Disruptive personalities," Dutch said.

"Exactly. And that's where I come in."

"And you are in hiding because . . . ?"

"We had a young lady, a very disturbed young lady, who was drowned trying to escape an auditing session. Unfortunately, she was the daughter of a Clearwater police officer. I was pursuing her when she drowned. Now the police want to try to blame the entire incident on the church, and they want to use me to do it."

"Typical," Dutch said. "Well, you don't have to worry about it up in these parts. I've got a bit of weight up here, politically speaking, and no out-of-state cops are going to come marching in and trampling all over our rights. We'll keep you out of sight and just let them wear themselves out running into stone walls."

Harry and Vicky landed in Gustavus at three that afternoon, just as Dutch's DC-3 was on its final approach into Homer, over five hundred miles away. Harry had arranged to rent a battered Jeep Wrangler through a one-man rent-a-wreck agency and it was waiting in the airport's dozen-car parking area.

"Nice wheels," Vicky said as she tossed her bags in the rear.

"The other choice was walking," Harry countered. He attached the Garmin GPS he had brought from home and downloaded the address of the cabins he had rented. "Says it's about three miles."

Harry pulled out his cell and called the state police in Anchorage. After five minutes explaining his situation, he disconnected and turned to Vicky. "They say there'll be a state cop in Gustavus tomorrow, and suggest we connect up with him when he lands. He'll be easy to find. He'll be on a state police helicopter. His name is Sergeant Jessie Reed."

"Okay, let's go see our digs and figure out where we can get some food," Vicky said.

Harry made another call and reached the owner of the cabins, who agreed to meet them in fifteen minutes. They headed toward town along Good River Road, a two-lane paved roadway with thick woods on each side.

"I feel like I'm being watched," Vicky said.

Harry pulled to the side of the road. "You are." He pointed into some thick brush where a female moose stood. The animal was about six feet at the shoulder and looked heavy enough to mangle their vehicle if they ran into it.

"Jesus H. Christ," Vicky said.

"I don't like having animals around that are bigger than my car."

"Let's get to the cabin so we can go inside and lock the door."

They continued on for five more minutes and turned into a gravel road that led to a cluster of rental cabins. The owner was already there, waiting outside his Dodge Ram pickup.

"You must be Harry Doyle," he said as Harry climbed out of the Jeep. "I'm Jeff Rutledge."

"Yes sir," Harry said, extending his hand. "And this is my partner, Detective Vicky Stanopolis."

"So you folks are up here lookin' for some villain, eh? Well, we got plenty of our own. Don't need to import any more."

"We're supposed to meet up with a state cop tomorrow. His name is Sergeant Jessie Reed. You know him?" Harry asked.

"I do," Rutledge said. "'Cept he ain't a he; he's a she. Don't arm wrestle her, though, 'cause you'll lose."

"Glad you told me. It would have been an embarrassing way to start off a police relationship."

"Let me show you the cabins. They're right down this path."

The path was about four feet wide and cut through thick brush with a secondary path every thirty yards or so, leading to a cabin.

"There's always moose in and out of here, so just be prepared for them. If you see one, back away and try to find something to put between you and it. The bigger the something the better, I might add. Another camper saw a brown bear today but said it wasn't aggressive, but that don't mean it won't be aggressive tomorrow, so just be aware. All the cabins have heavy anti-bear screening, but don't leave any food out. They have a tremendous sense of smell and an appetite that's beyond belief. They'll pretty much satisfy themselves with the dumpsters, but the dumpsters ain't always full. Oh, and if you go to the dumpsters, take a look first to make sure you're not interrupting anybody's dinner."

After a routine run-through of both cabins—water and electrical shutoffs, best escape route if the door was blocked—Rutledge wished them a good visit and went on his way.

Vicky stood in the middle of Harry's cabin, hands on her hips. "I don't want you to get the wrong idea, partner, and I know it's against regulations, but I want you to grab your stuff and move into my cabin."

"Are you that worried?" Harry asked.

"Let's just say that two guns are better than one, especially when you're dealing with something that can eat you."

Harry looked around the cabin. It was identical to Vicky's—it was basically one large room. It had a sitting area with a foldout couch and two armchairs, a well-equipped kitchen with a breakfast bar and four stools, an open bedroom with two queen-sized beds, and a full bath.

"Okay, I'll try to give you as much privacy as possible. If I'm missing something, let me know."

"Just don't walk around naked," she said. *If you do, I just might jump your bones*, she added to herself.

Homer reminded Tony of a 1990s television show that he had loved as a little kid. The show was called *Northern Exposure* and each week it began with a young moose wandering down a road dotted with small, rustic houses. He didn't remember anything else about the show, just the road and the moose, and a chubby Indian woman who played a small role. It was his favorite show . . . ever.

"Do you remember a TV show back in the nineties called *Northern Exposure?*" he asked Dutch.

"*Northern* what?" Dutch asked.

"*Exposure. Northern Exposure*. I think it might have been filmed here?"

"Never had a television show filmed here, that much I'm sure of," Dutch said.

Tony chewed this over. What the hell did Dutch know? "It was a great show," he said.

Dutch only grunted.

Dutch's commercial fishing operation—Malcolm's Ocean Fresh Halibut, a division of Vandermere Enterprises—was located on the Homer Spit and comprised a dozen commercial fishing vessels and a fish-processing plant. The Spit, as it was known locally, was a 4.5-mile-long piece of land that jutted out into Kachemak Bay at the southern tip of the Kenai Peninsula. The bay, like all of Homer, like all of the Kenai Peninsula, was surrounded by mountains, the upper regions of which were covered in snow year round, and one of which, Mt. Augustine, was an active volcano.

A Range Rover was waiting for Dutch when their plane landed at Homer Airport and it carried them on the short drive to the fish-processing plant which was located at the start of Homer Spit Road. Since many people's livelihoods were dependent on Dutch, he was treated with nothing short of reverence. Tony, moving in Dutch's wake, was an instant curiosity and also received a wary degree of preferential treatment. This included everyone. All except for Big Pete McGuire, Dutch's plant manager, who treated everybody, Dutch included, as if they were wasting his time.

McGuire was a house of a man, with bright red hair and blazing blue eyes, all coming out of a six-foot-four-inch body that looked to be carved from stone. He could have been anywhere from forty to sixty, so ageless were his features: square jaw, broad brow, bushy eyebrows, and a long, hooked nose that looked as if it had been broken more than once. Tony instinctively checked out his massive fists and instantly felt sorry for the men who had broken it.

"Hello, Dutch," Pete said with exaggerated gusto. "What the hell are ya doin' in this stinkin' fish house when ya could be home with that plump little Indian housekeeper of yours? I know what I'm doin'. I'm havin' such a good year I'm workin' on the Fourth of July, is what."

"You wanna know why I'm here, Pete? Let's go into my office and I'll tell you," Dutch replied.

Pete and Tony followed Dutch into a massive first-floor office with a wall of windows that overlooked Kachemak Bay and the array of mountains beyond. The rest of the office seemed to be dedicated to Dutch's personal memorabilia, including photographs from his days at Yale and with political figures ranging from George W. Bush to Sarah Palin.

Dutch sank into an overstuffed executive desk chair and waved the others into comfortable leather visitor's chairs. He leveled a hand at

Tony. "Pete, this is the young man I told you about on the phone," he began. "He has some bothersome people looking for him so we're gonna keep him out of sight for a bit. Understood?"

"No problem, we've done this before." Pete turned to Tony. "You've just gotta cooperate with us, son. If you're told to skedaddle for a bit, you just skedaddle for a bit." He turned back to Dutch. "How much work do you want him to do and what kind?"

"He's not here to work," Dutch said. "Give him what he needs to keep his mind occupied. If he sees something he'd like to try and it's not going to screw up your operation . . . well, you be the judge of that." Dutch spun around in his chair, much as a kid might. "If we think someone is on his tail, I want you to send him up to the hunting camp. In fact, take him up there so he can get an idea of what it's like."

Pete winked at Tony. "It's pretty plush," he said. "A little playground for millionaires who want to tell their friends they went big-game hunting but still had their special picnic lunches complete with champagne and foie gras. And you should see some of the secretaries and assistants they bring with them."

"Pete exaggerates," Dutch said.

"Pete does *not* exaggerate," Pete responded.

"That hunting lodge is sounding better and better," Tony said.

"Let's see what happens," Dutch said.

Harry and Vicky were at the Gustavus Airport when the state police helicopter landed at ten that morning. Sergeant Jessie Reed climbed out of the copilot's seat and walked toward the parking lot where an unmarked Jeep Cherokee, only slightly less battered than Harry's rental, sat waiting.

Reed easily made two of Vicky and spotted Harry ten pounds, none of which was fat. She was dressed in uniform with sergeant stripes on her pale blue tunic, a Sam Browne gun belt holding a Glock semiautomatic, highly polished steel-toed shoes, and a Smokey Bear hat. She cocked her head to the side and looked Harry up and down with steely gray eyes, then did the same to Vicky. "You the two Florida detectives I was told about?"

"We are. I'm Harry Doyle and this is my partner, Vicky Stanopolis."

"So you're Greek, eh?" Jessie said. "That sure musta been a mouthful to handle as a kid."

"It was practically Jane Smith in the neighborhood I grew up in," Vicky shot back.

For some reason the remark made Jessie smile. Ignoring Harry, she asked Vicky: "What can you tell me about the villain you chased up here?"

Vicky filled her in on Tony Rolf, the four women he had murdered, his ties to Scientology, his albinism.

"That's some spooky shit," Jessie said. "But if Scientology's involved, there can only be one dude they'd come to: Malcolm 'Dutch' Vandermere, a little pussy born with a silver spoon sticking out of his patrician ass, and a shit-eating grin on his lily-white pursed-lipped face."

"I take it you know the man," Harry said, fighting back a smile.

"Oh yeah, we've met. He owns a fishing fleet and a big fish factory in Homer, all bought for him by his daddy, and run by a big Irishman who's probably the best fisherman in Alaska, guy named Pete McGuire. Built like a brick, that one, and tough as nails—you'll know him when you see him, six foot four inches of muscle and a nose shaped like an S that he got one Paddy's Day when he wouldn't leave a bar I told him to get out of. He's been waitin' to pay me back for that one ever since." Jessie let out an evil laugh. "He tries, and that S is gonna go the other way on that Irish mug of his."

"If Vandermere is hiding our boy among his fishermen, how hard would it be to find him?" Harry asked.

"Not all that hard. It would just take time," Jessie answered. "He could also be hiding him in a very upscale hunting camp he runs back in the mountains. Hunting for rich pussies who don't know how to hunt, but want somebody to take 'em out, hold their hand, and bring 'em back with a trophy of whatever—buck, moose, bear, mountain goat. And all the time they get to stay in a fancy lodge and drink chateau whatever. It would be a helluva lot harder to find him there. They keep a pretty close watch on that place. Get a lot of celebs there: congressmen, judges, a few movie stars."

"But we could get there?"

"If we had to and we were sure he was there. That would sure break old Dutch's balls if we did. But let's go out to his place in Gustavus and see what we can find out."

They soon pulled up in front of Dutch's massive log home on Strawberry Point. Vicky took in the view of the mountains across the sound and let out a low whistle. "Some joint."

"Yeah, old Dutch doesn't deny himself anything," Jessie said. "Nothing but the best in wine, food, houses, and toys galore are good enough for Malcolm Vandermere." She grinned at Vicky. "I'm betting you think it's a tough way to live, eh?"

"Yeah, my heart really goes out to him."

They rang the doorbell and in less than a minute a short, round woman answered with a broad smile for Jessie. Jessie spoke to her in a foreign dialect that Harry and Vicky later learned was the woman's native Tlingit language. They switched to English and Jessie introduced them to her.

Her name was May Lightfoot and Jessie explained that she had worked for the Vandermere family—first Dutch's father and then Dutch—for nearly twenty years, which was most of her adult life. She had worked long hours and the Vandermeres had paid her only what they had to, which was typical of their employment practices, and she, like most of their employees, felt only the degree of personal loyalty necessary to keep her job.

"Was there a young man at the house this past week?" Jessie asked.

May gave her a worried look.

"This will be confidential," Jessie assured her.

May nodded her head.

"What was he like?"

"Strange," May said. "I would not want to be alone with him. He had the smell of danger on him."

"What was he called?"

"Tony."

"What did he look like?"

May gave a description so detailed it surprised both Harry and Vicky.

"That's our boy," Vicky said.

"Where is he now?" Jessie asked.

"Homer. Mr. Dutch says he will stay there, at least for now. I was happy to hear it. He is one who likes to hurt people. Sooner or later he will hurt someone again. It is written on his soul."

They thanked May and regrouped next to Harry's car.

"What do you suggest?" Harry asked.

"I think you should get your butts up to Homer. The best thing for you to do is fly up to Anchorage, rent a car, and drive down the Kenai Peninsula. May's not about to tell Dutch you're coming, so you should catch them flat-footed. In the meantime, I'll ask my boss if I can help you with this murder suspect who's loose in our turf. I expect he'll agree. Hell, I can't see why he wouldn't. If so, I'll call you on your cell with my ETA in Homer."

"Sounds good," Harry said.

"Yeah, I want to see you reshape the big bruiser's nose again," Vicky added.

"With pleasure," Jessie said.

Chapter Twenty-Four

Max Abrams was seated behind his desk at the Clearwater police headquarters when Ken Oppenheimer knocked on his door.

"Can I see you for a moment?"

Max looked him in the eye and fought back a smile. "Grab a seat."

"This is awkward."

"Not for me," Max said. "Happy Fourth of July; I had the day off and came in to clear up some paperwork."

"I know. I called to see when I could make an appointment to see you and they told me you were here."

Max shrugged. "Okay, I'm here. What can I do for you?"

"I think I'm being set up by Regis Walsh."

"I think you are too," Max said. "So, the question is: what are you going to do about it?"

"I don't want to be his scapegoat."

"Okay, let's say I don't want you to be his scapegoat either. Where do we go from there?"

"I have a long story to tell you. Can you get a stenographer on the Fourth of July?"

"I'll get you a stenographer and a three-piece band if you need it."

At eight o'clock that evening, Harry and Vicky were just sitting down to a plate of grilled haddock on the Gustavus town green when Harry's cell rang. He looked at the screen and saw the call was from Max Abrams.

"You're interrupting our festive Fourth of July dinner, Max," Harry growled. "How late is it there?"

"Late. And it's worth the interruption."

"Tell me."

"Ken Oppenheimer walked into my office today and gave me a sworn deposition ratting out his one-time boss and mentor Regis Walsh. I'm on my way to arrest the son of a bitch as we speak."

"Holy shit. We're leaving tomorrow to try and nab Tony Rolf in a place called Homer, Alaska. Can you send copies of everything you got from Oppenheimer to the Alaska state troopers in Anchorage, care of Sergeant Jessie Reed?"

"Will do. Let me give you a quick briefing for now and then I'll fax everything to the Alaska staties."

There was a broad smile on Harry's face as Max finished. "So Oppenheimer just walked in and handed you all this on the proverbial silver platter?"

"That's what you get from clean living," Max said.

"Maybe Rolf will give me a nice big kiss on the cheek."

"You be careful with that asshole. He's a complete psycho. And keep Vicky the hell away from him."

"Will do," Harry said.

"I wish I could be with you."

"I do too, Max. I do too."

"I just received a very strange phone call from an attorney named Jordan Wells," Dutch said. "Do you know him?"

"Yeah, I know him," Tony replied. "He's the legal gunslinger the church hires when things start to get heavy. He's a black dude and they say he's hell on wheels in court. I know he tied the cop who was after me up in knots."

"But that cop is still after you. That's why you're up here. Those knots must have been tied rather loosely."

Tony scowled at the comment but said nothing.

"Anyway, this Jordan fellow called to tell me that Regis is on his way to Anchorage. He'll be visiting the mission there. It seems the police in Florida are breathing rather heavily down his neck."

"Did he say it involved me?"

"No. It was more a heads-up that I might be hearing from him. He did mention someone named Oppenheimer. He said he'd been to the police and was cooperating fully. He warned that if I heard from him, not to consider him a friend."

"Oppenheimer is Mr. Walsh's assistant, and he has always been a backstabbing coward." *And a motherfucker I should have taken care of before I left*, Tony thought to himself.

"It doesn't sound as if Regis was a very good judge of the people who worked for him," Dutch said.

"He was too generous with them—generosity is his greatest fault."

Harry shut down his cell phone. "That was Max again," he said. "Before he could serve a warrant on Regis Walsh, the slippery bastard pulled a rabbit. He thinks he may be headed our way."

"Is he going to forward the warrant to us?" Vicky asked.

"He said if we can confirm that he's here, he's going to ask the Alaskan troopers to hold him and he's gonna come get him himself."

"It'll be like old home week up here," Vicky said.

"I think he misses us."

They were in the Gustavus Airport awaiting their flight to Anchorage. Harry had just turned in his rent-a-wreck and arranged for another in Anchorage.

Jessie swaggered in and came directly up to them. "Good news. My boss says I can hook up with you guys in Homer. Have you booked rooms there yet?"

"No, I was going to ask you for a recommendation."

"Good idea," Jessie said. "I gotta friend who runs a place called the Ocean Inn. I guarantee you'll be comfortable and you'll be five minutes from Dutch's fishing operation. If you like, I'll give her a call and set it up."

"I'd appreciate it," Harry said.

"You want two rooms or one?"

"Are there any big bears hanging around the inn?"

"Naw, you gotta go upriver for that."

"Two rooms," Harry said. "But close to each other in case we have any two-legged visitors."

They slept on the flight to Anchorage and had time for a leisurely lunch before picking up their rental car and heading south on the Kenai Peninsula. They were both beginning to get used to the long days of sunlight, and it proved to be an advantage when traveling long distances by car. Harry wasn't sure how he'd like driving here in the winter months where he'd be dealing with only a few hours of sunlight each day. But you certainly couldn't complain about the long days with the scenery Alaska laid out before you. He had never seen anything like it. The drive took them along the coast through deep forests and rushing rivers with snowcapped mountains rising in the distance. A brochure Vicky had picked up at the car rental office said they would travel along Cook

Inlet, across which they would see no less than three active volcanoes: Mt. Iliamna, Mt. Redoubt, and Mt. Augustine. The last to erupt was Mt. Augustine in 2006. They were also traveling during the end of the salmon run when massive brown bears were patrolling the rivers and glutting themselves on fish returning home to spawn; building up the layers of fat they would need to carry themselves through their long winter hibernation.

"So how do you want to handle it when we get to Homer?" Vicky asked.

"Let's have a look at Vandermere's fishing operation—but from a distance," Harry said. "I don't want to tip anybody off that we're here looking for Rolf."

"Sort of play it close to our vests until Jessie gets here, you mean?"

"That's what I was thinking. She knows the lay of the land and the players a helluva lot better than we do. If it looks like we're going to have to go out to that hunting lodge, I'd like to get our hands on some heavier weapons than our Glocks. Whoever is out there is sure to have access to some pretty good weaponry. I don't want to find us going up against high-powered rifles equipped with infrared scopes and night-vision goggles and us carrying nothing more than our nine-millimeter peashooters."

"Yeah, that wouldn't be fun," Vicky said.

"I'm hoping the Alaskan staties will provide some of their weaponry. If not, I'll buy what we need and sell it before we go back."

They drove on past the cutoff to Seward, named for William H. Seward, Abraham Lincoln's secretary of state, who was seriously wounded in the assassination plot and who remained with Lincoln's successor, Andrew Johnson, and eventually consummated the Alaska Purchase. Then they cut back to the coast onto the Sterling Highway and drove past the once-Russian village of Ninilchik.

When they passed over the Anchor River they got a glimpse of three brown bears fishing for salmon in the shallows, and within minutes they were inside the Homer city limits. There wasn't much to see there—a scattering of shops and restaurants, a few people walking down the main street.

Harry pulled in at Captain's Coffee Roasting Company, both to get a much-needed cup of coffee and to confirm his directions to the Ocean Inn. As he exited the car, he put his jacket on to cover the Glock on his hip and immediately came under verbal assault from a drunk passing by on the street.

"Why don't ya learn how to park yer fuckin' car? Oh, I see, you got a gun so you think you can park any fuckin' way you want, is that it? Well, it don't work that way here in Homer, you motherfucker." The man was clearly plastered and looking for trouble that Harry didn't need.

Harry raised the edge of his jacket to show the badge on his belt. "Watch your mouth," he responded as Vicky exited the car.

"Oh, big shot. Big badge, big gun, big cop—but you still don't know how to park yer fuckin' car."

Harry gave him a wave of disgust and he and Vicky walked into Captain's and took a seat. A heavyset man at a nearby table grinned at them.

"You just met the town drunk. Don't pay him no mind. I'm Sam."

"Harry." He inclined his head to his partner. "This is Vicky."

"Hello there, Ms. Vicky."

"Hi, Sam, how's the coffee?"

"Best in the world. But I'm prejudiced. I'm related to the owner."

Sam got them two mugs of coffee and asked if they were hungry. Vicky ordered a pastry after insisting that Harry eat half.

"Why do women always do that?" Sam asked Harry. "Do you think it makes them feel less guilty about ordering something sweet? And why do they feel guilty anyway? I could order a whole cake and I wouldn't feel guilty."

"If you ever find the answer, you could write a book and become a wealthy man," Harry said.

"Maybe I will. I'd like to be a wealthy man." Sam left to get Vicky's pastry.

"You think the whole town is like this?" Vicky whispered.

"I think all of Alaska is like this," Harry said.

After their coffee and snack, they drove through a small commercial district, past the town airport, to Kachemak Bay where the Ocean Inn was located.

"This is beautiful," Vicky said as they walked up to the office, which looked out at the bay and the snowcapped mountains beyond. "If I didn't know that Jessie picked this place, I'd think you were trying to seduce me."

"Maybe I'm just using Jessie to get your guard down," Harry said.

Vicky gave him a smirk that he couldn't interpret.

"Hi!" The manager, a perky middle-aged woman with bright blue eyes and a wide smile, came out of a back room with an armful of towels. "You must be Harry and Vicky, right?"

"We are," Vicky said.

"Jessie called about you and I've got two second-floor rooms that she suggested for you. They have great views and real squeaky outside stairs leading up to them. They're the only second-floor rooms in that building, so if you're both up there and hear the stairs squeaking, somebody's comin' up who shouldn't be. Jessie told me to tell you that. My name's Minnie, like the mouse."

"I like the bit about the stairs," Harry said. "Kind of an Alaskan burglar alarm."

"Exactly," Minnie said. "And Jessie asked me to tell you that she'd meet you both here tomorrow to go out for breakfast. She also said you shouldn't worry about weapons, she's got that covered."

Minnie signed them in and showed them the way to the creaky stairs and an outdoor hot tub should they choose to use it, then left them to get their bags up to their rooms.

Harry unpacked his bag and went next door to Vicky's room. It was the mirror image of his own, a leather sofa and reclining chair set up in front of a thirty-two-inch flat-screen television, a king-sized bed, and a master bath with a glassed-in black-tiled shower. Vicky had been right: if Jessie hadn't made the reservation it would indeed have had a seductive air about it.

"Pretty neat room, isn't it?" Harry said.

"It's fantastic." Vicky gave him the once-over. "You sure you didn't put Jessie up to this?"

"I wish I had."

"What's that supposed to mean?"

"I don't know." He pawed the floor with his shoe. "What do you want it to mean?"

Vicky hesitated. "I don't know either."

"I think we better leave it at that."

They drove down to the Homer Spit and eyeballed Vandermere's fish-processing plant. It was a discreet drive-by, typical tourist stuff, but it provided them with a lay of the land. It didn't give them any chance sighting of Tony Rolf but that would have been asking for too much. They went on to the end of the spit and found a seafood restaurant.

There was nothing intimate or romantic about Captain Pattie's Fish House; it was one large room overlooking the bay with long tables that guests shared. Diners waited to be called to a table where they were slotted in with others who had waited before them, as waitresses hustled platters of fish and crabs in a never-ending stream.

Vicky had a steaming platter of king crab; Harry ordered a charbroiled platter of fresh-caught haddock. The food was great, but when the meal was over they felt rushed and harried, and all they wanted to do was get back to their rooms and pack it in for the night.

"I might try the hot tub," Harry said as they walked to the car. "If I do, I'll let you know so you don't freak out if the stairs start to squeak."

"I wouldn't freak out. I'd just come out and shoot you."

"Nice to know you wouldn't panic."

"Not me."

Jessie met them at eight a.m. the following morning and drove them to Two Sisters Bakery on Bunnell Street, explaining that it was a favorite breakfast hangout for Pete McGuire and his crew.

"If your boy is hangin' with Pete, he'll be gettin' his breakfast feed there," Jessie said. "If he's out on a boat, then we're just shit out of luck until he comes back into port, and since Vandermere has a processing ship out in the Bering Sea, that could be a month from now."

"And if he's in this plush hunting resort back in the wilderness?"

"That would be best for us. We could go in and flush him out. I could get helicopters, whatever we need, given time."

"Would this Vandermere guy cooperate?" Vicky asked.

"Oh, he'd be madder than a hornet and he'd fuss and piss and moan all to hell, but in the end he'd cover his ass just like he always does."

"So the answer is yes."

"When all the pissin' and moanin' is over, the answer would be yes," Jessie said. "Basically, Malcolm 'Dutch' Vandermere, Skull and Bones '74, Yale '75, is one big pussy."

They entered Two Sisters and found a crowd of people waiting to place takeout orders. Jessie scanned those already sitting and spotted McGuire at a table with two other men. She pointed them out to Vicky and Harry but neither of the others were Tony Rolf.

McGuire must have sensed their eyes on him because he slowly raised his own until he was staring directly at Jessie, then Harry and Vicky. Jessie started for his table with Harry and Vicky close behind. She stopped and stared down at Pete McGuire, a self-satisfied smile on her lips.

"Hello, Pete, you're lookin' good," she said. "I especially like your new nose. It gives that Irish mug of yours some character."

A big grin spread across McGuire's face. "Do ya think so, Jessie? I was thinkin' that very same thing this mornin' when I was shavin'. And I also thought what I could possibly do for the lovely woman who gave me that nose, maybe give her one for herself. What do ya think of that?"

"But then I'd have to throw that big lovely Irish ass of yours in jail," Jessie replied. "And that would be a great pity."

"Why don't you marry me instead?" Pete said. "Sentence me to life without parole. And just think of the beautiful little kids we'd produce."

"Is that a proposal, Pete?"

"It surely is. And it's in front of witnesses."

Jessie shook her head. She continued to stare at him but remained silent.

"Think of the children," Pete said again.

"Think of the domestic abuse complaints," Jessie said.

"I'd never lay a hand on you," Pete said.

"I wasn't talking about you," Jessie said.

Pete threw back his head with a roar of laughter, then asked, "Are these the two Florida cops I was told to watch out for?"

"You're a smart one," Jessie said. "How'd you know?"

"Don't see many suntans quite that deep in Alaska."

"You'll be callin' that little shit you work for?"

"I will," McGuire said.

"Wish you wouldn't."

McGuire's eyes flitted to the two other men at the table, letting her know that even if he didn't, there were others who would. "What is this fella supposed to have done?"

Vicky chimed in: "Murdered four women. And that's just in Florida."

"We sure do get mixed up with a lot of crazy shit for a bunch of fishermen," McGuire said. "Watch your ass."

"Always do," Jessie countered.

They picked up three coffees and a bag of fresh-from-the-oven cinnamon rolls and headed back to the Ocean Inn.

Seated at a picnic table, Vicky leaned in toward Jessie. "I think I witnessed a marriage proposal back there."

Jessie blushed. "Think so?"

"I do."

"I'd marry the big lug at the drop of a hat."

"So say yes."

"I might do that if he asks again."

"Just go up and tell him yes," Vicky said.

Harry looked confused, maybe even a bit unnerved, by what he was hearing.

"Oh, for Chrissake," Vicky scolded.

"What?" Harry said.

Vicky just shook her head.

Dutch drove his Range Rover to the end of the trail that cut along Deep Creek, a spawning river that ran just south of the Russian village of Ninilchik then back into the Kenai National Wildlife Refuge. Before it reached the refuge, it passed through a two-hundred-acre parcel owned by Vandermere Enterprises which housed one of the most luxurious hunting camps in all of Alaska. At present, three corporate executives, one sitting US senator, and a well-known Scientologist movie star were in residence at the camp's 10,000-square-foot lodge. They had feasted on prime venison steaks and roasts prepared by the lodge's two chefs and consumed two cases of fine wines. None had picked up a rifle in four days.

A helicopter collected Dutch and Tony just southeast of Ninilchik and flew them to the lodge shortly after ten that morning. Dutch was fuming that Pete had not called him; that his warning about the two Florida detectives had come from one of Pete's subordinates. And now the Irish lug wasn't even answering his cell. Dutch thought about firing him but knew his fishing business would fail within the year if he did. What was worse was that Pete knew it too.

Tony was not aware of the situation and Dutch planned to keep it that way. He did not need any more loose cannons. Better to wait for Regis Walsh to arrive and let him deal with it. It might be time to start withdrawing his generous support. School loyalty and patronage to fellow Bonesmen could only be expected to go so far.

They landed at the lodge and Dutch was pleased to see the wide-eyed look of amazement that filled Tony's face. It was always the same for a first-time visitor. They never truly appreciated how well the rich lived until they came face to face with it.

"This is fucking unbelievable," Tony said. "I mean, I knew it would be fancy. Everything about you guys is fancy. But this is like a castle built of logs."

They stood at the base of the lodge looking up. It seemed to rise in tiers, each one larger than the last, each spreading out on another layer of land, each protected by electrified fencing to keep the wildlife at bay.

"Everything, of course, operates on our own power grid," Dutch said. "What you can't see are the iron gates that slide into place with the touch of a button on a computer screen. They cover all the doorways, all the windows, everything."

"And you what, have a secret way out once they're in place?" Tony asked.

"No need. The lodge is totally self-sufficient and self-sustaining. It has its own radio communication system, its own infirmary, and the ability to feed a half-dozen guests and staff for up to three months. If we were forced to close ourselves off to the outside world, to be trapped inside, so to speak, we would just sit back and drink some wonderful vintage wine until help arrived."

"Not a bad way to be trapped," Tony said.

"And, of course, we have one of the finest armories imaginable, filled with rifles which in the hands of a true marksman can take down a fully grown Alaskan brown bear."

The two men climbed the wide wooden stairs that led up to what was referred to as the Greeting Room. It was a forty-by-forty-foot room, the walls of which were lined with mounted animal heads; one full-sized brown bear standing on its hind legs, snarling mouth agape, front paws and claws extended; a fully mounted bull moose; deer heads with ten or more points; numerous hunting prints, many showing Indians and pioneers fighting animals with spears and knives; and animal pelts and rugs made from wolves, deer, moose, otter.

"How many kinds of animals are here?" Tony asked.

"If it's native to Alaska, it's here," Dutch said. "Come, let me show you your room."

Dutch filled Tony in on the other guests who were there. The senator and the CEOs made no impression, but the movie star left him wide-eyed. "He doesn't get up until midafternoon. Just tell him you work here if he asks. He probably won't. He doesn't have many interests beyond his own comforts. By the way, Regis Walsh may be stopping by today."

"What? Why?"

"I haven't the foggiest," Dutch said.

"Do you think something's gone wrong?"

Dutch only shrugged.

Chapter Twenty-Five

"Let's go get that slimy little son of a bitch," Harry said. "How long will it take to get a helicopter here, rifles, search warrant, and whatever backup you think we need?"

Jessie looked at her watch. "We've got lots of daylight left, so that's not a problem. We're only going after one man, and I don't think Dutch will be stupid enough to put his people up against us if we have a lawful warrant. Your Max Abrams has one from a Florida judge that he sent us, and since it involves four homicides, no Alaska judge is going to refuse to honor it. That will only take an hour or two and a quick fax from Juneau to Homer. Then it's just a question of one or two officers for backup and we're good to go. I'd say by three at the latest."

Harry took Vicky aside. He put his hands on her shoulders and looked intently into her eyes. "I want you to promise me something," he said.

"What's that?"

"I want you to deal with Rolf from a distance. Promise you'll do that. You let me handle him up close."

"What is this, Harry? When did I become some rookie cop who you have to protect?"

"It's not you, it's him. He's a psycho about women. If you get close to him he's going to want to cut you. He won't be able to help himself. Meg was good at what she did. She was very, very good. He shouldn't have been able to kill her, but he did. You are too important to me, Vicky. Just don't let him get too close to you."

"I'll do my best. That's all I can promise."

He squeezed her shoulders and she leaned against him. It was a brief moment of tenderness, but it was enough.

The helicopter brought Regis Walsh to the lodge at two p.m. Dutch immediately took him into the office without letting Tony know he was there.

"How serious is it?" Dutch asked.

"I gather there's a warrant out for my arrest," Walsh said.

"What are the charges?" There was a demanding edge to Dutch's voice.

"Apparently my assistant, Ken Oppenheimer, has told the authorities that I shielded Tony from them even though I knew he had killed at least one woman, possibly more. It's nonsense, of course. Ken is simply trying to justify his own errors in judgment."

"Did Tony kill the woman?"

"I have no way of knowing. I certainly don't believe he did."

Dutch let out a long breath. "I can't allow my company to become involved in a murder." There was a tremor in his voice.

"Nor could I allow the church to be involved with one," Walsh said.

"I think the police are going to be coming for him."

"That may be the best solution. Providing Tony doesn't survive the police assault."

"That would seem to be the best solution for everyone," Dutch said.

Dutch went down to Tony's room and found him staring out a window into the vast expanse of wilderness that surrounded the lodge.

"Do you get many wild animals close to the lodge?"

"Only when someone is careless with food," Dutch said. "We always warn guests about that, but sometimes people get careless. It only takes one encounter with a bear—a black bear usually—who wants the remains of a sandwich that was left out on a bedside table to make a believer out of a careless guest."

"I'll bet," Tony said.

"By the way, Regis is here. Would you like to see him?"

"Yeah, sure," Tony said. "Is anything wrong?"

"The police are sniffing around. I think it might be a good idea if you slipped back to Homer and let us get you on a fishing boat that will take you out to sea for a bit."

"Shit, I was really looking forward to staying here for a while."

Dutch thought for a moment that Tony might stamp his foot. He could be such a little boy when things didn't go his way. "Let's go see Regis," he said.

Regis was still in the lodge office and when Tony entered he moved quickly toward him and embraced him like a long-lost relative. It was a heartfelt scene and completely genuine on the surface and Dutch made note of it for future reference. Regis had far better acting skills than he had ever suspected.

"Dutch tells me the cops are on their way," Tony said.

Sadness filled Walsh's face. "Yes, the two sheriff's detectives who harassed us in Florida, the one they call the dead detective and his female partner, and some Alaskan state police officers they've enlisted up here. Also, you should know that Ken Oppenheimer kicked open the door by giving sworn testimony to a Clearwater police sergeant named Max Abrams who apparently has warrants out for both you and me. The whole thing is absurd, of course, but it has to be dealt with."

"That fucking Oppenheimer, that goddamn turncoat—you made him and this is what he does to you?"

Regis looked at Tony's cold eyes and knew without question that Ken Oppenheimer would be a dead man if Tony ever set foot in Florida again. It was truly tempting, but the aftermath would be far more dangerous to all concerned. He slipped an arm around Tony's shoulder in a gesture that exuded fatherly warmth. "The important thing right now is to keep you out of the hands of the police. I believe Dutch has a workable plan. We'll send you out with a hunting guide, who will take you back to Deep Creek, the river about a quarter of a mile north of the lodge. From there he'll head back toward Ninilchik. You'll have a compass with you and a radio so we can keep you informed about the police. Once you hit the river, it's just a question of following it west until you reach the village. You'll be picked up there and taken to Homer."

"What if the police show up before then?" Tony asked.

"The guide will lead them away from you, and when they stop him he'll just explain that he was out scouting a hunt planned for tomorrow. If they ask about you, he's instructed to give them a see-no-evil, hear-no-evil, speak-no-evil response. When they're gone he'll find you again. If they find you first, do your best to get away."

Dutch came over to them. "It's important that you stay out of police custody. We need time to set up a strong defense against the lies that Kenneth Oppenheimer is spreading about us and about the church."

"They won't get me," Tony said. "Do you have any camouflage clothing and a good hunting rifle?"

"Of course. Come with me and I'll get you outfitted and introduce you to your hunting guide."

Two Alaskan state police helicopters were waiting for them at the Homer Airport, along with two extra troopers. Jessie had equipped Harry and Vicky with bulletproof vests and rifles fitted with telescopic sights. She had the arrest warrants Max Abrams had sent ahead—one for Tony Rolf and one for Regis Walsh—along with a request that they be held for extradition to Florida.

Harry and Vicky had decided to use their own handguns and Jessie was familiarizing them with the rifles. "These are Savage 116 Bear Hunters. They take a .300 Winchester Magnum cartridge and hit with a helluva wallop. They also give a good kick to the shoulder, so just be prepared for that," she warned. "The scope is a standard Bushnell eight-power on a raised mount so you can use the iron sights beneath it as well. It's been sighted in but may be a touch off for you. I think it will be so slight it won't make a difference. Now, the weaponry they have at the lodge is a helluva lot better than ours. You can expect anything this guy Rolf is using will have more sophisticated attachments."

"Like what?" Vicky asked.

"Laser scopes, infrared scopes, basically scopes that paint little dots on you. Some of them are cheap and ain't worth shit, but some others are pretty sophisticated. So if you see a little red dot dancing across your shirt, hit the deck."

"Sounds like good advice," Harry said.

"Indeed," Vicky added.

Tony was dressed in camouflage clothing from head to foot. His boots and shooting gloves were made of camouflage cloth, his face was painted, his one-piece hunting outfit looked like tree bark with loose pieces designed to move like parts of a bush blowing in the wind. No section of his body remained uncovered. For a weapon he carried a Remington 700 .30 06 rifle with an eight-power infrared scope. In the right hands it could stop a charging brown bear at one hundred yards. In the wrong hands it would probably get you killed.

Tony was also carrying an eight-inch hunting knife with a razor-sharp edge. By the way he had caressed it, Dutch could tell it would be his weapon of choice. His personal switchblade was also tucked into his left hunting boot. For Tony it was like some people and their American Express Cards: he just didn't leave home without it.

Tony and Dutch stepped out into the hallway and ran right into the movie star, who was bleary-eyed and unshaven and stood there absently scratching his belly.

Tony was too startled to speak, not because he was face-to-face with a man he had seen so many times on the silver screen, but because that man was almost a head shorter than he and was staring up at him with a silly smile on his face.

"Hey, bro, we're off to the woods, are we?" The smile widened into the broad, sparkling gleam familiar to millions.

"Tom, how are you?" Dutch said, stepping forward.

"Oh, Dutchman, I am one starving, very hungry man."

"Well, get yourself on up to the dining room. I've got two four-star chefs just waiting to cook for you. In fact, Regis Walsh is up there ordering a late lunch right now."

"Regis! What the hell is he doing here? I haven't seen him since the dedication of the Flag Building in Clearwater. And why lunch? The hell with lunch, I need breakfast. You think your boys can rustle up an order of huevos rancheros? I became addicted to them on a gambling junket in Vegas last year."

"If you can hum a few bars, they can play it," Dutch said.

The dazzling smile returned. "Atta boy, Dutch," he roared, then turned back to Tony. "Go find out where all those deer are hiding, I wanna take back a freezer chest full of venison." He spun on his heels. "See you guys at dinner."

Tony watched him wander off down the hall. The man hadn't even asked his name, hadn't cared who he was. He just wanted someone to feed him.

"Let's go find the guide you're going out with," Dutch said.

The guide was a French Canadian named Chris Chagal, known to his peers as Frenchy. He had been raised in the woods of Labrador and had worked his way west across northern Canada until finally settling down at age forty as a hunting guide in the Kenai Peninsula.

Standing next to Tony he looked even bigger than his six feet, 230 pounds. He had a full beard of red hair that went down to his chest and covered all of his face except for two-inch patches beneath his eyes. His hands were big and brutish, his shoulders broad, and his protruding belly hard as rock. Frenchy's arms were as thick as most men's legs and his legs were like the trunks of trees. He had a scar on his left shoulder where a brown bear he thought he had killed had swatted him, sending him thirty feet through the air. Fortunately, the hunter he was guiding had shot the bear dead. He had never made that mistake again.

Dutch explained the situation: They did not want Tony taken into custody by the police. Frenchy was not to engage the police in gunfire. If they saw him with Tony, he was to separate from him and try to lead the police away from him. When stopped, he was to say that Tony was a guest at the lodge and he was guiding him on a hunt. The real goal, which he was not to reveal under any circumstances, was to get Tony to Ninilchik and then back to Homer.

"Am I to leave him to get to Ninilchik on his own?" Frenchy asked.

"Yes."

"Is he a skillful enough woodsman to make it all the way by himself? It's not an easy trip and there are—"

"We expect him to be able to handle it."

"I hope he understands what this will involve."

"He's been told," Dutch said. "Don't concern yourself with it."

"Let's mount up," Jessie said.

Jessie and the two other Alaskan state troopers boarded one helicopter and Harry and Vicky boarded the other. They lifted off from Homer Airport and swung northeast toward the Vandermere hunting lodge. It was a clear, bright, sunny day and visibility was almost endless. Beneath them they could see the occasional moose or deer, disturbed by the helicopters, moving off into the brush. Cars headed north and south along the Sterling Highway, paying little attention to the aircraft that flitted above them. Probably an everyday occurrence for them, Harry thought. Like Coast Guard helicopters in Florida.

Florida—it seemed a million miles away right now. Harry looked at Vicky with her deep tan, matching his own. He reached across the helicopter, extending his hand. She took it. He squeezed. "Let's get this bastard and go home," he said.

Frenchy and Tony moved out into the woods, slowly working their way north to Deep Creek, the river that would lead them to Ninilchik.

Frenchy raised his hand indicating they should stop. He spoke in little more than a whisper. "Deep Creek can be dangerous—shallow and then suddenly opening into deep holes. There are good crossing points, but you have to know them. I'll show you."

Tony noted that Frenchy was not dressed in camouflage and he asked about it.

"It's my job to lead the police away from you," Frenchy said. "If they come, you use the camo to hide yourself and I will move off and lead them away. When they're gone, you continue to follow the river to Ninilchik."

"Will I be able to do it alone?"

"The river goes there. You follow the river, you go there," Frenchy said. "It's easy."

"If you say so."

Frenchy placed a meat hook of a hand on his shoulder. "Don't worry. You just follow the river west. Go slow. Use your compass to be sure. When the police leave I will come find you. I promise. You have a good rifle. Only use it for bear and only if you have to. Camo will keep bear from seeing you, but they will still smell you. If you see a brown bear, find a tree you can climb and get up it. Brown bears don't climb. Black bears, they climb like bastids. They can come right up after you. But the brown ones aren't aggressive like that. Okay? Just go slow and easy now, and if the cops show up I'll lead them away and then I'll come back and find you. Okay?"

"Okay."

The state police helicopters started circling when the lodge was a hundred yards in the distance. The brush below was thick, the fir trees rising one hundred, one hundred and fifty feet in the air. Deep Creek lay seventy-five yards to the north and could be seen as patches of sunlight flashed across its surface through openings in the trees. All the troopers as well as Harry and Vicky scoured the ground for any sign of movement. The copters moved up to the river, one covering the north bank, one covering the south. They rose up and then dropped down again, trying to gain any good vantage point they could.

"Do you see anything?" Jessie called over her radio.

"Nothing," Harry responded.

"We're going to move toward the lodge, then back out again. Keep a sharp eye. They could be wearing camouflage. Over and out."

The helicopters elevated to clear the trees and swung toward the lodge. Harry couldn't believe the size of the place, all of it built in the middle of a wilderness for the indulgence of a few wealthy men.

"Movement, movement, ten o'clock!" Vicky shouted.

Harry looked down and saw someone heading east through the heavy brush. He moved up and pointed the figure out to the pilot. The helicopter swung down and hovered over a small clearing as the pilot got on the speaker and ordered the man into the center of the clearing. Harry radioed to Jessie and told her they had an armed hunter they were about to question. Jessie's helicopter swung back and both landed in the clearing.

Frenchy came out of the brush, his rifle held in both hands above his head, a large smile spread across his bearded face. "Hey, Jessie, Frenchy did something wrong? I surrender. Okay?"

Jessie walked toward him. "What are you doin' out here, Frenchy?"

"I'm scouting a hunt for tomorrow."

"What kind of hunt?"

"Deer—a big buck, I think. We got movie star who wants to take venison home."

"Why don't you just shoot him one? It would be easier."

"For me and for the deer," Frenchy said. "They usually look like Swiss cheese—they have so many holes—when our guests shoot them."

"It's a shame."

"Mr. Dutch, he says it's a business."

"We're looking for a man we think is here at the lodge," Jessie explained. "His name is Tony Rolf." She raised her chin toward Harry and Vicky. "These are two Florida detectives who have come up here after him. He's a bad man, Frenchy. He's killed four women that we know of, probably more."

Frenchy stared at her for a long moment. "Mr. Dutch don't tell Frenchy that. He just tells me to get him to Ninilchik. Fucking bastid, Frenchy don't help people who hurt women. Fuck Mr. Dutch. Frenchy don't work for him no more."

"Where is this man now?" Jessie asked.

"He's up at the river. He's got real good camo. He sit tight, you never see him unless he moves."

"Is he armed?"

"Yes, good weapon, Remington 700 with an eight-power infrared scope. I don't know how good he is with it, but the weapon is good enough to take all of you out." Frenchy shook his head in disgust. "I'll take you up there, help you find him."

"No," Jessie said. "It's our job, not yours. You tell Dutch we'll be up to see him as soon as we finish here. Tell him that if he leaves, his ass belongs to me."

"I tell him. I be happy to tell him dat."

Tony took the river crossing Frenchy had showed him and stayed close to the heavier brush, knowing that when he stopped he would be nearly invisible from both the ground and above. His rifle, which was covered in the same material as his clothing, was carried close to his body, with the barrel pointed down and the lens caps closed on the telescopic scope to avoid any glare that might give away his position. He only moved when the helicopters were both flying away from him, making his forward progress incredibly slow. But it was slow for his pursuers as well, and he knew the helicopters would eventually have fuel problems and need to return to Homer. That would be his chance to gain some ground toward Ninilchik, or for Frenchy to get back to find him.

Unless, of course, they had already told Frenchy he was wanted for murder and turned the guide against him. But Frenchy hadn't joined them, had he? He hadn't led them back to him. They were just stumbling along like they always were—like they were in Florida, like they were years ago in LA. He had always been able to get away, just as he would this time. And if they weren't careful, he'd take a few of them down before he did.

Harry spoke to Vicky through his headset: "Do you see anything?"

"No, I thought I saw some movement on the north side of the river but it was nothing, just some branches waving in the downdraft of the helicopter. I'm wondering if we'd do better with a couple of us on the ground."

"I'll ask Jessie what she thinks," Harry said.

"We can try," Jessie came back. *"Harry, why don't you have the pilot drop Vicky on the north bank where I'll be, and you hit the south bank with one of my people. That way, each of you will be with someone who's familiar with the territory."*

"Sounds good," Harry radioed back. "You guys watch your backs. If you see him, let us know and we will back you up. We'll do the same."

"Roger, over and out."

Tony watched from about thirty-five yards away as the helicopters deposited two cops on his side of the river and two on the opposite side. He intended to sit still and let them walk past him unless he had an angle that allowed him to take them out one after the other. He looked up at the two choppers back above him now. No, that would be foolish. He studied the cops more closely. Wait, one was that woman cop from Florida, Vicky Stanopolis, the one who worked with the guy they called the dead detective. They all looked so unisex here in the baggy field dress they were wearing. She sure as hell hadn't looked unisex in Florida. He remembered her from the marina where the other cop kept his boat. She usually wore tight jeans or slacks that showed off that shapely ass of hers. Oh yeah, he remembered that. The big broad with her must be that Alaskan trooper everyone said was so tough. She was supposed to have broken Pete McGuire's nose. If they got too close he'd take her out first. No sense in taking any chances, and he definitey didn't want the humiliation of being brought down by some tough bitch with a badge.

"He could be almost anywhere. We could step on him before we flushed him out," Jessie said. She squatted down and listened to the river moving past. "The current's fairly quick here so it gives some cover to the sound of our movements." The helicopter roared past overhead. "So does that. But it all works the same for him. We just gotta keep pokin' through the woods here and hope he gets antsy and makes a mistake."

"He's been pretty controlled so far," Vicky said. "He's surprised me."

Across the river, Harry alternated between keeping his eyes on Vicky and Jessie and searching the ground ahead of him. He hoped Rolf would be on his side of the water, as far away from Vicky as possible. He'd seen what that sick asshole did to women and he wanted to put him down before he had the chance to do it again. *That's a new one for you,* he thought, *actually wanting to take someone down. You've done it before, but like most cops you've never wanted it. When you started wanting it, it's time to start watching yourself; maybe even time to start thinking about packing it in.*

One of the helicopters swooped down low and the radio crackled in Harry's ears. *"I thought I saw some movement about thirty yards ahead of our people on the north bank,"* the pilot said. *"It's gone now—could have been an animal but I can't be sure, the brush is too thick there."*

Jessie motioned to Vicky, indicating something up ahead. She whispered, "Saw something move. Spread out, about fifty feet apart."

A shot rang out. Jessie grunted and staggered back; then a second shot, and she went down on her back. Vicky ran to her and dived headfirst next to her. There was a third shot that kicked up dirt about two feet in front of her head.

On the other side of the river, Harry fired into the area where he had seen a muzzle flash—two, three, four shots. The rounds coming at Vicky and Jessie stopped and Harry was up and running into the water, headed for the north bank. Covering fire came from the helicopters circling above.

Vicky watched Jessie gasping for breath. There were two bullet holes in her tunic, both heart shots. She ripped back the clothing and peeled off the kevlar vest. Jessie's chest had suffered two severe bruises but the bullets had not penetrated her skin.

Vicky got on the radio: "Jessie's okay. The bullets just knocked the wind out of her. Can one of you get down here to pick her up? I'll cover you."

"Roger, we're coming in. Get yourself to a more secure location. Our second chopper will provide us with backup cover."

Vicky ignored the instructions and waited until the helicopter had landed and two troopers were bringing a litter for Jessie before she broke away and headed for a thick brush pile. From her new location she could see Harry struggling against the river's current. He was waist deep and two-thirds of the way across—a sitting duck if Rolf had a clear shot at him. She scanned the woods, looking for any sign that would give his location away. Then she waved at Harry, motioning for him to get down.

She didn't feel him come up behind her, and then there he was. The eight-inch hunting knife slid up under her chin, the blade pressing against her throat, and she felt a trickle of blood running down her neck.

"Oooh, that is sooo sharp," Rolf whispered in her ear. "Just one little flick of my wrist and it will take your lovely head right off that beautiful body. And look at your boyfriend just struggling against the current, trying to get here to save you. Imagine how he's going to feel when he gets here and your lovely head is lying on the ground all by itself. And all that happens just before I blow his fucking head off. Why, it just might ruin his whole day, don't you think?"

"You are one sick motherfucker," Vicky rasped.

"And you have one dirty mouth on you, Miss Vicky. Didn't your mama teach you better than that? Mine didn't. That's why I had to kill her. Did you know her name was Vicky too? No, you didn't know that? Did you kill your mama? No, of course you didn't. You were one of those good girls, weren't you?"

Harry struggled up onto the bank, his rifle held in both hands.

Tony screamed at him: "One more step and her head will be on the ground next to her!" He smiled as he watched Harry stop dead in his tracks. "That water's cold, isn't it?"

Harry didn't answer, he just stared, looking for an opening.

"Now here's what I want you to do," Tony said. "You tell the helicopters to back off. That's number one."

Harry spoke to the choppers and they pulled away.

"Number two: toss your rifle in the river."

Harry did so.

"What other weapons do you have?"

"That's it," Harry said, thinking of the Glock in his shoulder holster.

"You're lyin', but I can't do nothin' about that now." Tony turned his attention back to Vicky and leaned in close to her ear. "When I killed the last one, I slid the knife in just under her left titty then up into her heart. I don't think she felt any pain at all. She just sort of slipped away, little by little, until that last little sparkle left her eyes and she was gone. It was beautiful, really. For me, anyway; I hope it was beautiful for her too. Do you think it was?"

"You sick fuck," Vicky spat out.

The roar was so loud it literally knocked them forward a step, and it was followed by an overwhelming stench of putrid breath. Tony spun around, his knife instinctively raised, his rifle all but forgotten. The Alaskan brown bear, which had been drawn in by the earlier rifle shots and the hopes of any easy meal, rose up on its hind legs to its full height of ten feet. It roared again, blocking out all other sound, and it bit down on Tony's head, driving its three-inch teeth into his skull. The murderer's screams only seemed to enrage the bear more, and it reared back and swung one giant paw, catching Tony on the shoulder and ripping out his arm as his body flew twenty feet down the riverbank.

Tony's torment filled Harry's ears as he rushed forward and grabbed Vicky. He threw her over his right shoulder in a fireman's carry as the bear loomed above him, then spun and raced back toward the water, expecting the animal to grab them from behind at any moment. He hit the water, headed for the south bank, and called over his radio for the helicopters to return and pick them up. Tony's screams and the bear's roars continued as he pressed himself against the rushing water to keep his balance. He glanced back over his shoulder and saw the bear had no interest in Vicky or him. It had followed its victim's body and was happily ripping and chewing on Tony Rolf as a geyser of blood spurted out. Tony's remaining arm still held the knife and he flailed weakly at the monstrous animal while it tore chunks of flesh from what remained of his body.

Harry continued to stare at the grisly scene as he reached the south bank of the river. "Bon appétit, bear," he said, then lowered Vicky to the ground and ran for the nearest chopper.

Chapter Twenty-Six

When the helicopter returned to the lodge from refueling, Max Abrams was on board.

Harry greeted him with a wide grin. "Just like you, Max. Show up when all the heavy lifting is done."

"I understand you had a trained bear do your heavy lifting for you," Max replied.

"They do things different here in Alaska. They feed their criminals to the wildlife. It cuts down on incarceration costs."

"I like it," Max said. "Be a good plan for Florida, good way for us to feed our alligators and all those big snakes we've got in the Everglades now. How much of Rolf were you able to get back?"

"Not much. After a while the troopers scared the bear off. Eventually they'll hunt him down and try to get more out of his belly to finish the autopsy. But they probably would have killed it anyway. Apparently they don't like to have bears in the woods that've developed a taste for human flesh, although from what I've heard, the damn things will eat anything they come across. And when they hear a rifle shot, it's like a dinner bell and they come running to see what there is to eat. If Rolf hadn't shot his rifle, the bear probably never would have showed up." Harry paused. "But I'm glad it did. Right before that bear ripped his arm off, Rolf had a knife to Vicky's throat."

"And he was telling me how good it was going to feel when he slipped it into my heart," Vicky added.

"Maybe they shouldn't shoot that bear after all," Max said.

"They should give it a medal," Jessie said, adding her two bits as she entered the room. "What kind of accent is that?" she asked Max.

"What accent?"

"Yours."

"You've never been to Brooklyn?" Max said.

"There really is such a place?"

"Are they all like this up here?" Max countered. "I thought Sarah Palin was something the comedians made up."

"Watch it, mister, we got more hungry bears up here."

Max raised his hands in surrender. "I've got a warrant to serve."

"And I have one too," Jessie said.

"Well, let's go have some fun."

Regis Walsh and Dutch Vandermere were smoking cigars in the lodge office, trying to sort their way through the current predicament. Tony was dead and that was a blessing. Without his testimony, much of what the authorities hoped to prove against either of them would be difficult. Regis had spoken with Jordan Wells earlier and the lawyer was confident that a jury—if it came to that—would be sympathetic to a plea of ignorance. And while ignorance of the law was not considered an acceptable defense, ignorance of another's evil actions was often looked upon with favor by jurors. The important point, the lawyer had stressed, was that Regis and Dutch remain supportive of and loyal to each other. Right now, the only person speaking ill of them was Kenneth Oppenheimer.

Max and Jessie entered the office together, leaving the door open behind them so Harry and Vicky could loiter in the hall and hear what was said.

"Mr. Walsh," Max began, "you are under arrest. You have the right to remain silent. If you choose not to remain silent, everything you say may be taken down and used against you in a court of law. You have a right to an attorney. If you cannot afford an attorney, one will be appointed for you. Do you understand these rights?"

Regis stared at him without speaking for nearly half a minute. "What am I charged with?" he asked at length.

Max handed him the warrant he had brought with him. "It's all in there, but it basically deals with your aiding and abetting Tony Rolf in the commission of four murders, your efforts to help him escape arrest after each murder, and so on."

"Tony killed four people?" Regis said. "When did this happen?"

"I'm not here to play games with you. Save it for court. Get up and put your hands on that desk while I search you."

"Are you going to handcuff me?"

"You bet your bippie I am," Max said. "You'll be wearing these bracelets until you get into an Alaskan jail. Do you plan to fight extradition?"

"Of course not. My home and my job are all in Florida, as is my attorney. The sooner I get back there and deal with this nonsense, the better."

"What were you doing here?" Max asked.

"Visiting a church facility in Anchorage and an old school chum here in Homer." He inclined his head toward Dutch. "And that is the last question I shall be answering."

Max patted him down and cuffed him behind his back. "My work is done here," he said to Jessie.

She nodded and turned to Dutch. "Malcolm Vandermere, you are under arrest for aiding and abetting the attempted escape of one Tony Rolf, who was an escaped felon wanted in Florida on four counts of first degree murder." Dutch's face became grayer by the second as she read him his rights.

"I want to call my attorney," Dutch said as soon as she had finished.

"Well, you just sit down at your desk and go right ahead. And do you think we could get us some coffee here while we're all waiting?"

"Just pick up the phone on that conference table, punch in a free line, and hit four. That will connect you to the kitchen. Tell them what you want and have them deliver it to the office. All our guests left when they heard about the unpleasantness of this morning, so the kitchen staff has nothing to do. If anyone is hungry, order lunch for your people. My treat."

Jessie smiled at the irony of his words. "Max, Vicky, Harry, anybody hungry? Sandwiches, coffee maybe?" she suggested.

"Sure," Max said. "I don't think I've ever been involved in an arrest where the perp bought me lunch. That's even better than feeding the perp to a bear. I do like the way you folks do your jobs up here," he said to Jessie. "It's very, very . . ." He paused, searching for the right word. "Progressive."

They dropped their prisoners off at the Homer City lockup to await their transport by air to a court in Anchorage. Dutch would undoubtedly post bail in the morning, as would Walsh upon his return to Florida.

"I want to stop at the fish-processing plant on our way to the Ocean Inn," Jessie said. "And I'd like you to go with me for moral support," she told Vicky.

"Sure," Vicky responded. She'd seen a man eaten by a bear today, what could be worse?

They pulled up in front of the processing plant and Vicky followed Jessie as she marched inside and headed straight for Big Pete McGuire's office. She pushed the door open and walked up to his desk. "I accept your proposal," she announced.

"What proposal was that?" he asked, his eyes twinkling with mischief.

"Your marriage proposal, damnit," Jessie snapped.

"Oh good," Pete said. "I was afraid you might be talkin' about the little ruckus that gave me this." He jabbed a thumb at his nose. "It still hurts like holy hell." He stood and held open his arms and Jessie walked into them.

"You seem to be in good hands—or arms. I'm going back to my hotel," Vicky said.

Vicky climbed into the car and looked at Max, then at Harry. "Jessie and Pete McGuire just got engaged," she said.

"Somebody better alert the NFL so they can draft their kids right out of nursery school," Harry replied.

They got Max a room overlooking Kachemak Bay and the Kenai Mountains and he said he was in need of a long nap and would meet them for drinks around five. Harry and Vicky climbed the squeaky stairs and didn't even make a pretense of going to separate rooms. They went straight to Vicky's room and started undressing each other as soon as the door closed behind them.

END

Acknowledgments

Special thanks to Nancy Williams, whose generosity and caring love are a constant source of amazement; to Beth Hovind, Tania Lewis, and Walter Kloepfer, for their valuable insights into Alaska; to Johnny Temple, for his steadfast support; and, as always, to the great lady who has been my literary agent for the past thirty-eight years, the incomparable Gloria Loomis.

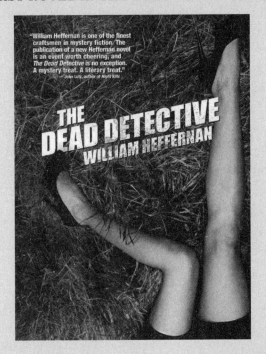